A Secret Summer

Rachel Louise Finn

Copyright © Rachel Louise Finn, 2021.

All Rights Reserved. No part of this book may be reproduced or transmitted in any form or by any means, electronic or mechanical, including photocopying, recording, or by any information storage and retrieval system without the written permission of the author, except where permitted by law.

ISBN: 9798708895837

prologue
That Summer

A red firework shot across the sky, closely followed by a blue one, lighting up the street. Eighteen-year-old Annie Pierce was in her bedroom, trying on dresses for the end of summer bonfire party in Jason Wright's back garden later that night.

She was almost ready and she knew that her best friends would already be out in her own back garden waiting for her to come out so they could start their pre-party drinks session.

Another firework thudded in the distance and Annie's dog whined from its place at the bottom of her bed.

"Shut *up*, Pixie." She sighed. "It's just a fucking firework."

Once she was finished admiring herself in the mirror, she slicked on another coat of lip-gloss and then turned to haul the box of alcohol up into her arms.

Getting Evan Johnson, the local pub owner, to give her the booze for free had been super easy. All she'd had to do was use that same bullshit story threatening to tell everybody that he was sleeping with the butcher's wife. He was far too easy. The picture Annie had taken on her phone was hardly worth anything - it was blurry and they'd practically pulled away by the time the flash went off. But he didn't know that and he was worried. Everybody knew that the butcher had a terrible temper.

Annie was just amused. She had bigger things to worry about than some bartender but he was good for keeping her in drink, and she really wanted to have a good time with her friends tonight. She had it all planned perfectly.

She swept out of her back door and into the garden, slamming the door as she went. Turning, she glanced up and made a face at her sister Chloe, who was watching from her bedroom window. She laughed when Chloe disappeared, shaking her head and dragging the alcohol towards the small shed she and her friends had agreed to meet up behind.

It was out of sight of the house, not that her mother would be able to do a lot if she caught her with a case of booze. Annie would be able to wriggle out of that one just like she was able to wriggle out of everything else.

When she finally appeared, her friends were already there as she'd predicted. They were always waiting for her. Annie was always running fashionably late. She liked to make an entrance. She flashed them all a bright smile, noting the adoring gazes and felt better. She hadn't even realised she had been worrying until it all went away there and then. She had problems, everyone did.

Annie wasn't just the Queen Bee of Baberton high school, she wasn't just beautiful and popular – she had issues too, you know! But those issues could wait. Tonight was about having fun and she would deal with it all some other time. Tomorrow was another day.

"Here's to summer, girls!" She announced, plonking the beers and wine coolers down in the middle of their little circle and pulling out a bottle as the rest of the girls helped themselves.

"This has been the best one yet. Let's see it off with a bang!"

The rest of the group cheered her mini speech and threw back their heads as they gulped a swig of their alcohol down.

Annie picked her four best friends Ruby Peterson, Kelly Sharpe, Sophie Baker and Imogen Ford from social obscurity when they were all eleven and just heading up into secondary school. Even at a young age Annie was addictive. With her doll-like face, raven hair and wide, bright eyes she was already a star. Everybody wanted to be her friend. She knew people loved her but her manipulation hadn't hit its peak yet and nobody was quite as wary of her as they would grow to be.

The four girls had no idea why she picked them - Annie did so for different reasons - but they were so grateful to have been welcomed into her inner circle. From the very start it was as though they were all VIPs in a town they had almost grown bored of.

There was Ruby with her long dark hair and painfully shy expression who Annie knew, instantly, that she could control.

There was Kelly, who was a year older than the rest of them, but who worshipped Annie like she was a princess and Annie loved to be worshipped. Loved to be obsessed over.

There was Sophie, with her great fashion sense and her fiery attitude - which Annie knew might cause a few problems but also knew would complement the group perfectly.

And then there was sweet little Imogen, with her blonde hair and her angel face. She was Annie's favourite because she always did as she was told and always gazed lovingly at Annie which boosted her ego... but she was also the easiest to talk to.

These four girls had no idea what a wild ride they would be in for when they met Annie, when they finally became her best friends. They all loved and hated one another just as they loved and hated Annie herself.

They were constantly vying for her attention, subconsciously feeling as though they had to get one over on each other and be better to get her to love them the most. Which is probably why they did whatever she asked, often without question, or without much arguing.

They had hurt people and they felt guilty but being Annie's friend felt worth it. It was wonderful, being part of her group. But it was also horrible because she would play them off against each other and tease them and keep secrets from them and sometimes she would ignore them for days and then act as though nothing was wrong.

But they always came back like wounded dogs with their tails between their legs. Because Annie was like a drug that people just couldn't get enough of.

Annie had another way of keeping these girls close to her, however. Annie liked secrets. She had this insane habit of being able to figure out the secrets their peers were keeping and using those secrets against them... and Annie had no qualms about doing this same thing with her best friends.

She knew about bubbly Imogen's sexuality struggle. She knew about wallflower Ruby's *scandalous* affair with one of their teachers. She knew about Sophie's eating disorder. And she knew about Kelly's addiction to her mother's prescription pain medication.

It was easier to keep people in line when you knew something about them that nobody else did. Even if they were your best friends.

Time passed and Annie kept drinking, probably drinking most of the case herself, but she felt in high spirits tonight. She'd had a long day of being forced by her mother to fill in last minute college applications, full of stress, and she was just looking forward to letting her hair down. Dancing, drinking, laughing, maybe making out with some cute boys... and waking up in the morning with no memory of what happened but knowing that she'd had a damn good time. That's all she wanted.

"Here's to us!" She giggled, holding up her bottle, half gone already.

Sophie Baker smiled, clinking her own bottle against Annie's. She was the smart one of the group and she never drank more than she knew she'd be able to handle. Sophie was always the reliable one. The one who made sure everybody else got home safe when they were too drunk to handle themselves. Tonight would be no different.

Sophie was looking forward to the party. She had the *biggest* crush on Thomas Playfair, a popular college boy that all the high school girls had a crush on. She was the one with the biggest chance, or she felt that way at least. He'd been paying her a lot of attention recently and Sophie was excited to see him while he was drunk, she'd even dressed especially for the occasion. He had a girlfriend, unfortunately, but the two of them were constantly arguing and were *definitely* on the verge of breaking up.

Sophie decided she would be there to be his shoulder to cry on if - no, *when* - that happened.

She and her little group had been best friends for around seven years and had started high school together. They were the most popular girls in their school. Love or hate them, everybody wished they could be them.

Sophie didn't see herself as superior exactly (like maybe Annie did) but she liked the perks that came with such popularity. She liked her friends, though she was the one who stood up to their ringleader most often. She and Annie always butted heads and they fought over absolutely everything. Boys, clothes, grades. Sometimes it felt like they were two wild dogs fighting over Alpha status.

Annie was the drunkest of the five girls by the time they started making a move over to Jason's party, which was only next door. It wasn't unusual for Annie to be the most gone of them all, she was the life and soul of the party, consuming so much alcohol that you'd think her tiny frame wouldn't be able to handle it all.

She'd be dancing and laughing and drinking all night and nobody would know how she was still standing. It was nothing out of the ordinary, they'd seen it all before.

Annie linked arms with Imogen Ford, who beamed back at the brunette, and they all moved towards the gap in the bushes that would lead them to Jason's garden, where the party already seemed to be in full swing. They could hear the music over the odd firework and merry voices filling the air.

Annie glanced behind her and saw the back door of her house opening, her sister slipping out into the night.

"Quick!" She squealed, giggling as she pulled her friends through the gap and into the party.

She and her twin sister barely got on these days. They used to be close when they were younger but as Annie got older and her popularity grew, she left her sister behind. Chloe was obviously upset, and probably jealous, but Annie kind of thrived on it instead of feeling bad.

"Hey, you!" Annie beamed, flinging her arms around Jason Wright's neck, knowing that beside her Imogen would be feeling jealous. Though whether that was jealous of Jason or Annie wasn't fully clear.

Annie had had a sneaking suspicion for a while that Imogen secretly *swung both ways*. She knew she'd had a crush on Jason Wright for years and she had seen the way Imogen gazed adoringly at her. Annie had hinted, for her own amusement just to make Imogen squirm, but she hadn't fully figured out how to take full advantage of this information yet.

She pulled away, squeal-laughing as she felt Chris Marshall come up behind her and grab her round the waist, spinning her off the ground. Chris was a complete creep, at least in Annie's eyes, but she played along anyway. Most of the time she liked to keep the college boys on side.

As Chris put her down, Annie turned to give him a playful shove. He just laughed and teased her. Annie's gaze was pulled over his shoulder by the feeling of eyes on her. Not just on her... practically boring holes into her skin.

Jamie Kirk. The college hottie who had never adored her the way she liked them to. Jamie had never fallen for Annie's bullshit and that irritated Annie. He was always standing up to her and calling her out.

She stared levelly back at him, meeting his glare. He was angry. Good.

He had a right to be, of course. He had only just gotten out of the hospital after his *oh-so-tragic* near fatal car accident... that Annie herself had caused when she messed with his brakes. She'd visited him in the hospital and made it very clear to him that she had done it, so that he would think twice about messing with her again.

She smirked as she turned her gaze away, turning back to Imogen and grabbing her hand to pull her deeper into the crowd. "Come dance with me!"

The hours passed in a colourful blur. The five girls danced and drank and laughed and revelled in their final freedom from the looming horror of the beginning of college, the biggest change in their lives so far. It would be strange not being at the high school anymore, though some of them would miss it more than others.

They all drifted to different corners of the party, interacting with everybody there. Everyone always wanted to talk to them.

Annie didn't see him at first and she wondered how long he'd been standing there. Charlie Baker. Lurking in the shadows at the edge of the woods. Was he here to find Sophie? No... judging from the way he was glaring at her, he was most definitely here to see her. *Fine*. Annie was in the mood for games tonight. Mainly due to the alcohol firing through her veins but wasn't she always in the mood for games?

She staggered away from Chris Marshall, thinking he was quite possibly the most repulsive guy she'd ever met and made a mental note to get her own back on him for drunkenly touching her up tomorrow.

The edge of the woods was a little out of sight and Charlie was standing behind a tree.

"Come to peep at all the under age girls, *Charlie?*" She trilled, blinking at him from beneath her false eyelashes. "Hoping one of them will get drunk enough to fall into bed with their poor, used up English teacher?"

The look on his face was reward enough and Annie laughed; a loud, drunken laugh. "I'm teasing. We're friends now, right? Friends tease friends."

Of course friends was a loose term for *'I've got you in my pocket and you'd better do everything I say or I'll get you thrown in jail'* but that was a bit of a mouthful.

"Piss off Annie." Charlie spat back through gritted teeth, his glare menacing through the darkness. "I'm not in the mood for any of your shit tonight. I'm only here to give you this." He shoved an envelope at her and turned to walk away but Annie grabbed him by the fabric of his jacket to stop him. He whirled round and yanked himself angrily from her grip, crossing his arms defensively over his chest and standing with his glare fixed on her.

She ignored him, opening the envelope and peering at the contents. Money. A lot of it. Her eyebrows shot up in surprise, something she would never have done sober, and she glanced at him.

"That's it. That's your lot. You're going to take this and you're going to leave me alone." He took a step towards her, uncrossing his arms. "No more grade changes, no more skipping classes and being marked as present on the register. No more free answer sheets… not one damn thing. I'm done with it. I'm done with *you*."

Honestly, Annie hadn't thought Charlie had it in him. He was always so nice and well-spoken that she'd assumed he would be more than easy to walk over… hadn't his mother walked over him? It was surprisingly easy to find that out and she planned to tell Ruby that he was the same way, an alcoholic with violent tendencies, wouldn't that keep her friend away from him once and for all? It had better.

"I want more." She announced, eyes still glued to the envelope, ignoring the spinning in her head. "This isn't enough to make it all just go away."

"I don't have that kind of money, Annie." He was getting angrier. *Good.*

"I don't think you understand how this works." Annie hissed, pocketing the envelope and turning her gaze on him. "I'm not just going to let this go. You're a dirty perv, Mr Baker. Everybody needs to know the truth."

She felt so dizzy that she felt like she might fall over against a tree at any second. Why had she had so much to drink?! *Idiot,* she thought to herself. What had she told herself? Control! *Always be in control.* Still, she continued to stand her ground. Staring Mr Baker down.

The argument didn't end there, though. He was furious, more furious than Annie had ever seen him, and when he reached out and grabbed her by the arm she had to admit that she was actually… a little scared. She turned and looked over her shoulder. Nobody could see them.

What was his problem? He was the one playing away with an eighteen year old, his own daughter's best friend no less!

He shook her slightly and said something that she didn't quite catch, but Annie didn't think she really wanted to know. She hadn't expected him to get this angry. Scared, maybe, at what she was threatening to do. Tense, anxious, nervous, worried, *compliant*... all things she had expected. Anger? Not one of them.

When, finally, he released his grip on her arm, Annie took a step back and shot him a glare. "You're going to pay for that."

"No, Annie. *You're* going to pay for that." He spat back at her, shooting one last glance towards the party, before turning and storming off through the woods.

Annie stood where she was, staring after him. *Whatever.* He'd sleep on it and realise that he was much better off doing what she asked. Creepy pushover English teachers probably didn't do so well in prison.

She turned at the sound of her phone pinging in her pocket, Charlie Baker completely forgotten, and checked her messages.

Annie had been receiving messages for the past year and a half. Strange texts, some threatening, some just *I'm watching you,* mostly just somebody acting like they were stalking her and she didn't know why they were doing it or who the hell they were... but Annie didn't like to feel like somebody else had an upper hand over her. By not knowing who the hell was watching her, she felt like she was losing a game she hadn't agreed to play.

"If you want to know who I am, meet me at your childhood tree."

More games? Ugh... Annie was far too drunk for riddles. But then, when she thought about it, she realised the answer was staring her straight in the face. Tree. Childhood. She and Chloe used to play under a specific tree in the woods when they were kids, back before Annie stopped giving a shit what her stupid sister got up to.

That was where this weirdo wanted to meet her? Meet, as in face to face? She was going to find out who this was *tonight?*

Annie, excited and dizzy, looked up and hurried off into the dark forest without even thinking twice about it.

It was pitch black and it would have been creepier if the raven-haired girl stumbling through the woods hadn't been too drunk to notice. Annie could feel her head spinning thanks to all of the alcohol she had consumed that night. She usually loved Jason Wright's parties but this one had taken a different turn.

A few different turns, actually. She was being watched and she knew it.

Annie Pierce didn't show weakness. Ever. She would never admit that she was scared... but she was still just an eighteen year old girl and somewhere inside she realised she'd been scared all along. Scared of what would happen if this person caught up with her.

She didn't want to become one of those stupid, pathetic girls who were just... nothing.

She didn't want to become Macey Cross, losing her popularity at the drop of a hat. To Annie, that was a fate worse than death.

She sat down, more like fell really, faint sounds from the party drifting through the forest. She was pissed off from her fight with Charlie Baker only five minutes earlier and she suddenly realised that she was on the verge of tears.

Annie Pierce didn't cry.

Crying was *weakness*. It proved you weren't strong enough, and she had promised herself she would never, *ever* give in to that. At that moment, she hated herself. It must have been the alcohol. It was making everything feel worse than it really was. Of course. That was it.

"Annie? What's wrong?" The voice was unexpected, and close, and Annie jumped. Her heavy eyes fell upon the face of Oliver Brown, Macey Cross's ex boyfriend. At first she thought he was imagining him because hadn't he moved to North Yorkshire a while back? What was he doing in town?

Annie didn't even care. Without thinking, she fell forward and flung her arms around him, just needing to feel like everything was going to be okay.

God, she was so fucking drunk and she hated it. She *never* got this out of control when she was drunk. It was a feeling she wasn't used to. Annie was *always* in control.

She started sobbing, a string of nonsensical words tumbling from her lips. She realised she was talking about the mystery texter, calling them a *"fucking stalker."*

When would they give up and leave her alone? What did they really want? It was unnerving and it made Annie feel like she was losing… which she didn't like or appreciate.

Annie hadn't hugged somebody because she needed comfort for a long time. For some reason it was a nice feeling and she wondered if it was time to just forget all about this weirdo. Go back to the party, clean herself up, and have a good time with her friends. Whoever it was would get bored if she didn't give them anything to react to. Right?

Then the sound of her phone broke through the silence and she jumped, leaping back and hitting the buttons. She squinted through her tears, staring at the words.

"I'm not going to wait here all night."

Oliver was forgotten as she turned and crashed through the trees, stumbling a little, but she knew where she had to go. There was a tiny clearing with a tree that she and her sister used to play beside when they were kids. They pretended to be explorers or something, she couldn't quite remember.

"Annie?!" Oliver's confused and irritated voice followed her but she didn't even react to it.

All she knew was that she had to get there, *if* she could remember the way in the dark while extremely intoxicated… Annie tried not to worry about that.

There was only one thought on her mind. Tonight, she was going to find out who was following her and make them regret it.

"Shit!" Yet another voice sounded through the darkness.

Annie stopped walking again, swaying. Who was that now?

"Who's there?" She snapped, narrowing her eyes as she scanned the area.

There was movement and the sound of branches being moved. Then a figure swam into view.

"Oh." Annie relaxed, rolling her eyes. "It's you."

Sarah Clarke. What an absolute bore. The girl was a complete headcase with absolutely no personality. She had always been so obsessed with Annie, probably wanted to be her or something. She'd been locked up in the loony bin for the last few months. Annie hadn't even known she was out yet. Though, of course, Annie was the reason she had even been in there. But whatever, not really. She didn't force those pills down her throat.

"What are you lurking out here for?" She demanded, getting dizzier by the second. "You weren't invited to the party."

"I'm not… I wasn't…" Sarah stammered and Annie rolled her eyes again.

"Yeah, whatever. I don't have time for this." Annie snapped, moving to rush past the girl, shoulder checking her in the process.

"I'm fucking sick of it!" Came the surprising shout from Sarah, followed by the even more surprising shove.

Annie stumbled, steadying herself on a nearby tree, turning to look back at the blonde. She smirked a little. "Well, look who's grown a pair." She chuckled, shaking her head. "You better watch yourself, *crazy*."

Sarah scowled back at her and Annie laughed. Loudly. Which seemingly triggered something in Sarah because the next thing she knew she felt a sharp pain in her shoulders as she was roughly shoved once more, and then she was falling.

She went down hard and fast and then there was a sickening *crunch* as the back of her head connected with a rock. "Fuck…" She muttered, but Sarah was already running away, she could hear the quick footsteps receding. She'd pay for that tomorrow.

Annie lay there for a while, feeling nauseous. Pain was shooting through her. She wasn't sure how long she was there for before she felt somebody trying to pull her up from the ground. Annie groaned and resisted at first but she eventually allowed herself to be helped back on to her feet.

When Annie was up, and focused, and realised that Poppy Hart had been the one to pull her up onto her feet, she scowled and yanked her hand away from the brunette's.

She *hated* Poppy, she was perfectly aware of that despite how drunk she'd managed to get herself.

God, her head wouldn't stop spinning... and it didn't help that it was now throbbing thanks to Sarah bloody Clarke. That bitch was going to pay for that one. Maybe, with any luck, she'd actually succeed at killing herself once Annie was through with her and everyone would finally be rid of her.

"I'm *fine*." Annie hissed, clenching her teeth and squeezing her eyes shut against the pain, wincing as she touched the back of her head. Was that blood on her hand? Fantastic... at least she'd have a reason to play up for sympathy from her mother tomorrow. That would really piss Chloe off.

She *almost* smiled at the thought but Poppy was still there so she rolled her eyes, turning her gaze on the older girl again. She was wobbling around and staring at Annie like she didn't even know where she was. How much had *she* had to drink? Probably a lot more than Annie by the look of her... and Annie had had a *lot*.

"Someone's enjoyed themselves." She mused, just thinking out loud, and glanced around. She was keen to get going because she was still on the hunt for this stalker freak.

She couldn't quite remember where the tree was, the one she and Chloe had played under as kids. A pang of longing shot through her when she remembered those days but she quickly pushed it away. Being drunk made her weak apparently.

Poppy didn't speak and Annie snorted, annoyed. "Cat got your fucking tongue, Hart?"

By this time Poppy wasn't even paying any attention to her whatsoever. She was looking round, as though she were searching for something, and Annie sighed heavily. She wasn't in the mood for this.

"God, lie down.." She muttered, annoyed, and tugged not so gently at Poppy's arm. She helped the brunette to settle down on the ground with her back against the tree.

"Did you hear that?" Poppy finally murmured softly, her eyes fluttering shut even as she spoke.

Annie ignored her "Stay here." She said firmly, glaring at Poppy because she was such a nuisance. "I'll... ugh, *god*, I'll come back and walk you home."

She winced again as a stab of pain went through her temples. Poppy wasn't even listening. Her eyes were still closed. Had she fallen asleep?

"Bitch." Annie muttered, standing up and stomping away through the woods. She'd probably come back and get Poppy home... play the good Samaritan. She wasn't *all* bad, after all. Something about leaving another girl unconscious in the woods all night didn't sit right with her.

She continued to trek through the woods, grabbing onto trees because everything was spinning.

What time was it?

She took her phone out and frowned at the screen, squinting.

Nope... too blurry... and Chloe hadn't even called her back.

Bitch.

Whatever… she didn't need her. Annie shoved her phone back in her pocket and instantly froze. Was that footsteps?

She stood very still, listening, holding her breath… but everything was silent. All she could hear was the thudding of her own heart in her chest, threatening to burst.

"Fucking hell." She muttered. Paranoid now too. *Awesome.* She started walking again, hoping that she was heading in the right direction.

The woods were eerily silent. Annie couldn't even hear the sounds of the party music floating through the forest anymore and, not that she would ever admit it, she was nervous. Anxiety and adrenaline were coursing through her entire body. Her head was buzzing with alcohol and she was unsteady on her feet.

A twig snapped somewhere behind her and she spun, caught off guard. Was that *them?* A tree branch rustled unnaturally as if in response.

"Who's there?" She called, suddenly feeling like she was in a horror movie. Maybe she should have brought Jason with her or something… but she could handle it. She could handle anything.

Anyway, this freak wasn't going to hurt her. They probably wanted to knock her down into social isolation (like that was even *possible!*) They didn't plan on throttling her.

"Oliver, if that's you, just go away!" She shouted, suddenly remembering he'd been right there not even twenty minutes ago, but no reply came.

God, she couldn't believe he'd caught her crying in the middle of the forest. She could believe even less that she had actually told him she had a stalker. Annie would have to remedy that as soon as possible. Tell him she was just drunk and stupid, maybe promise him a couple of dates or something to shut him up. *Everybody* wanted a date with Annie Pierce. She sure was an upgrade from Macey Cross.

Another rustling sound pulled her out of her thoughts and she became alert once again, spotting movement through the dark as her eyesight adjusted even more.

"Oh. *You.*" Annie sneered, rolling her eyes and placing her hands arrogantly on her hips. She tilted her chin up and jutted her jaw at the person who had come into view. "Didn't think I'd be seeing you again until it was time for you to pay up."

"I'm not doing this, Annie. You're mental if you think I'm going to give you another penny." Came the agitated response and, for a brief second, Annie thought she saw something deep in their eyes.

Fear. A dangerous thing.

"Oh, I think you will." She spat back, glaring venomously at the familiar face. "Unless you want *everybody* to know what you did!" She turned around, ending the conversation.

She was dizzy and she didn't want to look at them anymore, didn't want to continue this tonight. As long as they were here, her stalker wouldn't show themselves. Annie needed to find out who this person was and then she would be able to figure out how to stop them before they did some real damage to her life.

"I won't!" Came from the figure behind her, who clearly wasn't done yet.

Annie moved to turn again, ready to hiss a response, but she wasn't quick enough.

The next thing she knew there was a sharp, blinding pain in the back of her head as the cut she'd received from the rock after Sarah Clarke's shove was added to by the force of an even larger rock connecting with the back of her skull.

She fell to the ground, though she didn't scream. She was too surprised for that.

Darkness took her rather quickly and the last thing Annie Pierce ever heard was her killer's cry of frustration.

one

The town of Baberton woke with the sound of birds, their sweet song cutting through the cool morning air.

Imogen Ford woke with a groan. The light streaming in through her curtains only made her retreat further underneath her duvet. If she could just stay here all day that would be great. In fact, if she could just stay here for the rest of her life, that would be better.

The sound of a child crying broke through the birdsong and Imogen sighed, knowing that she couldn't exactly stay here and leave Brooklyn hungry and crying. Eric would be at work by now so it's not like she could just let him get their daughter.

Imogen threw the covers off and swung her legs over the side of the bed. God, she already knew today was going to be a long one. Pulling on her dressing gown, Imogen padded through to Brooklyn's room, smiling as she saw the little girl sitting up, tears rolling down her chubby cheeks.

"What's going on, silly girl?" She cooed as she leaned into the crib and gathered Brooklyn into her arms. "Let's go get some breakfast, yeah?" The baby's babbling brought another smile to her face.

Imogen wasn't sure what she would do without that little face. She hadn't had too many reasons to get up in the morning or to smile before the little girl had come along. Yes, she'd had Eric and he'd been amazing, but Imogen had struggled since the end of high school. Since that fateful night…

She snapped out of her thoughts and set about fixing Brooklyn a little bottle of milk. Looking down at that little face made Imogen feel a lot better than she had when she'd woken up minutes earlier.

Two dogs wound themselves around Imogen's ankles, waiting impatiently for her to be finished with the baby so she could feed them.

"Come on then." She chuckled, filling the bowls up by the back door, watching them dive on the food as if they hadn't eaten in years.

A few hours later, the phone rang. "Hey, honey." Imogen said with a smile, knowing already that it was her husband checking in on her.

"Hey, you." She could hear the smile on his lips too. "How are my favourite girls doing?"

"Oh, you know. Living it up, lots of cocktails." She joked.

Eric's laugh came back soft and amused. "Uh huh, I'll bet. I gotta run but I just wanted to check in, okay… did you take your meds?"

Imogen bit her lip and held back a sigh. "Yeah… I did."

Imogen had found out that she was schizophrenic when she was twenty-one, three years after her best friend Annie Pierce had vanished. God, so many years ago now. So many tragedies ago.

"Sorry, I know, I know…" He replied, knowing full well that it was a sensitive subject. He knew that Imogen didn't like that part of her and she didn't want it, but he definitely worried… he had seen her off her medication and after Brooklyn was born, things had been a bit difficult for her. So, of course he worried. Still, he didn't want to be pushy. "Babe, I've got to get going to this meeting, but I'll see you tonight, alright?"

"Okay… bye. Love you."

"Love you too."

The rest of the morning went on quietly and slowly. Brooklyn settled down and Imogen watched some television, half watching the news and half just scrolling on her phone. She saw Kelly Sharpe's updates on facebook and sighed softly.

Imogen missed her old friends but things had changed so drastically as the years dragged on. After Annie went missing, the group had all drifted apart and now they rarely spoke or saw each other. The only one Imogen saw most often was Ruby Peterson and that was only because she had a daughter around the same age as her own.

Kelly, though… she had spiralled completely out of control in the years following everything. She was all about drink and drugs and boys now. Imogen didn't like it but it's not like she could do anything. Kelly had always been far too stubborn to be told what to do anyway and Imogen had never really been one to do too much pushing.

She shut her phone screen off and sighed, turning to focus on playing with Brooklyn.

Three hours later, Imogen was sitting down by the river, Brooklyn in her pram beside the bench she was sitting on. She was gazing across the water, lost in a memory from years ago.

She and Annie used to come here. They would sit and talk for hours and listen to the water. Just the two of them in their own little world. Those were the days Imogen lived for back then. Annie had been so enchanting and Imogen had definitely been under her spell, completely.

Back then there had been five of them: Imogen Ford, Annie Pierce, Sophie Baker, Ruby Peterson and Kelly Sharpe. Annie was their leader.

They were the five most popular girls in school and everybody either loved them and wanted to be them or loathed them and maybe even feared them.

Imogen couldn't remember them being overly unkind, however she did know that she had done a few things she wasn't entirely proud of now looking back, at Annie's bidding... but Annie was *very* convincing. Sometimes it felt like she could make you do anything.

"Hey..." A soft voice from beside her broke Imogen out of her reverie and she looked up. Nina Everett. The second girl she ever loved... and lost.

"Hi." Imogen glanced at Brooklyn, checking she was okay, and then looked back up at Nina. "How are you?"

She'd always hated that question. *How are you?* It never felt sincere somehow but everyone always asked it anyway.

"I've been good… yeah. Not bad. What about you?" Nina gestured to the pram with a smile. "She's getting big.."

"Yeah, she really is… too quickly." Imogen worked up a chuckle as she glanced over at her daughter again, then looked back to Nina. She looked good and Imogen hated that it still caused a flicker of pain to shoot through her.

There was always that one, wasn't there? That one *what if?*

She wouldn't change her life for anything but sometimes Imogen had a terrible habit of living in the past, of pining for the old days, of getting too wrapped up in nostalgia. She had been that way ever since she was a little girl and she'd never been able to shake it.

"Do you want to sit?" She asked but Nina shook her head.

"Oh, no, thanks but I have to go and see my brother about something." Nina shrugged. "I'll… see you around though."

"Yeah, sure." A smile. "See you."

That night Eric came home from the newspaper and he seemed distracted. He was quieter and a little broody. Imogen asked him what was wrong but he didn't say anything and she eventually gave up and went to bed.

Sixteen hours later, the story broke.

They'd finally found Annie Pierce.

Her body had been found buried in the woods.

two

"Yeah, well you should have fucking told me!" Imogen snapped, rocking a fussy Brooklyn as she tried to get her to just drink her damn bottle.

"And what good would it have done? Look how upset you are!" Eric hated that he'd had to keep the story from her but he knew what Annie meant to her. Despite the fact that the girl in question had been his biggest damn bully growing up, he knew that his wife had loved her and he knew news of her body being found after all these years would hurt. Would sting. Could possibly *break* her.

Imogen sighed, shaking her head, struggling with Brooklyn as she put the unwanted bottle down. "She was my best friend, Eric."

"I know, love."

Imogen went quiet, looking down at Brooklyn before sighing and moving to hand her off to Eric. "I'm going for a walk."

"Immy--" But she had already put the leads on the dogs and was out the door before he could stop her.

* * *

Imogen found herself wandering down past the woods.

They were closed off due to Annie's body being found so she couldn't go in, not that she actually wanted to. They were giving her the absolute creeps to be totally honest.

Of course, after all this time, she hadn't really thought Annie could still be alive out there somewhere, she supposed she'd always known she was… *dead.*

But to *suppose it* and to *know it* for certain are two completely different things and Imogen wasn't sure how to process it.

She walked towards the houses, finding herself being pulled towards the Pierce family home. Not by the dogs, just by her subconscious.

She stood there for a few moments, sort of staring at the house. She felt a bit creeped out and maybe a little out of it as she looked at the building. So many memories.

Imogen tended to completely avoid this street in general. She'd barely returned since childhood, though she had seen the Pierce family around. It was always strangest seeing Chloe; Annie's identical twin sister.

"Hey…"

Imogen practically jumped out of her skin, turning. She hadn't even realised that anybody else was around, let alone right next to her. It took her a second to fully register the face. Ruby.

"Hey." She returned the greeting, trying for a smile and most likely failing miserably.

"You too, huh?" Imogen turned slightly and gestured towards Annie's house.

Ruby nodded. "Yeah…"

Imogen sighed, crossing her arms. "Yeah…" She echoed.

If she had to guess, they were both feeling the same pull of nostalgia today. Of sadness and unrest. Perhaps grief. Imogen knew that she was grieving, but she wasn't one hundred percent about the others. Some of their relationships with Annie had been complex. But they had all loved her. Right?

Imogen turned her gaze away, frowning as someone with a big camera came driving up the road, took a bunch of pictures and drove off again. Great. She could see tomorrow's headline already. *Mourners at the Pierce House.*

"Let's get out of here." She said, turning away completely and beginning to walk again. She didn't really care whether or not Ruby would follow but she just had to get away. It felt so heavy to be standing here and she couldn't take it anymore.

Ruby followed behind her and eventually fell into step beside her. The two walked in silence for a little while before Imogen looked up again. "How's Hope?" A change of subject was always nice, right?

Ruby smiled, nodding. "Yeah, she's great... shooting up now though, soon she'll be too big for cuddles."

Imogen couldn't help but chuckle. It was exactly the same thing she had thought not even the other day.

It had been strange at first, when Ruby had her daughter. Not because none of them had imagined her with a kid. No, Imogen had always thought Ruby was very maternal.

It was strange because the little girl's father was also Sophie Baker's father. He had also been their old English teacher back in high school. The two hadn't gotten together until after poor Sophie's body was found in the woods, years after Annie vanished, but it was still a strange situation to get used to.

The two of them seemed very happy though. Ruby seemed to brighten up Charlie Baker's dreary life after his wife left him and his daughter died. So Imogen didn't give it too much thought and she didn't judge. They were all adults now, right? Anyway… life was too short. Imogen and her remaining friends knew that better than a lot of other people.

"Are you alright?" Ruby asked. "Really?"

Imogen shrugged. "Yes… no… I don't really know. Y'know?"

Ruby nodded, looking very serious. "Yeah, I know."

three

Imogen was sitting in the living room, by the window, staring up at the sky. She had put Brooklyn down hours ago and she had been sitting here since, glass of wine in hand, just thinking.

She hadn't cried yet. She wasn't sure if she could. It was kind of like she didn't have any tears left, after crying them all out already when she was eighteen. She had cried over Annie a thousand times over and then, a few years later, Sophie too.

The door opened and she turned her head, seeing Eric coming into the room. She worked up as best a smile as she could, though it didn't likely hit the mark. Imogen wasn't really angry anymore, she was more... deflated.

"Hey." Eric's voice was gentle, soft, as he came over and placed a kiss on the top of her head, giving her a tiny squeeze.

"Hey." She replied, feeling exhausted. "Wine?" She gestured to the bottle sitting nearby and the other empty glass, as she stood up and moved over to the sofa.

Eric nodded, moving to fill up a glass for himself and then sitting down on the couch. Silence stretched between them for a few moments before he opened his mouth to speak again.

"Are you okay?"

Imogen shrugged. "I don't know." She said, having another sip of wine and sighing. "Not really."

It was probably obvious but Imogen just didn't know what to feel or how she should be feeling. Was she sad? Yes. Was she angry? Yes. Was she confused? Yes. Was she numb? A little.

"I mean... I always knew that..." Imogen trailed off, the words dancing in her head - *that she was dead.* Of course she'd known, they all had. Annie wasn't the type to just up and disappear despite her impulsive seeming personality. She liked the attention too much for that, she wouldn't just vanish and fade out of everybody's memory.

Still, it had been nice to sort of be able to pretend that she had convinced herself that could be true. That maybe Annie had skipped town without a word so that, through her vanishing, she could keep her name on everybody's lips. It was easy enough to convince herself that Annie would have gotten a thrill out of that. Knowing that everybody back home would be going crazy for years wondering what happened to her.

Now she couldn't do that.

Now she had to admit that Annie was dead.

She had to admit that Annie was dead and somebody knew she had been buried underground for the last six years.

Imogen's thoughts hadn't really taken her there before now. That the night of Jason Wright's end of summer party, somebody had *murdered* her best friend and buried her in the same woods they used to explore when they were children.

A wave of nausea suddenly washed over her. Oh, God... Annie had been *murdered* that night. By *who?* Was it somebody she *knew?*

"Immy... Im, just breathe, okay?" Eric had reached out to take her wine glass off her and set it to the side, moving to crouch in front of her with his hands on her knees.

"Breathe..." He mimicked breathing in and out slowly and eventually Imogen managed to get a hold of herself enough to copy him.

Breathing in, *one, two, three.*

Breathing out, *one, two three.*

"I'm alright... I'm fine." She said eventually, running her hands over her face with a sigh. This was all so awful and she suddenly felt overcome with exhaustion.

"I just want to go to sleep, okay?"

Eric nodded, not saying anything as he moved to stand, setting his own glass on the table, reaching for his wife's hand so he could help her upstairs.

four

"Come on, Brookie…" Imogen pleaded, bouncing Brooklyn gently on her hip as she tried to get her to drink from the bottle. The little girl was screaming, clearly hungry but also clearly not realising that she could quite easily remedy that problem if she just took the damn bottle.

Maybe that meant it would be easy to wean her off entirely in the next couple of months but for right now it was a bit of a nightmare.

"I know, I know.." Imogen sighed, carefully sitting down on the couch to see if it would be easier to feed her daughter without standing.

She thought idly about how nice it must be to just be able to scream whenever you felt like you had to.

When did people stop doing that? Imogen wondered.

Brooklyn eventually took the bottle and Imogen smiled lightly, mostly in relief. She was still reeling from the last couple of days and her patience was thin.

Annie's parents had finally decided to hold a funeral, in a week or so. Imogen was already dreading it.

When Annie disappeared, though there was an unspoken knowledge that she was likely dead, the Pierce family hadn't had any sort of funeral or memorial service. It was their way of holding onto the hope that Annie was still alive.

Now those hopes were dashed completely and Imogen felt for them. She really did. They were all such a big part of her childhood, even Annie's sister Chloe despite the fact that Annie had mostly just poked fun at her.

Imogen hadn't really seen Chloe properly in... years. It was too difficult. To look at her face and see her beloved best friend. There were differences between the two girls of course, but for all intents and purposes they were identical twins, and Imogen had always found it too eerie. Too sad. She felt bad about it but she also did her best not to think about it.

It was just easier that way.

The day passed by in a bit of a slow blur as Imogen did her best to fill the time, and her mind, with caring for Brooklyn and some planning for when she went back to work next month.

Imogen wasn't sure if she was looking forward to going back to work or not. She was worried that she wouldn't be able to concentrate. She was a primary school teacher and she loved it but she hadn't been back to work since before she had Brooklyn. A year before, in fact.

Imogen didn't like to think back on that time because it was painful.

It was embarrassing too, a little, because she had gone completely off the deep end. She had stopped taking her schizophrenia medication when she fell pregnant, though kind of against doctors recommendations, because she didn't want to affect the baby.

This was a year or so after Sophie Baker had turned up *dead*.

It had been such a horrible tragedy. It was the first time Imogen felt her old friend group thrust back together due to something awful.

After Annie, they'd all drifted apart. After Sophie, they'd all felt a sick pull back together. They didn't stay together, of course, it was all just extra painful, like setting an unhealed blister on fire.

Imogen was the one who had found Sophie. Her body lying there in the woods after falling down an incline and breaking her neck. Sophie's beautiful pale face lit up in the sunlight and her strawberry blonde hair spread around her head like a halo. She really was an angel.

Imogen had sort of snapped after that. It was a break triggered by the trauma, but her mind had gotten all twisted.

It had started as dreams. Nightmares, really. The image of Sophie's decomposing body standing in the corner of her room screaming, while the flesh peeled from her bones, haunted Imogen's nights.

Then, it started to seep into her waking hours too and she would see Sophie standing on street corners or walking through the crowd in the middle of town. Imogen would run after her, pushing people out of the way, but by the time she rounded the corner Sophie would be gone.

Before she knew it, she'd been running all over town, chasing a hallucination of her dead friend.

Her mind became so paranoid due to these hallucinations that she started to believe that everybody was lying to her. That everybody was saying Sophie was dead when she was really still alive.

She could *see* her, after all!

A lot of stuff from that time was a bit blurry. Time ran into itself and she barely slept as her schizophrenia took over. She remembered stealing from the corner shop, arguing with a man at the bus station, getting high. Most of the time she'd just been hiding in odd places or walking around, panicked and stressed, wondering why nobody else was seeing Sophie when she was *right there*.

This lasted for a few months until eventually she'd completely freaked out on poor Charlie Baker, ranting about Sophie and how everybody was lying. She'd probably said a lot of distressing and upsetting things but she hadn't thought about it.

Then she'd taken off and had gotten lost in the woods, until she'd stumbled upon the place where she had found Sophie.

She ended up in a hospital for a few weeks, and diagnosed with schizophrenia.

Later, when she found out she was pregnant, Imogen had been scared that she'd hurt her unborn baby. She stopped her medication cold turkey but was eventually convinced to go back on it and luckily nothing was wrong with Brooklyn and the rest of the time went smoothly enough.

* * *

Now that Annie's body had finally been found in those same woods, it kept bringing back the images of Sophie too.

Imogen knew her mind was just making connections due to the fact she'd lost two friends in the same sort of way.

Though obviously Sophie had a terrible accident and Annie... well, somebody had buried her under the dirt so obviously somebody *killed* her in the first place.

It was so horrible to think about, it made Imogen feel cold and numb.

She could be walking past this person every day and not even know it. Imogen had gone over everybody who was at the party that night in her head. Over and over, trying to figure out if she'd missed anything at the time... but she just couldn't imagine any of those people doing something like that. *Murder.*

Yes, Annie could be a little bit difficult to handle sometimes. She had been manipulative and played with people, but she was the Queen Bee of Baberton High. She had a reputation to uphold, right?

Imogen still, after all this time, found herself making excuses for Annie's behaviour. Annie had been nothing but a bully, really. When she looked back on it all, on some of the things Annie had done or said, or made her friends do or say, it made Imogen cringe. She was ashamed that she had blindly followed Annie's lead, done anything the girl asked without question.

Imogen had loved Annie in more ways than just her best friend, she'd been *in love* with her, and Annie had known it too. She'd used it to her own advantage - hell she'd even *kissed* Annie once out at the ice rink, then the other girl had laughed in her face - and Imogen *still* found herself making excuses.

It frustrated her but Imogen would always love Annie and she would always feel the pain of her loss. She was the biggest and best part of her childhood and after Annie vanished, Imogen had felt lost and more alone than she had ever felt before.

The doorbell went, pulling Imogen out of her thoughts as she stood from where she'd been playing with Brooklyn, and moved over to answer it. She peered through the spyhole and smiled to herself as she unlocked the door and pulled it open.

"Hey!" Imogen beamed, stepping to the side so her friend could come inside. "What's up?"

Sasha Miller smiled back at her as she moved inside, shrugging her shoulders. "Hey, you." She leaned in for a half-hug before she moved past Imogen to fuss over Brooklyn. "Just thought I'd stop in and see you guys." She looked up at Imogen. "How are you doing?"

Imogen was tired of that question but Sasha was her best friend these days and she shrugged, moving to collapse on the couch with a sigh. "I'm okay.... I don't know. It's weird, you know?"

Sasha nodded, looking sympathetically back at her before she turned back to focus on little Brooklyn, playing with a pile of blocks in front of her. Brooklyn watched closely, entranced.

She always loved when Sasha came to visit, she was one of her favourite people, which Imogen thought was adorable.

Imogen and Sasha hadn't always been this close. Back when they were in high school, Annie had kind of had some sort of vendetta against Sasha. She'd pushed and bullied her and even told Imogen this big lie about how she'd seen Sasha cheating on her boyfriend Harvey Newell at some party Annie had been to. Harvey was a nice guy so Imogen was upset for him.

She didn't realise Annie was making it up at the time, she didn't think her best friend would do something like that to her.

So, at Annie's urging, Imogen had marched right up to Harvey and told him what Annie saw. Though of course, Annie said that Harvey would believe Imogen over her, so she convinced Imogen to lie to Harvey's face and say *she'd* witnessed the cheating herself.

Harvey was heartbroken and ended things with Sasha there and then in a dramatic, public fashion, and then Harvey and Annie ended up dating for a while. Sasha was angry after that and had it out for her, thinking Imogen had purposefully set her up, but Imogen thought she was just upset she'd been caught.

It wasn't until after school when Annie was still just missing, and she and Sasha met on the dancefloor of local nightclub AJ's, and drunkenly talked it all out that Imogen finally realised what had happened. That Annie had taken her for a complete fool.

She'd apologised profusely but Sasha had put it in the past already, and she was in a good place now anyway. She'd left all that Annie high school bullshit behind her.

After that the two kept in touch and eventually they were as close as you could be.

Sasha was probably the one person besides Eric that Imogen told everything to.

Sasha looked up from where she sat on the floor beside Brooklyn, studying her friend's face briefly. "You're allowed to not be okay, you know." She said gently.

Imogen smiled a little, though it probably didn't reach her eyes, and nodded. "Yeah… I know… thanks." She did know that… right? She thought she did, anyway.

She was quiet for a few moments before she spoke again. "It's just weird, you know? I mean, I think we all knew that she was..." *Dead*. She still hadn't said it out loud. She hadn't said *Annie's dead* or *Annie was killed* out loud. In her head it was easier but saying the words made them seem more real.

Sasha nodded because she understood what Imogen was saying. Truthfully, the whole town had probably known on some level that Annie was most likely dead, but there had always been that glimmer of hope without a body, no matter how many years passed.

"Anyway, it's just... strange to have it confirmed, I guess." Imogen continued, shrugging as she kept her gaze on Brooklyn, who was intensely focused on a specific block. "I don't know what I'm feeling." She admitted.

"That's alright." Sasha replied, looking up at her from her position on the floor. "It's bound to bring up all sorts of horrible, conflicting shit. You know? I don't think you need to put a label on it."

Imogen nodded. She knew that Sasha was right and she knew that it would take time. Sophie's death still weighed heavily on her soul and now Annie was confirmed dead too and it was just... a lot.

"At least they're together..." She said quietly, looking at Sasha, who knew what she meant and smiled softly, reaching out to reassuringly pat her knee.

"Right." Imogen stood up. *Enough moping,* she decided. "Want some tea or coffee?" She asked, heading for the kitchen before she threw a look over her shoulder. "Wine?"

"Wine." Sasha agreed with an amused chuckle.

five

The next day, Imogen went round to Ruby's. They'd arranged a playdate for Brooklyn and Hope which she was quite looking forward to.

Imogen thought it was nice that her daughter could play with the daughter of one of her best friends.

Even if they weren't as close as they used to be, she and Ruby were definitely still on speaking terms.

It was Kelly that Imogen had barely seen in years. The girl had gone a little wild. Well, more than a little, but she supposed she couldn't blame her.

The door opened and Imogen was face to face with Charlie Baker. It was still so weird, she just saw him as her teacher, as one of the grown ups who'd been around when they were younger. She knew a lot of people had given Charlie and Ruby hell for their relationship but Imogen just thought they were brave to continue in spite of it all. It wasn't really anybody else's business, not even hers.

"Hey." She smiled, moving inside carefully as Charlie opened the door wider to let her in.

"Hi." He smiled back, reaching for his jacket from the coat rack beside the front door. "I was just heading out." He smiled down at Brooklyn, then looked back up to Imogen, offering her one more smile. "Have fun."

"Bye!" Charlie called as he reached for the door again and slipped out into the afternoon.

"Don't forget your--!" Came Ruby's voice but Charlie was already gone. She sighed, rolling her eyes but she wasn't annoyed, just a little amused. "He's always in such a rush." She said, smiling a little but it didn't look one hundred percent genuine.

Imogen worked up a chuckle, but she felt a pang of sadness. She knew that it was because Charlie kept himself busy and on the move so he didn't have to think about poor Sophie. Imogen couldn't imagine losing Brooklyn, especially like that, so her heart did go out to him. Still, he'd seemed more of a mess before Hope was born. It seemed that Ruby and the new arrival really kept him going.

"Eric's at work, I take it?" Ruby asked as she and Imogen moved through to the living room where Hope was playing with some toy animals. Imogen took Brooklyn out of her pram and set her down beside Hope, smiling as the two of them got stuck into the game.

"Yeah." Imogen nodded, following Ruby towards the kitchen area, glancing over her shoulder at the girls before she turned back, leaning against the doorframe. "With... *everything*... they're pretty busy at the newspaper."

Ruby hummed, nodding, as she put the kettle on and grabbed them some cups for tea. "I can imagine."

Imogen didn't want to keep talking about it. About Annie. It made her sad and it made her think of Sophie and that day she'd found her and just... it made her want to cry. All of it. Imogen was scared that if she started, she wouldn't ever stop.

"Have you seen Kelly recently?" She found herself asking, though was surprised she'd bothered. She hadn't heard a thing about or from Kelly since well before Annie's body was found.

"Nope." Ruby shook her head and sighed. Ruby and Kelly had been very close back in the day, and now it seemed like Kelly was close to nobody. "As far as I know, she's not even in town. She's in London with some bloke."

"Seriously?" Imogen made a face, moving to sit down at the dining table as Ruby set their mugs of tea down. "Hmm."

"Yeah… I think she met him on a night out and they just took off. You know Kel… impulsive is her middle name."

"True." Imogen nodded, though she couldn't help but feel like Kelly was just acting too recklessly. She didn't want to end up attending *another* funeral.

Still, it wasn't her place anymore, so she did her best not to overthink about it.

"Anyway, how's the book coming?" Imogen moved the subject along, deciding that was probably the best thing.

"Oh, it's great, actually." Ruby smiled in response, launching into details about her new story. She'd always been such a creative person, since school. She was always scribbling stories down in her notebooks and Imogen had always known she'd be a writer when she was older. It was just meant to be.

The afternoon passed by nicely. Imogen had a great time chatting and catching up with Ruby, it was just what she'd needed. The kids had a great time too, making a complete mess of the living room and nearly tripping Charlie up when he came home and didn't notice their toys.

Imogen left still smiling and feeling a little better than she had all week. It was an incredibly welcome change.

***

When Eric got home that night, he was glad to see Imogen looking lighter. She was in the kitchen cooking pasta for dinner, humming away to herself. He smiled as he came up behind her and wrapped his arms around her waist.

"Good evening, my beautiful wife."

Imogen laughed, turning her head slightly so she could see him. "Hello, my handsome husband."

If Brooklyn was old enough to really understand what they were saying, Imogen had no doubt she'd be sitting in the corner pretending to gag right about now, and the thought made her chuckle.

"How was work?" She asked, turning her attention back to the dinner, stirring in the sauce and the veggies.

"Work was...." Eric hummed, flicking the kettle on so he could make himself his usual post-work cup of coffee. "It was hectic." He said, glancing over at her.

Imogen wondered if he was too anxious to say anything specific in case she went off at him again or something. She knew there was more to print than Annie's body being found but she also knew that the local paper had it pretty high on their list at the moment.

"Yeah? I'll bet Nikki's loving it." She said, focusing on the pasta.

Nikki Clayworth was Eric's top writer, and also his ex-fiancee. Imogen used to be so, so jealous of the other blonde but ultimately she and Eric had been so wrong for each other and Imogen and Eric had been so right. Things tended to work themselves out in the end.

"Oh, yeah, you know Nikki. She thrives off stress." He chuckled, leaning in to press a light kiss to her cheek. "I'm gonna go get changed." Eric added, studying her face for one moment longer as if making sure she really was okay, then he turned away. He gave Brooklyn a quick kiss before he headed for the stairs and went on up to change for dinner.

* * *

That night, Imogen was trying to read the final chapter of Ruby's last book, but she couldn't concentrate. She had read the same sentence fifteen times and she was driving herself mad.

Eventually she just closed the book and lay down, turning the light off and lying there in the dark.

Eric was already asleep beside her and Imogen listened to his soft breathing for a while. It was comforting to know he was there but she still couldn't switch off.

She tossed and turned for what felt like forever, until the small stupid hours of the morning, and eventually she just slipped out of bed with an irritated sigh and crept down the stairs.

She settled herself on the couch in the dim glow of the fairy lights she'd strung up on the wall behind the sofa, sipping a cup of tea and trying to figure out what was keeping her up.

The answer was obvious enough in the end.

Annie.

Sophie.

Imogen felt guilty for enjoying herself, for having a good day.

She grabbed her phone to text Sasha, who turned out to still be up herself. That wasn't unusual though, Sasha had been a night owl her whole life.

They texted back and forth for a little while and Imogen told her about her day, and eventually about why she couldn't sleep. About how she'd been feeling, about the guilt.

Sasha, as usual, listened and offered advice, and did what she could to put her mind at ease. When she stopped responding, it was evident she had fallen asleep and Imogen set her phone aside and just sat with her thoughts for another few quiet moments.

Eventually Imogen drifted back upstairs and fell asleep curled up beside Eric.

six

A week later, Imogen was staring at her reflection in the full-length bedroom mirror. She was wearing a black knee-length dress and shoes and her hair was pulled back from her face.

Today was Annie's funeral.

She didn't know what word to attribute to how she was feeling. Sad. Anxious. Numb. All of the above? This whole thing just felt so completely surreal. After Sophie's funeral, Imogen had hoped she would never have to go through another one of these again. That was a problem with getting older though, wasn't it? More and more funerals.

Though of course, if Annie had been found *when* she died, they would have all been eighteen. Which Imogen thought was far too young to die. Far too young to have to attend your best friend's funeral. Far too young.

Annie wouldn't ever grow old. She wouldn't ever have a son or daughter who would play with Imogen and Ruby's own. She would never build a career or get married.

Truthfully, Imogen had been dreading this. She didn't really want to go. It meant saying goodbye, accepting that Annie was really gone forever, and she had never really wanted to do that, even if deep down she had sort of somehow known that Annie wasn't ever coming back.

For two whole years after Annie vanished, she had just sort of assumed that her friend would just... come bouncing back into town one day.

Maybe assumed was the wrong word but she had hoped for it. Vehemently. With all of her being, she had hoped for it.

Much like with Sophie's, Imogen didn't know how she was going to get through Annie's funeral. It was one thing to have the possibility, however slim, that your best friend had simply run off somewhere in the back of your mind, it was another thing entirely to actually be told, to know for certain, that her body had been found buried in the middle of the woods.

Under some tree.

Just shoved under the dirt like she was nothing. Absolutely nothing.

She stared at herself in the mirror, took in her outfit. The dress, the tights, the shoes, even her hair tie. All black. All gloomy. Nothing like the Annie Pierce she had known, who was so vibrant with colour and life.

Imogen didn't realise that she had started crying until Eric walked into the room to tell her it was time to go. She hid inside his strong arms for a while before it really was time to leave otherwise they would be late.

People stared at her enough, she didn't need to give them another reason by turning up late. She'd spent a long time feeling like an oddity, a circus sideshow and she was tired of it.

After Annie went missing, the spotlight was on the friends she'd left behind. It was all anybody could talk about and there were stares and whispers for years after.

Then again, when Imogen found Sophie's body in the woods years later.

Imogen pulled herself carefully out of Eric's arms and wiped her eyes. "I'm alright… we should go."

Imogen almost didn't want to get out of the car when they parked, and then walking into the church was horrible. She wished she had Brooklyn to hold in her arms for comfort but her daughter was with her mother.

She held Eric's hand tight as they walked along the pews to sit down. She glanced over at Ruby and offered her a sad smile, which was returned. She'd seen Kelly sitting at the back somewhere but the other girl hadn't looked at her.

Imogen glanced over her shoulder and scanned the room. She recognised everybody's face.

There was Jason Wright, neighbour to the Pierce family and the guy who had thrown the party that fateful night. Jason's long time girlfriend Cassie Jones sat next to him, holding his hand to comfort him. Imogen could remember Cassie not liking Annie but Jason had been like an older brother to the twins so it was nice that she was here.

Sitting in the same row was Thomas Playfair, Chris Marshall, Kyle Flynn, and Jamie Kirk. Jason's best friends since their own high school days. The five of them were still very close, as tight they had been when Imogen was still in school as far as she could tell.

She didn't really keep in close contact with them anymore. If they saw each other in the street, they'd exchange a smile or a brief greeting but these days it never usually went much further than that. It was the same with most of the people she had known back then.

Kyle had been Annie's boyfriend at the time that she went missing. His father was a police officer for the local department. She'd heard that he was one of the officers on scene when Annie was found so she couldn't imagine how Kyle's head was doing right now.

Imogen looked around the room a little more, her gaze landing on familiar face after familiar face. It seemed like *everybody* was here, even some people she wouldn't have expected to see in a million years.

There was Sarah Clarke, the quiet, shy girl who used to be in their class. Imogen could remember that Annie didn't seem to like her for some reason. Imogen thought she was alright, nice enough, but she definitely had some issues considering she attempted suicide back then they were about sixteen.

There was Poppy Hart, sitting with her sister Jasmine in the middle row. Poppy and Annie had gotten into a physical altercation in the middle of town one day, that same summer that Annie went missing. Everyone had witnessed it. Imogen couldn't even remember what Annie had said now but it ended with Poppy punching Annie in the face, giving her a bloody nose. She remembered that Annie had been fuming and she'd vowed to get her own back.

There was Austin Ramsey, who was sitting next to his sister Daisy. Daisy didn't look like she wanted to be there at all and Imogen didn't blame her. Daisy wasn't Annie's biggest fan either, to put it lightly.

Austin and Daisy had sort of been outcasts since they had moved to town, years before Annie vanished. Daisy had been too weird and Austin had been too volatile.

Imogen had always felt bad for them but Annie always told her that she had too much empathy for people who didn't deserve it.

Daisy looked up suddenly and met Imogen's gaze. Imogen felt caught and, embarrassed, quickly averted her eyes. When she chanced a sneaky glance back, Daisy wasn't looking anymore.

Breathing a tiny sigh of relief, she continued her curious sweep of the room.

There was Hannah Clarkson, with her bright red hair, sitting beside Thomas Playfair. Latched onto his arm like a limpet, an image that Imogen had seen many, many times since she was in high school. Every time Imogen saw her, it seemed like she hadn't changed much. Hannah was rich, spoiled, and high maintenance and always had been.

There was Oliver Brown and his fiancee Macey Cross, sitting together near the back. Macey had big dark sunglasses covering her eyes. Imogen wasn't sure why because there was no way she would be upset.

Macey had been the most popular girl in school before Annie. Annie had always wanted to be in Macey's place so she had hatched a scheme to humiliate Macey and knock her off her throne, and then Annie herself ascended that same throne and took over as Queen Bee of Baberton High.

Imogen was surprised to even see Macey here but she supposed a lot of people would be here simply due to morbid curiosity. Annie's disappearance had been highly public at the time and everyone who had been at Jason's bonfire party that night sort of felt something about it. Connected in some way, perhaps. Or maybe that was just how Imogen felt.

Oliver was sitting with his arm around Macey's shoulder, his lips moving like he was talking to her. Oliver had moved away to live with his father when they were all sixteen, but she was sure he'd moved back the day after Annie disappeared. She hadn't expected to see him either.

Sasha slipped into the seat next to Imogen and Eric, offering Imogen a little smile. She smiled back, glad that she was here.

Imogen glanced towards Ruby again but she was sitting with her head on Charlie's shoulder, not looking back.

As she continued to look around the room, scanning the faces around her, it suddenly occurred to Imogen that somebody in this room, right now, could have done it.

She could be sitting in the same room as Annie's killer.

She could be *looking* at that person right now.

The thought made her shiver and she instinctively leaned closer to Eric as the service began.

seven

Imogen supposed she didn't hate wakes as much as she hated funerals. Everybody tended to try and make them as happy as they could, telling funny stories about the deceased and remembering how much they had loved them. That's what she remembered about Sophie's wake.

That's not what Annie's was like.

Everybody who decided to show up was sitting around the room, talking in hushed tones to the people they had shown up with. There wasn't too much mingling.

No big cries of recognition as people from the past came back together.

No *god, how have you been's* or *do you remember when's.*

Most of the people in town didn't really have the best memories of Annie. Not like Imogen and Ruby and Kelly would. Or her family. Annie had been loved and revered by people but she'd also been loathed and feared. She had caused a lot of problems. Imogen could probably run off a list of things for every single person in this room.

Jamie Kirk was sitting with Jason Wright and Cassie Jones, scowling into a glass of whisky. Imogen wasn't sure why he had bothered coming to this part. Or at all, really. He *hated* Annie.

Dakota Pike was sitting at the table next to them with her friends Lacey Dixon, Abigail Tate, and Madeline Benson. They were about five years older than Imogen was. Sometimes, back in school, when Annie wanted more... sophisticated company than the girls, she would hang out with Dakota's group. Imogen was always so jealous of that, like they were stealing Annie away. It seemed so silly now.

Annie's family was sitting by themselves at the end of the room, at a big table. Mrs. Pierce looked inconsolable and Mr. Pierce looked angry. Chloe just looked like she wasn't really here. Not present. Imogen knew what that was like.

After checking in with the Pierce family, giving their condolences, she and Eric drifted over to where Ruby and Charlie were sitting. It seemed like the safest option.

Sasha had had to run back off to work but Imogen was glad she had been here at all and she'd told her she would call her later. When this was all over.

She checked in with her mother after she sat down, making sure everything was alright. Which of course it was but Imogen was still in that stage of being a bit of a helicopter mum. She couldn't really imagine herself ever not being, honestly.

"What a day, huh?" Eric said after she hung up.

Imogen nodded, making a face as she put her phone away and glanced up at Ruby and Charlie. "Will you guys be staying long?" She asked.

Charlie shook his head. "No, my niece can't stay at the house for too long so we've gotta get back for Hope." He explained.

"Even if she could stay, I don't know if I would want to stay for that long..." Admitted Ruby, who glanced towards Imogen and shrugged. "I feel bad, but..."

"No." Imogen shook her head. "I'm the same... I wasn't even sure if I should come to this bit, but then I thought it would be rude not to." She sighed but felt a little better when Ruby nodded in agreement.

Imogen glanced across the room, meeting Jamie Kirk's gaze. He was quick to look away again and she turned back to Ruby, lifting her glass of wine to her lips.

"Feels like 2015 all over again."

Ruby nodded in agreement. She felt it too.

The door opened a few moments later and Kelly Sharpe walked in. The room went silent, not that it had been buzzing with noise in the first place but there was definitely a bit of a lull. The hum of whispering had abruptly stopped.

Kelly rolled her eyes and made her way over to the bar. Of course. Straight for the alcohol.

Imogen wished there was something she could do to reach Kelly but the girl had been so far away for so many years now. Even a little bit before Annie disappeared, Kelly had been changing somewhat. Imogen didn't know why and she'd never thought to ask.

"Yep! It's me! Stare away!" Kelly's loud voice drifted across from the bar.

Imogen looked up again and noticed that the raven-haired girl was now standing facing the room, drink in hand, arms lifted as she addressed all the staring faces.

Imogen could relate, of course, but she really didn't think this was the time or the place and it annoyed her a little that Kelly would come here of all places and act like this.

Charlie was up on his feet before anyone else could really react quick enough to decide what to do. He took Kelly gently by the arm and led her quickly from the building.

She started laughing. "Mr Baker to the rescue!"

"Now is *not* the time, Kelly." Imogen heard him say as he pushed her carefully out of the door. When Charlie came back inside, Kelly wasn't with him. He placed the drink he'd wrangled from her grip on the bar, ignored the people looking at him, and made his way over to the table the Pierce's were sitting at.

Charlie Baker and Harry Pierce, Annie's father, had been good friends for years. Imogen remembered that much, out of all their parents, those two were the closest.

He talked to them for a while, likely apologising on Kelly's behalf and checking they were alright. Eventually everyone stopped staring and people started to drift out of the door themselves, heading for home.

Charlie came back a short while later, joining in on the conversation the table had lapsed back into, and then it was time for everyone to head off.

Imogen swung her handbag onto her shoulder, following everybody out. She could hear people talking around her but one conversation in particular caught her attention.

"Well, she's officially dead and buried." A brief pause. "Again."

She was aghast, thinking what an absolutely disgusting thing that was to say.

Imogen turned and scanned the remaining people in the room but she couldn't figure out who had said it. She couldn't place the voice either but it irritated her and she was sure it showed on her face.

How fucking disrespectful.

As the door swung closed behind her, Imogen heard her phone go off, alerting her to a text message.

She pulled it out of her bag but she was distracted by Ruby turning and speaking to her.

Her phone in her hand, she put her free arm around Ruby in a goodbye hug.

"We'll get the kids together again soon, okay?" Ruby said as she and Charlie set off towards the car. They all waved and Imogen and Eric turned to go the opposite way towards their own car.

Imogen finally looked down at her phone, her smile fading into nothingness as she read the words in the text message.

"I know who killed Annie Pierce."

eight

Imogen was sitting in the living room, watching Brooklyn playing on the carpet in front of her. The television was on in the background, some cartoon, but Imogen wasn't really aware of too much going on around her.

Her thoughts had been superglued on that message she had received after the funeral yesterday. She hadn't even been able to sleep.

Who was it from? Had somebody seen something? Heard something? Why wouldn't they go to the police instead of sending her a random text? Was it just some sick prank? The questions were driving her insane.

Imogen hadn't done anything about it yet. She was too shocked, too confused. She hadn't told Eric. She hadn't told anyone.

She knew that she probably should. She also knew that it was most likely a disgusting prank.

But what if it wasn't?

What if somebody, somewhere, somehow... knew something about what happened to her best friend six years ago?

Imogen made up her mind quite impulsively as she reached for her phone, scrolling straight to the message from the unknown number.

She stared at it for a few long moments and then she started typing.

"Who is this?"

Imogen wasn't sure why she was expecting an immediate response. Like in a movie or something. As it went, nothing happened for a few hours.

Imogen was driving herself crazy trying not to think about the message, trying not to check her phone every five seconds and failing. She did her best to focus on her daughter and on the present moment, trying to convince herself it was all just a sick joke. Telling herself not to take the bait.

Still, she leapt for it when the phone finally went off again.

It was a phone call, not a text.

It was Sasha.

"Damn it." Imogen muttered, immediately feeling bad about her lack of enthusiasm because of course she was happy to talk to Sasha, but her mind was so set on this that the disappointment was intense.

'Hey, you." Imogen answered the call and did her best to sound normal. "What's up?"

"Just wanted to check in. Y'know, after yesterday." Sasha replied.

It was nice of her and Imogen would probably have done the same thing if the roles were reversed but she also didn't really want to think about the funeral.

Honestly, she didn't want to think about any of it.

The funeral, Annie, Sophie, memories of the past, that text…. It was a lot.

"Yeah… thanks. I'm alright." Imogen nodded, leaning back against the couch, her gaze on Brooklyn. "What about you?"

They talked for a little while and Imogen eventually started to feel better, less stuck on the message.

She relaxed into a regular conversation with her best friend until it was time to go and feed Brooklyn so she said goodbye to Sasha and hung up.

As Imogen looked down at her mobile phone so she could hit the end call button, a wave of ice seemed to suddenly wash over her.

She had another text from the same number.

"I'm someone who knows everything that happened that summer. Do you want my help or not?"

Imogen stared for a long moment. She hadn't given much thought to the days or weeks leading up to the day when Annie had met up with the girls to go to Jason's, before Imogen lost her in the crowd and woke up the next morning to find out that she was missing.

Should she have?

Was there something everybody had missed?

Well, there had to be considering somebody had murdered her best friend, buried her in the woods, and gotten away with it.

Imogen's fingers moved to type out a reply before she could stop herself.

"Yes. Tell me."

The seconds ticked by agonisingly slowly as she waited for another reply to come through.

She moved to feed Brooklyn, who was beginning to fuss, and kept looking at the screen every few moments.

Eventually, her mobile phone lit up and a new text message flashed on the screen.

"Start with Thomas Playfair."

nine

Imogen had spent the past two hours thinking about the last message she had received. She just couldn't shake it off.

Thomas Playfair? It didn't make sense to her, he was probably the last name she'd ever expect to come up. Other than Jason, anyway. What did they mean by start with him?

Thomas was one of Jason's best friends. One of the "College Hotties" as they all used to be so fondly dubbed back in the day. A few years older than Imogen and her group and one of the most popular guys in town.

She wracked her brain, trying to pull up every memory she could about Thomas and Annie. Were they even friends? They were on the same kind of level, sure, but it's not like Imogen could remember them all spending time together when they weren't all at one of Jason's parties.

Start with Thomas Playfair.
Start.

Did this person mean that Thomas was involved in what happened to Annie? Did he know something? Or, and this thought chilled her to the bone, was Imogen being contacted by the killer themselves, trying to set somebody else up for the murder now that Annie had been found.

Imogen had to admit that the timing was suspicious. Why now? If this person had witnessed something, why the hell would they wait until now to say something? Annie had been missing for *years*. Her disappearance had been all over town, in papers all over the country even! If somebody knew what had happened to her, why were they only coming forward now... especially if they were innocent?

Imogen groaned, closing her eyes and pressing her face into one of the couch cushions. This was beginning to give her a headache.

She still hadn't told Eric about any of this. She knew he would only worry or tell her to go to the police or ignore it. Imogen didn't feel able to ignore it. Not this. Not when it was about Annie.

She *had* toyed with the idea of going to Lauren Hayes for help. Lauren was a police officer who had moved up here during Annie's disappearance to help with the case, and stayed after falling in love with Imogen's mother, Brooke. However, Imogen was pretty sure that Lauren would also tell her to ignore it and leave it to the police.

She just couldn't, though. This whole thing had already wormed its way under her skin.

An hour later, she was busying herself in the kitchen, cooking dinner in an attempt to distract her crowded mind.

Eric walked in the door after work, immediately chuckling as he moved into the kitchen. He pretended to look amazed to see her in there.

"What's this? My wife, *cooking?*" Eric joked, laughing as she reached out and playfully shoved him, pretending to be offended.

Imogen had never been the best cook, and she had never really enjoyed cooking either. Her specialty was beans on toast or pasta so her bad cooking skills had become a running joke between the two of them.

Imogen rolled her eyes at him. "Ha ha, you're so funny."

"I know." Eric shot back, grinning at her in a way that only further amused her.

"Asshole." She muttered jokingly, making sure she was loud enough for him to hear.

Eric feigned shock and moved to the dining table where their daughter was colouring, covering his hands gently over Brooklyn's ears.

Imogen just laughed, shaking her head at him in amusement as she finished up the food.

"Come on, grab a plate."

"I'm not sure if that's safe but I'm hungry so I'll risk it." Eric teased, getting himself another playful smack on the arm, which only caused more laughter to erupt from him.

* * *

That night, Imogen lay awake until it was well past four am. She kept tossing and turning, staring at the clock beside the bed as the seconds ticked by.

Once again, her thoughts wouldn't stop tangling together up in her head. She couldn't shut off and it was driving her crazy.

Imogen even took an extra quetiapine pill, which usually had a drowsy effect on her, but no such luck tonight. She supposed her system was too used to the medications by now... or her body was just refusing to give in.

Either way, she felt like she was going mad by the time five am came around.

It was around this time that Imogen finally made a decision.

She was going to find out what happened to Annie the night she went missing - *was killed*.

It was still difficult to think of it as the night she died... the night she was *murdered*.

Imogen told herself she would entertain these messages, whoever they were from. This person seemed to know something, which was more than the police had had in years, and Imogen was desperate to know what happened. Who would kill Annie?

Imogen fell asleep not long after that, as if that's what her brain had been waiting on all along.

The next morning, Imogen decided to take Brooklyn out for a walk. She pushed the buggy through town, enjoying the warm sun on her skin as she walked, and ended up at the park.

Baberton's park was a beautiful expanse of green grass containing an abundance of trees, flowers, and a little pond. As well as a children's play area in the middle, which was where Imogen tended to find herself these days.

When she was younger, she and her friends would come and hang out in the hidden corners of the park and secretly drink Bacardi Breezers, pretending they were the biggest rebels on the planet, laughing and joking and feeling utterly untouchable.

Imogen spotted a few people playing football on the grass nearby and the image took her right back to being in high school. She remembered all the college football games she and her friends had sat through. Imogen had never been interested in football but Annie always wanted to come and watch the boys running around in their shorts and none of her friends were going to say no.

It took Imogen a moment or two to realise that the guys kicking the ball around were the same guys she had watched kicking what could even be the same ball a few years back.

Jamie Kirk was sitting on the sidelines, underneath a tree, acting as referee. He hadn't been able to play football since the car accident that messed up his leg. If she remembered correctly, he had been lucky to get away with his life after that. Apparently he'd been driving too fast, at least that's what the police concluded.

Still, Imogen knew having to sit on the side and watch his buddies all play the game you wanted to play professionally couldn't be easy.

Kicking the ball in the space in front of him was Jason Wright, Kyle Flynn, Chris Marshall… and Thomas Playfair.

Imogen's thoughts immediately flashed to the text message and then to the decision she had come to the night before.

Pushing Brooklyn's buggy over to a nearby bench, Imogen sat down to wait until the game was over. She watched as they kicked the ball around and pretended to just be sitting there with her daughter instead of having an ulterior motive... not that Imogen knew what she was going to say. Or if she was going to say anything at all.

Eventually, the game seemed to come to an end and the guys began to drift in different directions. Imogen noticed Jamie throw a glare her way but it was so brief she thought maybe she had imagined it.

"Hey, you." Jason's voice sounded in front of her and Imogen looked up, realising that he was there.

"Oh, hey." She smiled at him, watching as he moved to interact with Brooklyn.

"How old is she now?" He asked, and it struck Imogen just how long it had actually been.

"She's going to be two in a few months." Imogen said and chuckled at Jason's expression of shock.

"Where does the time go, eh?" He shook his head.

Imogen nodded in agreement, making a face. "Yeah, tell me about it."

"Kinda seems like just yesterday we were all running around town causing chaos." Jason said, moving to swing his backpack onto his shoulder.

A laugh came from behind the bench she was sitting on and Imogen turned her head, realising that Thomas Playfair was standing there, drinking from a bottle of water.

"Chaos is right." He joked, giving Jason a look.

Imogen supposed their two groups had caused different sorts of chaos but she didn't really want to talk about the crap that Annie would get up to. Imogen liked to remember the good things about her friend over the bad.

"What is *she* doing?" Chris Marshall didn't seem to even acknowledge Imogen's presence as he snatched up a water bottle and nodded across the grass.

Imogen followed his gaze, seeing Daisy Ramsey standing over by the duck pond, camera aimed in their direction.

"She was taking pictures of the game." Jason shrugged.

"Creepy bitch." Chris made a face, gulping from his water bottle. "She didn't ask, she should delete them."

Jason made a face. "Leave it alone, man. It's harmless."

Chris rolled his eyes but he grabbed his jacket and turned away, wandering off in the opposite direction, Jamie trailing behind him.

Imogen was relieved. Everyone knew that Daisy liked to take pictures around town. As far back as Imogen could remember, photography had been Daisy's most identifiable hobby. She was pretty good at it, too, from what Imogen had seen.

"I better get going or Cassie will think I've run off." Jason joked, giving Imogen a little smile before reaching out to clap Thomas on the shoulder. "Good game, man. See ya next week."

Thomas returned the goodbye and then moved to grab up his jacket and the ball, which was apparently his.

Imogen sat there feeling awkward, the anonymous messages swirling around in her head as she did her best not to stare at him and come off like a complete weirdo.

What was she supposed to say?

Was she supposed to say anything at all?

Imogen started to doubt herself, wondering if it really was better to ignore all of this and just... get on with it.

Annie was gone and Imogen was just one woman. The *police* could handle the how and the why of her best friend ending up under the ground, right?

Still, Imogen knew that she wasn't likely to be able to just let this go and before she knew it, she'd drawn Thomas back into conversation.

"So... do you guys still do this often?" She asked, looking from her daughter to Thomas, now standing in front of her.

He looked up and she wondered if he was surprised she had spoken but then he nodded, offering her a smile.

"Every week, yeah." He told her, nodding as he glanced towards Brookly, giving her a smile. "She's getting big, huh?"

"That's nice… you know, that you're all still close." Imogen said, before nodding as she looked at her daughter. "Yeah. Too big too fast." She chuckled.

"Yeah…" There was a short silence before Thomas spoke again. "We were thinking of you guys, y'know… since the funeral."

Imogen glanced down at her hands, picking at her nails before she shrugged and lifted her gaze again. "Yeah… thanks."

"It's mad." He spoke again, sounding slightly awkward maybe. "Y'know… Annie…" Thomas cleared his throat.

Imogen didn't know what to say. She was used to this sort of thing, though. People talking about Annie, bringing her up in front of her and her friends. It had happened a lot more after she went missing but she was still used to people shooting glances her way or whispering about the missing girl's best friends… she supposed it would be dead girl's best friends now.

"Yeah." Imogen eventually replied, looking up at him. "It's still pretty hard to believe."

She studied his face, noticing a hint of something she couldn't quite place. "Were you close?" She asked suddenly, noting the surprise on his face as he shifted his gaze back to her.

"What?"

"Annie…. were you guys close?" Imogen asked again, looking steadily back at him.

Thomas lifted a hand to his nose, scratching the end of it as his gaze shifted to the ground. "No, uh… not really, no. I mean, y'know, she was always around… but so were the rest of you." He shrugged. "I wouldn't say *close.*"

But there was something in his expression, or maybe his voice, that Imogen wasn't sure she believed.

"Thomas!" The call came from somewhere behind and Imogen turned, looking over the back of the bench.

Hannah Clarkson was marching towards them. Imogen glanced at her dangerously high heels and wondered how she wasn't getting stuck in the soft ground she was stomping across.

"Hey, Han.." Was Imogen imagining it or was there relief in his tone?

Hannah immediately moved up to Thomas and slid her arms around him, almost possessively. She gazed evenly back at Imogen and then turned to look at Thomas. "We gotta go, babe. Daddy's waiting in the car."

"Right, yeah… cool." Thomas smiled, leaning in to press a kiss to her temple. Imogen noticed the slightest tension shifting in Hannah's shoulders and frowned lightly.

"See ya later, Imogen." Thomas said, his voice normal again. He no longer looked uncomfortable or like he was put on the spot as he slung an arm around Hannah's shoulders and turned to walk off across the park with her.

"Yeah, see you." Imogen replied weakly, moving to take care of Brooklyn who was suddenly fussing, wanting to wobble around on the grass.

As she lifted the baby out of the buggy, Imogen noticed Hannah had glanced over her shoulder and was staring at her.

She was pretty sure she heard Thomas's voice drifting back towards her too, though only two words were really discernible.

"...about Annie..."

ten

Imogen kept telling herself she was just being completely paranoid. She was, right? She was being crazy and irrational and seeing things that weren't there. It was all because of that text. The text had put Thomas Playfair in the forefront of her suspicious mind in regards to Annie and then she had projected.

Right?

She was sitting on the sofa, nursing a cup of tea, with a book sitting open on her lap but she couldn't really concentrate long enough to read it.

Imogen hadn't received another text from the anonymous number but every time her phone went, she jumped for it, just in case.

Nothing.

Maybe it really was all just a prank. A sick joke by someone who didn't like them back then or something. It seemed more and more plausible as the time ticked by without any more contact.

Imogen felt kind of foolish as she sat there, thinking. But then she remembered the way Hannah had looked at her when she practically walked Thomas away, the expression she'd been wearing.

Then the words *about Annie* that Thomas had muttered at the same time

It could have been innocent but due to her already heightened suspicion, Imogen wasn't entirely sure that was the case. Had he been telling Hannah that Imogen had been asking him about Annie?

It's what made the most sense and she knew it could have been entirely conversational. Annie was a hot topic around here again, after all.

Still, there had been a certain edge to his voice that Imogen couldn't quite shake off.

She closed the unread book on her lap and stood up. Imogen knew she would only drive herself mad if she kept sitting there letting her thoughts run away with themselves.

She walked into the kitchen, dumping out the contents of her mug, and leaving the empty cup in the washing up bowl. Imogen stood and stared at it for a moment before she turned and trailed back out of the kitchen.

Imogen wandered back into the living room. The house was so quiet and she wasn't used to that, not since Brooklyn had been born. Eric had the day off work and had taken their daughter to lunch with his younger sister Molly. They would probably be out for ages knowing those two. They were very close and sometimes Imogen was jealous of that bond.

Her whole life, Imogen had always wanted a brother or a sister. Her mother had had her very young and then the years afterwards had been difficult due to her having untreated schizophrenia. Which Imogen would, of course, later inherit.

Imogen had been raised by her grandparents after her mother tragically tried to drown her in the bath as an infant. Imogen had only found this out by accident, when she was sixteen and found an old diary of her mother's up in the attic of her grandparents home.

By this time, her mother had been back in her life for years and though it was difficult to find out about, Imogen didn't hold a grudge for very long. Especially not when her own troubles with the very same illness started. Luckily, she was treated very quickly from the onset. After she'd cornered poor Charlie Baker in the street ranting about Sophie being alive, he'd gone in search of her mother and this had helped get her into the hospital.

Imogen's mother was fine now. The medication really helped keep her stabilised. It wasn't all sunshine and rainbows but she was doing well.

Imogen moved over to her phone to call her mother after the thoughts had crossed her mind, but when she reached the sofa where her mobile sat, it went off. As if it sensed her coming.

"Hannah knows something about Annie."

Another message from that same number. Imogen frowned as she scanned the words. Hannah.

The look in Hannah's eyes as she'd walked away the other day played in Imogen's mind again, and the next thing she knew she was reaching for her keys and leaving the house.

* * *

Imogen walked into The Hot Spot, one of the many local cafes. It had always been one of the most popular hangout spots, ever since Imogen could remember, and it was still going strong.

She looked around, scanning the tables for the familiar shock of Hannah Clarkson's dark red hair. It was always easy to spot her in a crowd. The other woman usually stuck out, but not in a bad way. She was drop dead gorgeous and her clothes were all designer, and she went nowhere without her signature sunglasses, come rain or shine.

Daddy's money had carried her through her whole life.

Imogen thought it was all a bit pretentious and she always had but that wasn't really relevant.

As soon as she spotted her, Imogen made a beeline for the table the redhead was sitting at. It was stupid but red hair always brought her mind back to Sophie these days. Frustrating since plenty of people had red hair.

Hannah looked bored when Imogen stood in front of her. "Do you need something?"

Imogen frowned gently as she looked back at Hannah. "Um." Truthfully, she had no idea why she was here or what she wanted to ask. She had seen that text and was out the door before she could stop herself.

Hannah looked up from her phone. "Well?"

Imogen felt her cheeks heat up slightly. "I want to talk about Annie."

Hannah's gaze narrowed just slightly, and she stared back at Imogen for a few moments. Imogen felt like the rest of the cafe had melted away, her focus intensely on the other woman as she waited for some sort of a response.

"What about her?" Hannah's expression had become hard to read, almost flat.

Imogen blinked, a little thrown off by the sudden change on Hannah's face. "Well… look, I've just heard some things." She half-lied, wondering if she could trick anything out of the other girl.

Hannah frowned. "What kind of things? From *who?*"

Was she imagining it or was there something in Hannah's tone? Something… guarded? Angry? Worried?

Imogen didn't know how to play this. She wished she hadn't been so impulsive. She had never been good at improv.

"Well… I mean, yesterday, Thomas…" Imogen was immediately cut off.

"Thomas?" Hannah's voice was now like ice. "What about Thomas? What did he say?" She narrowed her eyes. "What did he tell you?"

Imogen paused. *What did he tell you?* Was she taking it far too literally or did that sound like there *was* something to tell and Hannah was afraid he'd already told it?

She didn't say anything else because what could she say? Thomas, frustratingly, hadn't said anything to her and she didn't know enough to hint at anything.

"I don't have time for this. Leave me alone." Hannah snapped, turning her body away from Imogen so she was sitting sideways in her chair now, completely shutting the blonde out.

Imogen hovered for a moment or two and then, embarrassed, she turned and wandered aimlessly out of the cafe. She stood out on the street for a few moments, frowning to herself.

Well, that had done absolutely nothing.

Imogen took a few steps to her left and ducked into the tiny alleyway beside the Hot Spot, leaning her back against the wall with a sigh. What was she supposed to do?

She stood for a minute, glad that she was out of sight of the street. She'd just needed a moment to collect her thoughts. This really did seem hopeless. She didn't even know what she was doing.

Just as Imogen opened her eyes and was about to step back out onto the street, Hannah Clarkson's voice reached her.

"What the hell did you say to her, Tommy?"

Imogen froze. She felt unable to move for a few long moments and then she carefully inched down the wall of the alley, sucking in a small breath as she peeked her eye around the corner.

Hannah was standing outside the cafe, a few paces from the door. She must have thought Imogen was already long gone.

Imogen slid back round the corner, fully concealed again, not wanting to be noticed, especially with what she had just heard.

"Well, she knows *something*, idiot!" Hannah snapped into the phone.

Imogen frowned, both at the words Hannah said and the tone she used when she was talking to her boyfriend.

So, the texts were right? They really did have something to do with this? Could they have something to do with what happened to Annie that night?

Imogen was half tempted to storm out of the alley and confront the other woman then and there, but she stayed where she was, wanting to listen for anything else Hannah might say.

However, that seemed to be all she was going to get, as the next time Imogen peered round the corner, Hannah was nowhere to be seen.

Imogen finally peeled herself away from the wall and took off down the street.

Not in the direction of home, though. She was heading in the direction of Thomas Playfair's house.

eleven

Thomas wasn't very happy to see her and Imogen supposed she couldn't blame him. Especially if he was guilty of what she suspected him of.

It hadn't been believable at first but the more Imogen heard and saw from Thomas and Hannah, the more suspicious she became, and the more she believed the anonymous texts.

"Imogen, I'm not doing this right now..." Thomas sounded tired.

Imogen didn't really care. "You're going to, Thomas. I need to know what the hell is going on."

He stared at her, shaking his head. "*Nothing* is going on." He paused, before adding. "You're starting to sound paranoid."

Imogen glared at him. "Don't you dare." Everybody in town knew about her schizophrenia. They all knew about her past paranoias and her episodes.

Thomas lowered his gaze. At least he had the grace to look ashamed.

"Look..." He said, his voice softer now. "I don't know what you want here." Thomas looked at her again, shrugging almost helplessly. "I really don't."

Imogen stared at him silently for a few long moments, thinking it over. The texts. The way he and Hannah had scurried away in the park and the look Hannah had given her. The things Hannah had said on the phone.

"Did you kill Annie?" The words were out before she could even stop them. Not that she wanted to. Imogen wanted to know what he was going to say, she needed to know.

Thomas stared at her, mouth slightly open, looking aghast. "Wh--what?!"

Imogen eyed him suspiciously, trying to read every little detail of his expression.

"It's a simple question. Did you?" She paused. "Did *Hannah?*" Maybe he was covering for her and that's why she was so defensive.

"Imogen, you're way off the mark here."

She frowned. "Am I? Then what did Hannah think you told me?"

He looked at her, confused, and she tilted her head, looking back at him steadily. She wasn't sure where this confidence had suddenly come from but she was desperate to know what happened to her best friend.

"I heard her on the phone. She thinks you told me something in the park. What is it?"

Thomas turned and she thought he was about to walk away from her, which would simply confirm his guilt in her mind.

He paced a step away, then paced back again, shaking his head. "No... No, Imogen, you've got it wrong."

Imogen looked at him. "Then just tell me."

There was a silence as Thomas seemed to weigh up his options.

"I didn't do anything to Annie." He said, eventually. "Neither did Hannah."

Imogen gave him a look that said she wasn't sure whether or not she could believe him.

"It's true!" Thomas sighed, frustrated. "Look... that summer..." He paused and Imogen blinked back at him, waiting.

"That summer, Annie and I... we were together." Thomas continued, lifting his gaze.

Imogen stared at him. the words not really registering properly with her at all. "What do you mean?"

Thomas frowned at her like she was stupid. "I *mean*, Annie and I were together." He paused. "*Together*-together."

"No, but..." Imogen shook her head, frowning along with him. "No... she... Kyle!" God, she couldn't string together a proper sentence, she was that stunned.

Thomas shook his head, groaning as he turned to sit down on his couch. She could tell he didn't want her to know this, or he wasn't very proud of it. Maybe it was both.

Annie had been dating Kyle Flynn that summer and they were mad about each other so, to Imogen, what Thomas was saying didn't make sense. Thomas had also still been dating Hannah at that time.

"We were having an *affair,* Imogen." Thomas emphasised.

It was Imogen's turn to lower herself into a nearby chair, a little stunned at this revelation. Then again, why was she so surprised? Annie did and got exactly what she wanted, always. Thomas had been one of the most popular guys around. Just Annie's type.

The silence stretched between the two of them for a few long moments before Imogen spoke again. "Hannah knows?"

Thomas nodded, looking down at his hands. He was tapping his foot, obviously uncomfortable.

"Yeah, Hannah… she saw us that day. That morning. The day…" Thomas trailed off and didn't finish the sentence but it wasn't difficult for Imogen to deduce the last two words. The day *Annie disappeared.*

"She *saw* you?" Imogen was stunned again, but it made sense. Suddenly Hannah's expression in the park the other day, the phone call to Thomas outside the Hot Spot, it all clicked into place.

"Yeah, she went and confronted her that afternoon. It got heated."

"That's a motive…" Imogen murmured, not having meant to say it out loud.

Thomas shot her a quick glance. "No." His voice was sharp. "We had nothing to do with it."

"Then why not tell the police?!" Imogen exclaimed, frustrated.

"God, Imogen, think about it! Why didn't we tell the cops? You just said it yourself! It looks like one or both of us had a motive to… to do that to her."

"Kill her." Imogen stated bluntly.

Thomas went quiet, nodding. Imogen wondered just how close he and Annie had gotten during this affair. He almost looked sad.

"And we didn't. Imogen, we really didn't. We're protecting each other because of what it would *look like*. Not because we actually *did* anything. I swear."

Imogen didn't know what to believe or what to think. She just shook her head, unsure what to say.

"If anyone had a motive, it was Kyle." Thomas's next admission threw Imogen for a loop, not that she wasn't already there, spinning round and round.

"What are you talking about?" She asked.

"He was having an affair too, you know." Thomas stated, folding his arms.

Imogen frowned. "What? No, he wasn't. He wouldn't…" Would he?

Thomas simply shrugged. "Maybe you should go and ask Dakota Pike who her son's father is."

Imogen blinked. Her head felt full. "What?"

At that moment, the front door swung open and in marched Hannah Clarkson, a tower in her high heels. She took one look at Imogen and turned on Thomas with fire in her eyes. "Are you kidding me?"

"I have to go." Imogen muttered, snatching her bag back up and sliding past Hannah carefully. She threw a glance back over her shoulder towards Thomas. "Um. Thanks."

As she closed the door behind her, she could hear Hannah launch into a tirade against Thomas.

Imogen had no idea what to think as she hurried away from Thomas's place, eager to be gone before Hannah got any ideas about following her out.

Had Annie been cheating on Kyle with Thomas? Had Thomas been cheating on Hannah? Was *Kyle* cheating on Annie?

From what Imogen could remember of their relationship, Annie was head over heels for Kyle and Kyle was the same way. Right?

Imogen's phone buzzed in her pocket and when she reached for it she saw that it was from that anonymous number again.

"Annie's summer was more eventful than you ever knew".

Imogen frowned, staring down at the words, and then her head snapped up. She looked around, turning a full circle. She didn't see anybody but the timing of this message set her on edge.

Were they watching her? Were they following her?

"You know she loved to keep secrets."

The phone went off again in Imogen's hand and she nearly dropped it in fright.

She felt anxious, panicky, breathless. Imogen did her best to try to remember and put into practice those soothing techniques her therapist had given her but she wasn't sure she could calm down right now. Especially not if someone was *following* her.

Imogen shoved the phone back into her bag and took off down the street again, faster this time.

With every step, she imagined she was being followed. Her mind conjured up the image of a shadowy figure tailing her round every corner.

She knew she was being silly. There was no way somebody was watching her. Right? How would they even know where to go? How would she not be able to see them?

Imogen slowed her pace, doing her best to begin focusing on her breathing. *In and out. In and out.* The way she had been told in therapy.

Her panic began to ease and she kept her gaze focused ahead of her as she continued to walk in the direction of home. Imogen made a point of not looking over her shoulder, though the urge to do so was gnawing at her.

She was letting her imagination run away with itself, she knew that. As usual.

Imogen turned her phone off and shoved it away into her pocket again. She didn't want to deal with any more of this right now.

She needed time to think. Time to process what she had just found out... and figure out her next move.

twelve

The rest of the night passed in a little bit of a blur. Imogen felt like she was sleepwalking through the minutes, just killing time.

Eric would talk to her and it was like it would go in one ear and out the other. She would fake a smile and pay as much attention to Brooklyn as she could but Imogen didn't altogether feel like she was there. Like she wasn't present.

Shortly before they went up to bed, Eric came downstairs from checking on Brooklyn. Imogen was busying herself with putting away the dishes as he stood in the doorway watching her for a few moments.

"Are you okay?" He asked, making her jump a little because she hadn't even realised that he was there.

Imogen nodded, looking over at him. "Sure... why wouldn't I be?"

Eric shrugged, crossing his arms and leaning against the doorframe. "You seem distant." He paused. "Did you take your medication?"

Imogen slammed down the bowl she'd been about to put away and luckily it was one of Brooklyn's plastic ones so it didn't smash.

"Of course I did!"

"I was only wondering." Eric said carefully.

"Well, I'm sick of people wondering. Yes, I take my meds. Yes, I'm distant. My best friends are *dead!*" She snapped, turning to move past him into the other room.

Of course, Imogen was also being harassed by some anonymous weirdo but she didn't know if she wanted to tell him that. She didn't want to put that burden onto him and she knew that he would only tell her to go to the police.

Imogen didn't know if she even trusted the police. What good had they done, after all?

She knew that it wasn't fair to be going off on Eric like this. He hadn't done anything wrong. She was simply letting her paranoia run away with her and letting her stress lead her.

She just couldn't understand what was happening. She couldn't understand who was doing this. She couldn't understand what she was supposed to do, what she *could* do.

Worst of all, Imogen was starting to wonder if any of this was even real.

Was she really getting messages from a random number who knew all sorts of secrets about *that summer...* or was she in the beginning stages of another episode?

It would be so easy to just show Eric her phone and have him confirm that the texts were there but she was too afraid to do that, just in case he said they weren't. In case he confirmed her worst fear.

That Annie's body being discovered had triggered another Sophie-esque mental break.

"I'm going to bed." She sighed, turning to move past him and making for the stairs, taking them quickly and shutting herself away in the bathroom for a moment.

Imogen stared at her reflection in the mirror, trying to see if there were any answers written there. In her expression, something… but she didn't get anything.

Imogen sighed, splashing water on her face and then turning to head through to Brooklyn's room, giving the sleeping baby a gentle kiss, careful not to wake her, and then she turned and moved into the master bedroom, slipping beneath the covers and trying unsuccessfully to concentrate on finishing Ruby's book.

* * *

The next day, Imogen had made her mind up once again. She had woken up determined to seek out Dakota Pike or Kyle Flynn - whoever she found first - and find out if this was all true.

It was slowly starting to feel like everything that Imogen thought she knew was a lie and it was really messing with her.

She had to find out everything she could about Annie's last summer. Her apparently incredibly secret summer. Imogen thought they told each other everything but she was starting to see that wasn't quite true.

Imogen pushed Brooklyn's buggy through town, window shopping and just meandering along. She was exhausted, not having slept very well the night before. No surprise, really, considering.

She had done her best to convince herself that she wasn't completely losing it. It hadn't been easy but this was real... it was all real. She just had to keep holding on to that.

Imogen turned the corner, heading up the high street towards the park. It seemed that she walked through there every day. Brooklyn seemed to enjoy the route, she got to see so many people and colours and *things*. Imogen got great pleasure out of watching her daughter experience the world.

"Woah!" Came a voice, a chuckle quickly following.

Imogen looked up. She hadn't even realised that she was drifting away into her own little world. Her mind was a million miles away.

Standing in front of the buggy was Chris Marshall. Imogen had nearly run over his toes.

"Sorry!" She exclaimed, shaking her head at herself. "You alright?"

"Yeah, yeah." Chris laughed, nodding. "All good, I don't think anything's broken." He teased.

Imogen forced up a smile. Chris looked at her curiously, as if he could tell she was faking.

"Are *you* alright?" He asked.

Imogen nodded. "Uh, yeah... yeah, I'm fine." She shrugged a little. "Tired, you know..." She nodded towards Brooklyn, though it wasn't really the reason she was losing sleep.

Chris nodded, moving his gaze towards Brooklyn again. "Right, yeah... is she a big fusspot, then?" He chuckled, looking back up at Imogen.

As she looked back at him, Chris seemed to hesitate. Like he wanted to say something, thought better of it, and then changed his mind again.

"I'm sorry… about Annie." He finally said, causing Imogen's stomach to lurch. "Must be tough."

Imogen bit her lip and nodded. "Yeah. It is." She said, glancing away a little anxiously.

There was a slightly awkward silence and Chris was about to take a step away when Imogen realised that he had been at the party that night with them all too.

"Did you see anything?" She found herself asking before she could really stop the words coming out. The look Chris gave her said that he really didn't understand what she was getting at and she couldn't blame him considering she hadn't given any context to the question.

"Sorry, I mean… you know. *That night.* Someone *killed* her and *buried* her… I just keep thinking *somebody* must have seen *something.*"

Chris blinked back at her, clearly taken aback by the words. She could see him processing it, his mind whirring round and round back to that night.

"I mean… not really." He finally shrugged, causing Imogen to feel a little disappointed. "I was trashed that night… I was so drunk I barely even remember it." He admitted. "It was so long ago."

Yeah, it was so long ago, but it was bleeding through into the present and Imogen couldn't just let it go.

"Sorry." She said, and he quickly shook his head.

"No.. no, I mean you're not wrong. Someone has to know something, right?"

Imogen nodded, glad that he was agreeing with her and not looking at her like she was a headcase.

"So, you... really don't remember much? You don't remember if anyone was acting... weird?"

Chris shrugged. "Nope. Like I said, I was totally smashed. I don't think I would have even noticed if anyone was."

"Okay." She couldn't deny that she was disappointed. Imogen supposed she wanted to unearth something that would just tie everything up in a neat little package.

Sadly, Imogen knew that that's not how the world worked.

"Anyway, I better get on." Chris said, looking back at her with a slightly forced smile. A clear ending to the conversation.

Imogen worked up a smile back, nodding. "Yeah, yeah." No big deal. They barely spoke these days and he didn't know anything. "I'll see you 'round."

Chris nodded. "Sure." Then he moved to walk around her and Brooklyn's buggy, slinking off into the small crowd around them.

Imogen sighed as she looked down at Brooklyn, who was occupying herself chewing on the ear of her stuffed animal. "Well, that was pointless, huh?"

Drifting across the road and into the Coffee Bean cafe, Imogen spotted Sasha sitting at a table in the middle, sipping a coffee.

She made a beeline for her best friend, smiling as she sat down in the empty seat opposite her. "Hey!"

Sasha looked up, jumping slightly. "Jesus!" She laughed, clearly taken aback. "Way to sneak up on a girl!"

"Sorry." Imogen chuckled, amused as she reached into her baby bag and then handed Brooklyn a snack to keep her occupied. "Thought you'd be working today."

Sasha nodded, leaning over to fuss at Brooklyn for a moment. "Yeah, I was meant to be. Did you not hear?"

Imogen frowned. "Hear what?"

Sasha made a face. "Shit. Well, there was a fire. In the boutique."

"What?!" Imogen's mouth dropped open, aghast. "Was everyone okay?"

Sasha worked at the little boutique up the high street that Isabel Pierce, Annie's mother, owned.

Sasha had taken another sip of coffee before Imogen had asked the question so she paused to swallow, nodding. "Yeah, yeah... no, everyone was fine. They caught it before it got out of control. It was through the back."

"God." Imogen shook her head. The last thing the Pierce family needed was more trouble.

When Imogen looked back up and saw the thoughtful look on Sasha's face, she tilted her head slightly. "What is it?"

Sasha shook her head. "Nothing..." She was quiet and then she shrugged. "It's just... they're pretty sure it was intentional."

Imogen stared at her. "Wait, what?" She frowned. "Like... someone set fire to the place on purpose?"

"Yeah." Sasha nodded, biting her lip. "And... it was weird, I saw Chloe lurking around out the back, by the bins.."

"Chloe?" Imogen frowned again as another memory shook loose from the depths of her mind.

Annie telling her about the lighter that Chloe would play with constantly, the fires she threatened to start, and then a week later an abandoned shed being set alight in one of the fields.

Annie was adamant this had been her sister, though nobody was ever caught.

"Yeah. She just looked a bit weird." Sasha shrugged. "I guess she always looks a bit weird these days."

She wasn't entirely wrong. Since Annie - and honestly maybe for a while before - Chloe had been... *reserved* would be the nice way of putting it. *Weird* would be the less nice but still pretty accurate way.

"That's so crazy." Imogen shook her head. "The last thing that family needs is more drama."

Sasha nodded in agreement. "Anyway, at least I get a day off." She joked. "You want a hot chocolate?" Sasha asked, after looking down and realising she had finished her coffee.

"You know me too well." Imogen grinned, chuckling as Sasha hurried up to the counter to buy their drinks.

Chloe, Kyle, Dakota, Thomas, Hannah, and Annie all drifted to the back of Imogen's mind as she just let herself enjoy the afternoon chatting and laughing with her best friend.

thirteen

"Do you remember how mad it would make Annie when Kelly would dress up like her?" Ruby asked, looking up from the photo album on her lap.

"Oh, God, yeah... Kelly wanted to be *just* like her, didn't she?" Imogen made a face. It had been embarrassing to witness at the time. Kelly's obsession with Annie and with being just like her.

Now, though, Imogen supposed she was old enough to know that kids were like that sometimes. Kelly had idolised Annie a great deal.

"Annie told me once that she wanted to kick Kelly out of the group.." Ruby admitted. "Just because she couldn't take the copying." She shrugged. "I don't think she would actually have done it though."

Imogen was a little surprised by this revelation but also, on the other hand, entirely unsurprised.

Annie had never really liked competition and maybe she would have seen Kelly's over the top adoration of her as some sort of threat.

"It's a shame, isn't it?" Ruby asked and Imogen immediately knew, without having to clarify, that she meant the way Kelly had ended up now.

Imogen nodded. "Yeah. I wanted to reach out for a while but... it didn't seem like she would have appreciated it."

Ruby shook her head. "I did reach out. She told me to go fuck myself." She sighed, dipping her voice on the word *fuck* so that Hope and Brooklyn didn't overhear.

Imogen frowned. "Jeez." Truthfully, it didn't really surprise her but she felt bad for Ruby. She and Kelly had been close.

Ruby looked over at the kids playing on the carpet and she sighed, closing the photo album that the two of them had been flipping through.

It was kind of nice, having somebody to reminisce with. Someone who had been there and who understood. Imogen was glad that she and Ruby hadn't lost touch altogether.

"I'm sure she'll figure it out. Eventually." Imogen said, shrugging. She hoped so, at least, but really part of her wondered if Kelly was too far gone.

Ruby nodded, agreeing but Imogen could see on her face that she wasn't completely sold either.

The conversation moved on and Imogen was glad for it. Thinking about Kelly and how her life had turned out made her unhappy, and also made her feel a little guilty.

* * *

Later that night, Imogen was sitting in the living room nursing a hot chocolate and flipping through her own photo album.

The one with all the pictures from her childhood days with her old friends.

She used to look at these photos so often, pining after the past and the way things used to be. Reminiscing and losing herself in the memory of it. Imogen probably romanticised a lot of the past, but she was sure that was fairly common.

She turned another page, pausing on a photograph of Kelly, Annie, Sophie and Ruby that she had taken. She smiled lightly, but it faded just a little as her gaze scanned across Kelly's expression.

Imogen had never noticed it before, but in that moment Kelly had been staring at Annie. Not just staring. *Glaring.*

Imogen frowned at the image, leaning a little closer. There was definitely an edge to Kelly's gaze. Right? She looked irritated. Angry, maybe.

The more she looked, the more obvious it was. If you weren't really looking though, you would just see four friends standing together for a picture.

She kept trying to think back to the day the picture was taken. Had they had a fight? Was Imogen imagining the look because the texts were making her see everybody as a suspect?

Turning a couple more pages, Imogen sighed. Was she just seeing things that weren't there? Was she making connections that didn't exist? Imogen felt tormented by her own mind sometimes.

Still, Kelly had been unusually obsessed with their friend. It was clear that she had wanted to *be* her. Is it possible that she wanted it so much, she killed for it?

Imogen shook her head and closed the photo album, frowning at herself. Of course not. This was Kelly Sharpe she was thinking about. She wasn't a psycho killer, she'd been their friend!

Imogen stood up, hot chocolate forgotten, as she went off in search of painkillers to ward off the incoming headache she could already feel on its way.

She stared at her reflection in the mirror.

So many names were spinning round and round in her head.

Thomas Playfair.
Hannah Clarkson.
Kyle Flynn.
Dakota Pike.
Chloe Pierce.
Kelly Sharpe.

Is it possible that one of them is responsible for what happened to Annie?

Did one of those people want her gone so bad, for whatever reason, that they *killed* her that night?

fourteen

The next morning Imogen had once again woken up with a rush of determination. She had decided that she was going to follow the clues. Thomas and Hannah had pointed her in the direction of Dakota Pike and Kyle Flynn, so that's exactly where she was going to go next. No getting distracted this time.

Eric had a late start that day so he was still home when she got up, padding into the kitchen with a little smile. "Morning."

"Morning, love." He smiled at her over his shoulder. "Hungry?"

Imogen shook her head. "No. Thanks though." She eyed the eggs and bacon, feeling like if she ate anything she would just bring it back up.

The morning was slow and nice, but Imogen had this impatient knot swirling around in the pit of her stomach. She was anxious to get started and anxious for what the day might bring.

Finally, she kissed Eric goodbye and waved him off as he headed out to the garage to take his jeep to work.

Imogen's mother was babysitting Brooklyn today so she got her daughter all dressed and ready, packed her a little bag of toys and nappies and everything, and then headed out to her own car.

She settled Brooklyn into her car seat and then got in herself.

Imogen didn't drive too often nowadays, mostly because she was anxious that she would end up having some kind of episode at the wheel and cause an accident.

Her doctors and family told her it was irrational considering she was medicated and stable, but she couldn't shake it and so a lot of the time Imogen would walk.

* * *

"Hi, baby!" Imogen's mother beamed excitedly as Imogen walked into the house with Brooklyn.

She chuckled. "I know you're talking to Brooklyn, not me, and I'd like you to know I'm a little offended."

Brooke waved a dismissive hand, giving Imogen an amused look. "You know you'll always be my baby too, kid."

Imogen grinned, putting Brooklyn down on the carpet and watching her go straight over to her mother and Lauren's cat and start messing with its tail. The cat, used to this, simply gave the little girl a look and walked away towards the kitchen in search of food.

Imogen and Eric had named their daughter Brooklyn after Imogen's mother when the woman had gotten into what could have been a fatal car accident the night after Brooklyn was born.

She had been driving back home from the hospital and had been hit by a drunk driver.

Brooke had been in a coma for two days and the doctors had made her prognosis sound very bleak and so, heartbroken, Eric and Imogen had decided to name their daughter Brooklyn.

Brooke had miraculously opened her eyes the next afternoon but the name had just sort of stuck by then.

"Okay, I'll be back to pick her up at, like, half four?" She looked to her mother questioningly and Brooke nodded.

"That's fine. Lauren is home early today so I think we're all going to play out in the garden. Have a little picnic, enjoy this good weather."

Imogen smiled, nodding. "That sounds nice, she'll like that. Take pictures." She moved over to Brooklyn and leaned down, kissing the top of her head. "I'll be back later, little bug."

Imogen left her mother's house, petting the cat on her way out the door, and went back out to her car.

She pulled away from the curb, not wanting to linger too long outside her mother's house in case she noticed and wondered if something was wrong. Imogen parked back up a couple of streets away, checking her phone.

No more texts, which was disappointing but it just meant she needed to stick to her instincts. Follow the clues until she found where they were leading.

Imogen turned the engine back on and pulled away from the side of the road.

Next stop, Kyle Flynn and Dakota Pike.

She found Dakota first, sitting on a bench in the park.

The brunette was looking down at her phone but she was obviously keeping an eye on the swingset nearby, where Imogen could see her son Luke playing with another young boy. He had to be about seven now and Imogen was struck suddenly by just how much time had passed.

Dakota looked up as Imogen sort of hovered awkwardly nearby, and she smiled when she recognised her. "Oh, hey!"

Imogen smiled back. "Hi." She moved closer, feeling more comfortable to sit down on the seat next to the other woman. "How're you?"

Dakota nodded. "Good, yeah." She gestured to the swings. "Wanted a nice day in to read my book but Luke was adamant he wanted to come and play with Dale."

Imogen smiled, looking over to the boys playing on the swings again. They were lying on their stomachs, twisting the chains around as far as they would go, and then lifting their feet off the ground and letting the chains untangle and spin them out.

Imogen felt a wave of nostalgia tug at her as she remembered doing the exact same thing when she was young.

"I don't blame him." She chuckled. "They're having a blast."

Dakota nodded. "Yeah. Oh to be a kid again, huh?"

Imogen remembered thinking how much she longed to go back in time. To go back to when she was a kid and everything was easy, and she was out running around town all day, every day, with her friends.

Now though, she knew that she wouldn't change her life for anything. Eric, Brooklyn. She wouldn't be without them.

"What about you?" Dakota's voice brought her back out of her thoughts. "No baby today?"

Imogen shook her head. "Oh, no. My mum's got her today. I just know I'm going to pick her up and she's going to be hyped up on sugar and swimming in new toys." She joked lightly, though it wouldn't be far off. She was always getting spoiled when Imogen dropped her off at Brooke and Lauren's.

Dakota laughed. "That sounds about right."

Imogen thought how easy it was to just simply start a conversation when you were older. As a kid, she'd never have just walked up to somebody on the playground and sat down to start a random chat, even if she knew of them.

Things always felt so much bigger when you were younger. So much more dramatic and end-of-the-world-y. The things that mattered back then didn't tend to matter too much nowadays.

Still, she knew this conversation was set to get harder.

Imogen studied Luke as best she could, trying to see Kyle in his features but he just looked like Dakota so it didn't really help sway her either way.

She was quiet for a little while, trying to decide if there was some natural way of bringing up Annie or Kyle but she was pretty sure there wasn't.

Of course, as usual, Dakota brought it up first. It seemed the discovery of Annie's body had become the hottest topic in town.

"Hey, I'm sorry about Annie." She said, and Imogen looked up at her.

"Thanks." She hated thanking people for that. It didn't feel right. "You were her friend too though, right?" Imogen knew that Annie had hung out with Dakota and her friends back then sometimes. Imogen had always been so jealous, worried Annie preferred the other group because they were older, cooler, all smoked.

Dakota made a face, though she tried to hide it. She didn't do a very good job though and Imogen frowned as she looked back at her. "What?"

Dakota shook her head. "No... nothing."

"Doesn't look like it's nothing." Imogen said, unable to help herself.

Dakota sighed, glancing over at the swings again. The boys were trying to see who could go the highest now. Imogen wondered if Dakota looking at Luke was some minor confirmation of the affair with Kyle, her son being the result, but of course she couldn't be sure.

"We just didn't always get on, that's all." Dakota shrugged. "You know what she was like." She glanced at Imogen. "Doesn't mean I'm not sad for her."

Imogen was quiet for a moment, trying to decide how she was going to bring the whole thing up. Was there some subtle way?

Eventually, she decided there wasn't time to be subtle. She wouldn't get anywhere that way.

"Did you guys not get on because of Kyle?" She blurted out the question, watching for Dakota's reaction.

The other girl looked surprised. She hadn't expected it and she eyed Imogen a little suspiciously.

"Did she tell you then?" Dakota asked, sighing as she slumped back a little in her seat, looking over at her boy again. "It wasn't serious."

So, it was true then? Imogen blinked, sort of stunned even though she had worked herself up to believing it more. She shook her head. "No. Thomas Playfair told me."

Dakota looked surprised again, then a little irritated. "Why would he do that?"

Imogen shrugged. He'd done it because she had pretty much accused him and Hannah of murdering Annie but she wasn't about to admit that. She still couldn't even be sure if he and Hannah weren't suspicious. Why were they still together if Hannah was so angry about Thomas's affair?

"Look, Kyle and Annie had a few issues. He found out she'd cheated on him." Dakota said.

"So, what, he decided to cheat back? Like revenge?" Imogen wondered, but Dakota shook her head.

"No. It wasn't calculated. He didn't mean for it to happen. I was just talking to him about it." She said, looking back at the blonde. "It just happened."

Imogen turned to look at the boys playing again. "And Luke is his, right?"

Dakota sighed. "No. Luke's *mine*. Kyle doesn't want to know."

Imogen frowned at that. What kind of person could create a child and then just pretend they didn't exist and continue along happily? Imogen could never imagine leaving Brooklyn with Eric and never being part of her life.

"I'm sorry."

Dakota shrugged. "It's no big deal. We're doing just fine on our own."

Imogen looked at her, regarding her with a little bit of respect for the things she was saying. She really didn't sound too bitter, just grateful that she had Luke.

"Did you see Annie the day she died?" Imogen found herself asking.

Dakota turned to give Imogen a funny look. "Well, yeah. I was at the party."

Imogen shook her head. "No, I mean... before. Or... after." She trailed off, feeling awkward.

Imogen watched as the words registered in Dakota's mind. She saw the annoyance flash across her face, the indignation, and she couldn't blame her.

"After?! Are you asking me if I fucking *killed* her?" Came Dakota's biting response.

Imogen shook her head. "No, I..." She trailed off again because what could she say? She kind of was. Wasn't that what this whole thing was about?

"Look, Imogen." Dakota stood up, shaking her head.

She was angry and Imogen felt like a child being told off by its mother.

"Yes, I saw Annie that day. She came storming into the cafe and started screaming at me in front of everyone because she figured out Kyle had cheated. She was furious that I'd done that, and I suppose I can't blame her, but I also can't blame Kyle. That girl was a *nightmare*."

Imogen had never liked people around her calling Annie names or being that way towards her. Especially after her death. Imogen wanted to preserve Annie's memory. The good parts. She wanted her to rest in peace forever as the angel girl Imogen had viewed her as. Deep down, she knew that she had always worn rose coloured glasses when it came to Annie but she wouldn't consciously acknowledge that. Not yet, anyway.

"Luke wasn't even one year old and there she was standing in front of us screaming and telling me I was going to live to regret it." Dakota continued. "I was furious. I thought she needed knocked down a peg. But no, Imogen, I did not kill her."

"Sorry." Imogen mumbled but Dakota had already turned and started moving towards the boys on the swings. She watched the three of them move off in the direction of a nearby ice cream van.

Imogen sighed. She felt bad but she hadn't really learned much. She felt like she wouldn't get anywhere else with Dakota though, so she stood up and turned to walk across the park, back in the direction of her car, going off in search of Kyle.

Kyle still lived at home with his police officer father, so Imogen decided she would try there first.

He worked part-time at the police station too, in the mail room, but Imogen hadn't wanted to go to the station and start poking around in case Lauren caught on.

She hovered outside for a few moments before forcing herself to raise her hand and knock.

At first she thought nobody was home because it took a while to get an answer. She knocked again and then turned to walk back down the driveway but it was at that moment that the door opened.

"Imogen?" Kyle sounded confused, probably wondering what the hell she was doing here.

"Hey." Imogen paused, probably looking like a complete idiot as she tried to figure out what to say. "Can I come in?"

"Why?" Kyle asked, keeping hold of the door as he looked back out at her.

Why? Imogen blinked at him, shrugging. "I..." She paused briefly and decided there was no need for subtlety. She was in this deep enough as it was already. "Because I'd rather not talk about your affair and the night Annie was killed out here on the front steps for all your neighbours to see."

Kyle was frowning as he stepped out of the way, jerking his head back slightly in a *hurry up and get in then* sort of gesture. Imogen glanced over her shoulder and stepped inside.

Kyle's dad's house was big and modern, with bright white walls and thick fluffy carpets. It had changed a lot from when Imogen had last been here, probably almost seven years ago now. Back then, it was all lemon walls and wood floors. Back then, Kyle's mother had been alive too.

"What is this about exactly?" Kyle looked over at her, frowning.

Imogen wasn't sure where she wanted to start with this. She knew she kept jumping in without a plan but she felt like she was running out of time. Time for what exactly, she had no idea.

"Did you cheat on Annie with Dakota Pike?" She found herself asking.

"That's not really any of your business." Kyle replied, still frowning as he looked back at her, arms crossed over his chest.

Imogen stared at him. "It is if it's the reason my best friend ended up in the ground."

"Whoa, whoa, whoa." Kyle held up his hands, shaking his head. "What are you on about?"

"I know Annie found out." Imogen told him. "I know she was angry. Maybe at the party, you guys had a fight, and something happened…"

"Hold the hell on here." Kyle interrupted, scowling at her. "Bullshit. You've just made up this little fantasy in your head, huh?" He shook his head. "Last I checked, you're not the cops."

He was angry and she could see that but Imogen wondered if he was *so* angry because she'd figured him out. Because the jig was up.

"Should I be calling the cops?"

"Jesus, Imogen, *no!*" Kyle shook his head, staring at her like she was absolutely insane. "Where are you even getting this shit?"

Imogen blinked back at him. "Somebody *killed* her! They put her in the goddamn ground that night."

He looked down, looking uncomfortable. *Good,* she thought.

"Somebody killed her, somebody in this town, somebody I know. I need to know who and I need to know why." Imogen continued.

Kyle sighed, looking back up at her. His shoulders dropped slightly as he untensed, his expression softening though only a little. "Well, you're looking in the wrong place with me."

"Prove it."

"How am I supposed to do that?" Kyle asked. "I can't shove us in a time machine and show you."

"I don't know, Kyle. Convince me. Tell me about that night."

"What about it?" He was getting impatient.

"I don't know." Imogen wished she'd come up with a plan. "Were you arguing about it?"

Kyle rolled his eyes. "No, she was making a point that night to not speak to me at all. She'd already cornered Dakota in the cafe and she'd already screamed at me earlier that day."

"So, you guys did fight?" Imogen pressed.

"Yes, but I barely saw her at the party. And I went home early because she put me in such a foul mood. You can ask Jason or, you know what, you can ask my father because he was still watching TV with my mother when I stumbled through the door."

Imogen chewed lightly on her lower lip as she digested the information. Was Kyle's dad the kind of man who would cover for his son even if it meant lying? No. She didn't think so. He was one of those all around trustworthy blokes. He was a by-the-book cop, too.

"Fine. I will." She heard herself saying before she really made the decision to even speak.

Kyle rolled his eyes again. He was being quite aggressive but Imogen knew she couldn't actually blame him for that because if someone barged into her home and started accusing her of murder she would probably be the same way.

"Great." Kyle moved towards the door and yanked it back open, pulling it all the way back to the wall, and stared at her. "Now get the hell out of my house."

fifteen

Imogen left Kyle's house with a sigh. She felt pretty unaccomplished. She hadn't gotten any closer to figuring out what actually happened to Annie.

She knew Annie was cheating on Kyle and Kyle was cheating on Annie. She knew Hannah had found out about the affair and Annie had found out about the other affair.

Neither of these things had gotten her any closer to the actual truth of how Annie had died, despite the fact she did think both sides had plenty of motive.

She drove through the streets feeling glum and no closer to anything than she'd been when she left the house that morning.

As she drove, she turned her music on, blasting Taylor Swift and singing along in an attempt to release some of the tension and anxiety that had settled on her shoulders.

It didn't completely work and by the time Imogen pulled up outside her house she was feeling even more despondent.

She decided that she was going to spend a few hours at home by herself relaxing, maybe take a nap, and then she would go and pick up Brooklyn.

As she grabbed her phone, however, the screen lit up and she noticed that she had a text message. Her breath caught in her throat as she saw it was from *that* number.

"Where did Annie go after arguing with Dakota? You should ask your beloved Nina."

Imogen read the message five times, the words not fully computing in her brain at first. What did Nina have to do with anything?

Nina and Annie hadn't always gotten along, Imogen knew that, but Nina steered clear of her back when they were all in school. Annie used to tease Nina sometimes but that was just normal kid stuff, right?

Imogen hadn't started dating Nina until after Annie was already missing.

Imogen had never given her sexuality a lot of thought as she was growing up. She would look at girls and she would look at boys and she would find herself equally attracted to both but it wasn't something she ever consciously sat and thought about.

Imogen knew now that she was probably forced into the closet by compulsory heterosexuality and the social biases she had grown up around, through no real fault of her own or the people around her.

Of course, she had loved Annie as more than a friend. Annie was beautiful and magnetic and Imogen had been addicted to her. Her heart shaped face, her smile, the mischievous glint in her hazel eyes.

She had eventually started to kind of feel like Annie had known about her crush on some level. Just little things she would say sometimes, weird comments and remarks, sly jabs. But Imogen blindly ignored all of it, too caught up in idolising Annie in a way.

Nina, however, had always been openly gay since they were all in school. She had never hidden it after coming out at a young age. She was unashamed of who she was and Annie sort of took to picking on her like she picked on many others who weren't quite up on her level.

At the time, Imogen had convinced herself it wasn't that big of a deal. She'd been uncomfortable and thought it was wrong to bully people but she had also managed to explain it away, justify Annie's behaviour because she had loved Annie. It was that simple.

After Annie had disappeared, Imogen had been lost. She didn't know how to cope with not knowing where her best friend was or what had happened to her.

One day, she had been sitting beneath a tree in the woods, by the lake, crying. Nina had stumbled upon her there and, after some awkwardness, tried to comfort her.

After that, the two started spending more time together and over the months, Imogen realised she was crushing hard on Nina.

It was then that, with Nina's help, she finally acknowledged her bisexuality and she came out to her family and then started officially dating the other girl.

The relationship obviously didn't last but she was Imogen's first love and what they had would always be special to her, especially because Nina helped her come to terms with such a large part of herself.

Imogen knew that Nina hadn't been at Jason Wright's party that night. She hadn't even been invited and it wasn't her crowd. She'd never gone to one of those parties.

Did Nina see Annie the day she died, though?

Imogen chucked her phone back down onto the passenger seat beside her and pulled the car away from the curb again, thoughts of a nice, quiet nap at home banished all of a sudden.

She couldn't expect to get all the answers right away. Not when this all seemed to be some big game. A chase around Annie's antics that whole summer, which seemed to have led to this one fateful night.

Maybe she had to stop being so hard on herself, so impatient to get all of the answers. She had to be more patient and follow the clues no matter how long it took or if they pulled her in directions that didn't make any sense to her.

Patience, however, had never really been her strong suit.

Imogen drove through the streets, trying to figure out if she even remembered where Nina lived now. It had been so long since she had even really needed to know Nina's flat number.

Eventually, she pulled up outside the block of flats, idling on the street for a few moments before cutting the engine. She sat there in her car for a few more minutes, anxiety tugging at her.

Imogen couldn't imagine any interaction between Nina and Annie being very helpful to where she was ultimately trying to get to, but she had to play the game by whatever rules this anonymous person set.

Though it would help if she knew those rules herself.

Eventually, Imogen forced herself to get out of the car and moved up to the flats, pressing the buzzer for number eight.

There was a long silence and Imogen thought that maybe she wasn't even home but eventually the voice crackled through to her.

"Hello?" Nina asked, her tone betraying she obviously wasn't expecting anyone.

"It--" Imogen's voice broke and she quickly cleared her throat, feeling stupid. "It's Imogen."

A brief pause and then she heard the sound that signalled the doors unlocking.

Imogen pushed the door open and made for the stairs, heading up to Nina's front door. When she got there, the door opened before she could reach out and knock. Nina must have been watching through the spyhole.

"Hey." Nina smiled at her but she looked confused. "Something wrong?"

Imogen shook her head. "No." She paused. "I mean, I don't know."

Nina frowned at that, looking back at Imogen carefully for a few seconds before she moved aside and gestured for the blonde to come in.

Imogen stepped in and looked around. She had never actually been in Nina's flat. When they dated, they'd all still lived at home and after they broke up, there wasn't any reason for her to come around. They were still friendly but not really friends.

"Do you want anything to drink?" Nina asked. "Juice? Water? Tea?"

"Um, yeah, tea would be good. Thanks." Imogen followed her towards the kitchen, lurking in the doorway as she watched Nina flick on the kettle.

"So, what's up?" Nina asked, turning to look at Imogen, crossing her arms and leaning casually against the kitchen counter.

Imogen didn't really know where to start. *How* to start, even. Did she just go all out and lay the whole truth on the other woman?

"I've just been... thinking about Annie." She said.

Nina was looking back at her and she could see the mild confusion in her expression. "What about Annie?"

Imogen shrugged. "The day she died."

Nina turned to grab some mugs from the cupboard and the milk from the fridge. "Well, I think that's natural."

Imogen could hear the question in her tone still. *Why are you talking to me about it?* It was fair enough considering they hadn't gotten on and Imogen and Nina hadn't really been that close in a while now.

Imogen nodded, reaching for her mug of tea once the kettle had boiled and Nina had finished making them.

"Do you remember much about that day?" She asked, trying to sound casual.

Nina looked at her, shrugging. "I mean... I guess so?"

Imogen took a sip of her tea, feeling her heart speed up. "I know you weren't at the party." She watched Nina nod. "But did you see Annie during the day?"

She studied Nina's expression and thought she saw some discomfort written there. Nina looked uneasy while she lifted her own tea to her lips, but whether it was due to simply thinking about Annie or something deeper Imogen couldn't tell.

"Why?" Nina's response wasn't exactly what Imogen had been hoping for. It seemed almost defensive to her.

"I just--" Imogen paused. What should she say? "I'm trying to figure things out."

Nina frowned, not understanding. "What things?"

Imogen shrugged. "I don't know, just her... her last day."

"What, are you going around town asking everyone if they saw her?" Nina shook her head. "What good will that do, Imogen?"

Imogen felt a bit embarrassed because technically she supposed that's kind of what she was doing.

"No, it's..." She tried to protest but didn't know what to say and felt silly.

Nina didn't say anything, just sort of looked down at the counter as she lifted her cup again.

It frustrated Imogen a little. It felt like she was deliberately dodging the topic or trying to downplay it.

"Did you see her or not?" She blurted out.

Nina gave her a look and Imogen could tell she was surprised by the fact she'd asked again, pressing the issue.

Imogen worried once more that she was losing it a little. That she was going too hard on all this Annie stuff. That her mind was working against her.

But she had to know.

"Look. I need to know, okay? I can't explain but I have to know what she did that day." She paused. "It will help me move on." It wasn't the whole truth but it was close enough that Imogen figured it would do.

Nina shook her head, putting her mug down on the counter and running her hands over her face. "Imogen-"

Imogen didn't say anything else, she just watched and wondered why Nina seemed so uptight about it. It made her feel a little scared that it meant something horrible. Like maybe Nina was more involved than she knew. Was that what this anonymous texter had been getting at? No. Surely not. Imogen knew Nina more than anyone else. Nina wouldn't hurt a fly. Quite literally. She had seen it with her own eyes.

There was a slightly awkward silence and Imogen eventually opened her mouth to say something just to fill it, but then Nina finally started talking.

"I did." She admitted, shrugging as she moved to sit down at her dining table. "I saw her that day, way before the party though. In the afternoon."

Imogen bit her lip gently, nodding.

So Annie had spent the morning arguing with Dakota and Kyle, making out with Thomas and being caught by Hannah, and then the afternoon had seen her run into Nina.

It was a rough timeline but it was better than absolutely nothing.

Imogen was already confident that Nina wouldn't have any sort of motive for Annie's murder, like the other names on the list.

There was no way. This person had probably only brought up the fact they knew Nina had seen Annie that day because they knew it would shake Imogen up a little. Not that she could figure out *why* they would want to shake her up in the first place. Were they helping her or were they working against her?

"Was she with anyone?" Imogen wondered. Maybe she had been seen with the person who would later go on to kill her.

Nina shook her head. "No, she was by herself." She looked a little uncomfortable again.

That afternoon, Nina had been walking through town, feeling a little moody.

She and her current girlfriend Emma Williamson had just broken up and she was beating herself up about it.

As she walked, she spotted Annie Pierce a short distance ahead of her down the road.

A bolt of anger surged through her as she remembered the previous day, the vicious taunting that Annie had given her. The names she'd called her. The shoves against the wall.

Nina wouldn't normally do something so impulsive but she was frustrated about her break up and frustrated by Annie's existence and so she found herself heading straight for the raven haired girl.

"You!" Nina snapped, getting Annie's attention. The other girl turned to look at her with a frown which only irritated Nina further.

"Ugh, what do *you* want?" Annie's reply only added fuel to the already growing fire in Nina's stomach.

"What do you think?" Nina snapped, crossing her arms across her chest as she glared at the other girl.

Annie looked back at her, cool and indifferent. She shrugged. "I don't know. Which is why I asked."

"You're really just going to pretend as if yesterday didn't even happen?" Nina felt like she should pull back but she was beyond that point now.

Annie frowned at her as if she was completely clueless. "What the hell are you talking about?"

The memory of Annie taunting her and making fun of her newly dyed pink hair tips sprang back into Nina's mind and she stared back at the girl, anger bubbling in her chest. "You're unbelievable."

Annie rolled her eyes. "And you're a freak. I don't have time for this."

As Annie turned away to walk off, Nina felt another flash of fury and before she knew it, it had taken over her body entirely. She stepped forward, towards Annie, arms outstretched now.

It was like she couldn't stop herself as her hands connected with Annie's back, giving the other girl a harsh shove.

The motion pushed Annie off balance and Nina watched as she went flying into the road and straight into the path of an oncoming vehicle.

Luckily - or unluckily as she remembered thinking at the time - the car screeched to a halt.

Annie stood and she was clearly shaken as she snatched her handbag up from where it had fallen to the road, and hurried back towards the pavement.

The few people around were watching and the car lingered before it sped off again, deciding that since nothing had happened they weren't about to stick around.

"You." Annie's voice snapped her out of her thoughts as she stormed towards her, getting up in her face and shoving her shoulders. Nina stumbled backwards. "You are going to *regret* that."

Without thinking, Nina shoved Annie back again, and shook her head. "No, Annie. *You* are going to regret *that*." She snapped and then immediately turned and fled the scene.

As she walked home, Nina's anger subsided quite quickly and morphed into mild horror at her own actions and thoughts.

She glanced down at her hands. They were shaking. Had that actually just happened?

Nina looked over her shoulder, as if she was afraid that Annie was going to be coming after her right now, but she was nowhere to be seen.

Nina turned back again, feeling sick. What if that car had hit her?

Oh, God.

Annie was going to *kill* her.

Present

Imogen stared at Nina for a few moments as she took in what she had just heard.

Nina and Annie had *argued* that day. More than argued. Nina had *pushed* her in front of a car!

"I didn't mean to do it, it just happened." Nina said desperately as she looked up and met Imogen's gaze.

"I don't understand." Imogen shook her head and glanced away.

Nina frowned. "She had been so vile to me the day before and then she just acted like it didn't happen. I was upset. I was *angry*."

"Yeah, no shit you were angry." Imogen interjected, shaking her head as she looked back at Nina. She almost didn't even recognise this woman sitting in front of her.

"Look, it was horrible, yeah, but she was fine. She walked away." Nina stated. "And I didn't see her again."

"Are you sure?" Imogen found herself asking though she wished she hadn't.

Nina stared at her. "How can you even ask me that?"

Imogen shook her head. She didn't know.

Did she think that Nina was capable of hurting Annie? No, but ten minutes ago she wouldn't have thought she was capable of that level of anger either.

"I don't..." Imogen shook her head again, putting her empty mug in the sink and stepping towards the door. "I have to go, I... have to pick up Brooklyn."

Before Nina could say another word, Imogen had rushed through the living room and out the front door.

As she got into the car, her phone vibrated, a sensation that had started to make her stomach sink.

She opened the message.

"You really can't trust anyone."

sixteen

Imogen woke the next morning with a headache. She groaned. So much for the painkillers she'd taken before passing out, she thought as she forced herself upright, stretching.

She didn't hear Brooklyn so she took the opportunity to quickly get ready for the day. It wasn't often that she got to get herself all washed and dressed before Brooklyn got up. Usually, she had to do everything in between tending to the baby.

Her thoughts kept drifting towards Nina and her interaction with Annie that day. It was scary but Imogen also knew what anger could do to you.

She was scared that Nina could somehow be involved.

Had she gone after Annie later that night in hope of revenge? Had she been lurking on the outskirts of the party?

She shoved the thoughts away, needing her brain to just stop going round and round over this for a while. She needed quiet

When Imogen left the bathroom and eventually drifted towards her daughter's room, she nudged the door open with a slight smile, ready to see that chubby face looking back at her.

Instead, she found Brooklyn's cot empty.

Imogen froze.

She stared at the empty space where her daughter should be for a little too long.

She was wasting time.

Imogen turned and made for the door and then for the stairs, her thoughts racing.

Had she forgotten that Brooklyn was with her mother and Lauren? No.

Imogen's thoughts were pulsing through her mind, her body in complete panic mode.

Had whoever was texting her come into her house during the night and taken her baby? Did this person want to use her as leverage?

Did they even exist? Had *Imogen herself* done something to her baby that she just didn't remember?

Was what she'd feared the other day really true? Had she genuinely lost her mind?

Did she take her medication?

Imogen's bare feet smacked against the tiles of the kitchen floor as she came running in from the living room.

Brooklyn was sitting in her high chair at the kitchen table, chewing a teething ring and babbling away to herself.

Eric was standing by the cooker, the smell of bacon and eggs wafting through the air between them. He was keeping an eye on the pans in front of him, humming away happily to himself.

Imogen's panic level slowly began to subside. She sucked in a deep breath, telling herself to calm down.

Eric turned around, smiling obliviously over at her. "Morning, love. I hope you're hungry."

Imogen felt like she'd stopped breathing and was trying to figure out how to breathe normally again.

She blinked at Eric, moving to sit next to Brooklyn's chair, reaching over to fuss with her. Just to make sure she was really there.

This was real. It *was*, right?

"Yeah.." She nodded, clearing her throat as she fought to regain control. "I thought you would be at work already." Imogen told him, glancing up at the kitchen clock to double check the time.

It was definitely long past the time she would have expected him to be home. It was eleven. God, had she really slept that long?

"I took the day off." Eric told her, plating up the bacon and the eggs and turning to move over to the table where his two favourite girls were. He put a plate in front of Imogen.

"I know you've had a hard week, so we thought we'd let you have a lie in. Didn't we?" The question directed towards Brooklyn, his smile colouring his tone.

Brooklyn giggled back, waving her hands in the air.

Imogen couldn't help but smile despite the fact that her heart was still hammering away like mad in her chest. "Thanks."

Eric shovelled a forkful of eggs into his mouth, looking from Brooklyn to Imogen. "Are you okay?" He asked, suddenly realising there was something written on her face other than just the gratitude of having a long lie in.

"Yeah." Imogen nodded quickly, chewing a tiny piece of bacon. "No, I'm fine. Just, um. Weird dreams last night."

"Nightmares again?" He reached out and placed a hand over his wife's, wanting to comfort her.

Imogen smiled. "Yeah. But it's alright. I'm good." Imogen told him, reaching over to interact with Brooklyn, who was just obliviously happy.

It was best that she didn't tell Eric about the panic she'd felt. Better to keep the fact she'd immediately jumped to Brooklyn being kidnapped to herself. It would lead to having to tell him about the messages which would, in turn, lead to telling him about the fact she was starting to question reality. Again. He didn't need that and she could handle it.

Eric nodded, satisfied enough with her answer to continue munching away at his breakfast. Imogen wasn't too hungry but she forced herself to eat. *It was good for her. She had to look after herself.* One of the many mantras of therapy.

After putting their empty plates in the sink for later, Imogen moved to take her medication.

She could feel Eric watching her but she pretended not to notice.

Then Imogen moved onto the living room floor, sitting cross-legged in front of Brooklyn so she could play with her toys with her.

She told herself to forget all about the panic of the morning. To forget about the texts and her suspicions and forget all about Annie. Just for a while.

Imogen wanted to enjoy a nice day with her family. It wasn't too often that Eric took days off and she wanted to make the most of it.

The day actually turned out to be really fun and Imogen actually did forget all about her panic and her paranoia and her mission to find out what happened the night Annie disappeared.

Eric drove Imogen and Brooklyn out of town for the day, heading for one of their favourite reservoirs. They took their dogs Buddy and Lolly, and went for a lovely long country walk.

It was beautiful and Imogen took lots of pictures of everybody so she could fill up her next photo album.

Imogen wanted Brooklyn to have all the memories that she possibly could. She wanted her daughter to be able to look back on her life. Imogen was big on photos and memories and preserving the past. She liked being able to look back on her life. Maybe it was because she'd had such a difficult time knowing what was real.

Nothing was more real than a photograph, right? A moment encased in time forever.

The water was calm as they walked the path. Imogen could see ducks and swans ducking and diving. A real picture of peace and she felt a wave of contentment wash over her. If only it could stay like this.

The air was mild and Imogen was bouncing Brooklyn in her arms, pointing to butterflies and flowers, showing her the world, while Eric walked the dogs alongside them.

"Look! They've got babies!" She grinned, pointing across the water, over to a mother duck and the ducklings skirting behind her.

Eric smiled, looking over at his wife holding Brooklyn so she could see, though who knew what she was really looking at. Her gaze was everywhere, enchanted by the new place.

"I should take more days off, shouldn't I?" Eric chuckled, looping an arm around Imogen's waist as they turned back in the direction of the car.

Imogen looked up at him with a grin, opening the door for the dogs and moving to settle Brooklyn into her car seat.

"You really should." She said as she slid into her own seat, clicking the seatbelt in place.

* * *

Imogen curled up under the covers that night feeling a long way from the way she had when she'd woken up that morning.

She stepped out of the shower where she'd been for the last half hour or so, enjoying the hot stream of water cascading over her skin, practically massaging away any lingering stress.

She stood in the bathroom looking in the mirror, feeling so content from what a nice day they had all had together. It was one of those perfect days she was sure that she would remember for years to come.

Brooklyn had conked out early from all the excitement of visiting the reservoir.

Imogen smiled as she peeked into her daughter's room, having already gotten herself dried from the shower and dressed for bed. The little girl was sleeping soundly so she carefully eased the door shut so as not to wake her.

Eric was half asleep beside her already. He did try his best to always be there but there were many times when Imogen fell asleep alone or woke up alone.

His job was important, he ran the whole newspaper now, and she was proud of him but some days she had to admit that she just missed him.

She turned off the light and melted down under the duvet, closing her eyes with a content sigh. She felt Eric moving closer and she cuddled up to him.

Just as she was about to drift off, happily having managed to forget about Annie and Nina and everyone else, her phone buzzing on the side table shook her out of her near-slumber.

She opened her eyes with a sigh, feeling Eric roll away from her with a light groan, still pretty much asleep but clearly disturbed by her jolting awake in his arms.

Imogen was just going to ignore it because it was late and she wanted to sink into dreamland but she found herself rolling over and reaching out, grabbing the phone from the side table and opening her bleary eyes to look at the screen.

She had a text message but it didn't say anything. It was from that anonymous number.

Imogen sat up, frowning. They hadn't written anything this time, they had just sent a picture.

A picture of Charlie Baker and Annie Pierce.

seventeen

Imogen had barely been able to sleep after receiving the message last night.

The picture kept popping back into her head every time she tried to push it out. The image of Charlie Baker and Annie Pierce in the woods. It looked like it was taken the night Annie died. She was wearing the same clothes. It looked like they were arguing.

Imogen's thoughts felt all foggy. She didn't know what she was supposed to do with this information, or what this information even meant.

Did it mean *anything?*

Should she tell Ruby?

Should she confront Charlie?

Confront Charlie about *what*, exactly? Confront him over a photo of him standing in the woods?

Yes. With Annie. Who was wearing the same top she was the day she died. Looking angry as hell.

Imogen couldn't understand it. Charlie wasn't even there, was he? She opened the message again, clicking on the picture and zooming in. It did kind of look like Jason's back garden, the bit that backed up onto the woods that Annie eventually died in.

Maybe Charlie had just come looking for Sophie and ran into Annie before she went missing and she was being her usual aggravating self.

Not that Imogen would *ever* admit that Annie could be aggravating… but Annie *could* be aggravating and argumentative and difficult. Even to adults. So maybe that was all this was.

But if that was true, why did Charlie never, ever mention this to the police? The cops had interviewed all of the friends and their parents multiple times over.

Not once did Sophie's father ever say he'd been around the area that night. That's something you would say, isn't it? If you had nothing to hide?

So, what if he *did* have something to hide?

Imogen sat there for a few moments, thinking it over. It seemed so unlikely. Good old unassuming Charlie Baker. English teacher. Her best friend's father. Now her best friend's boyfriend. He had always been around, hadn't he? If they went to Sophie's. If they were at school.

The more Imogen stewed on it, the more she felt like a dog with a bone. Like she just couldn't let it go. It was an itch that wouldn't be satisfied until she scratched the hell out of it.

So she stood up, text Ruby that she was bringing Brooklyn over for a play date with Hope, and she left the house.

* * *

"Sorry, I hope you don't mind the last minute intrusion." Imogen said as she swept into Ruby's house after her friend greeted her at the door.

"Of course not, no." Ruby shook her head, smiling. She looked happy and Imogen felt bad that she was probably about to drop this bombshell on her and her life.

"Come in, I'll get some tea started." Ruby closed the door behind Imogen and led her through to the kitchen.

Imogen plonked Brooklyn down on the carpet with Hope so they could both play together, and she moved through with Ruby.

In the dining room, Charlie was sitting at the table reading this morning's newspaper.

He glanced up and offered Imogen a little smile as she walked in. She smiled back, or attempted to, but her heart was pounding as she looked at him.

Did you kill my best friend?

It's not like she was going to just come out and say it like that, but still. The words were dancing around in her head, all shaken up like they were in a snowglobe.

Imogen hopped up on one of the seats. There was a perfect view of the children's playing area from here. She had to admit Ruby and Charlie's place was something to be jealous of.

It was spacious and it was beautiful and bright; the perfect space for children to grow up in.

Of course, after Sophie, Charlie and his ex wife Jenna had sold the house. Too many bad memories, she supposed. It had been kind of bittersweet since Imogen had spent so much time there. Had so many sleepovers. So many hang outs with the whole gang in Mr and Mrs Baker's house.

Of course, she knew it was worse for Sophie's parents.

Imogen's fingers curled around the cup of tea that Ruby slid in front of her. "Thanks." She smiled.

There was an awkward chill running through Imogen but it didn't seem like anybody else noticed. Charlie kept his eyes on his newspaper and Ruby looked bright as a button.

"I know I say it every single time, but they're really just getting *so* big." Ruby chuckled, looking through towards where the girls were playing.

Imogen couldn't help but chuckle in return, turning to look over her shoulder with a smile. "Yeah, tell me about it."

Every time Imogen looked at the kids, they were like little markers, showing the passage of time.

Imogen looked back over the last few years and it was like the time had flashed by. Just like that. It never felt like it when you were actually in it, but when you looked back over your shoulder, the time was just gone.

She turned back with a slight smile, though her stomach was still churning a little. Charlie turned the page of the newspaper, the crinkle giving Imogen some serious sensory overload.

Her grip tightened on her cup of tea as she did her best not to look over, but unable to stop herself glancing towards him.

What was he hiding?

Imogen blinked, looking up. She had missed whatever Ruby had just said and both she and Charlie were staring at her.

"Are you okay?" Charlie asked.

"Sure." Imogen shrugged, fairly unconvincingly, and noticed the look Ruby gave her.

She sighed. "Just… a lot on my mind."

Ruby lifted her mug and sipped her tea, leaning her elbows on the counter. "Wanna talk about it?"

Imogen shrugged. "It's just... Annie stuff."

Charlie cleared his throat, shifting in his seat as he turned the page of the newspaper again. Was it her imagination or was he focusing a little too intently on the page?

"Yeah, just--" Imogen said quietly, shrugging. "You know... the night she.. was *killed*."

Ruby nodded, her expression knowing and sympathetic. She could understand because she felt the same way as Imogen did. Annie was so present in her mind now that they had found her body. Both Annie and That Night.

Imogen blinked at Charlie. He was doing a very good job of not looking up, of not reacting, of not showing anything on his face.

"What about you?" Imogen wondered. "Charlie?"

He looked up, surprise clear in his eyes. "What about me?"

Imogen stared at him for a moment. "Do you think about it?"

"What?" Charlie shook his head as if he didn't understand what she was getting at.

"The night she died. Was killed." Imogen corrected herself. "Do you think about it?"

"Immy, what-?" Ruby started but Charlie had already opened his mouth to respond by the time she did.

"I worry about it." He said, shrugging.

"What's for you to worry about?" Imogen's reply was a little too quick and she knew she was going a little hard on him but suddenly all she could think about was that picture of him glaring at Annie in the woods on that fateful night.

"Imogen, please--" Ruby again, but Charlie shook his head and held a hand up.

"No, hey, it's okay…" He folded his arms on top of the newspaper. "I *worry* about how it affects the mother of my child. *That's* what I have to worry about. I worry about Ruby."

Imogen was quiet for a moment before she reached for her phone, opening the image and just sliding it across the counter.

Ruby reached for it as Charlie craned his neck to get a better view.

Ruby sighed, shaking her head. "Imogen. What are you doing? Where did you get this?"

Charlie leaned back again, crossing his arms. That was defensive, right?

Imogen eyed him carefully, though she was confused as to why Ruby wasn't more concerned or surprised about the picture.

"That's the night Annie died… isn't it?" Imogen persisted.

Charlie nodded, which only surprised her more than anything. She had been expecting him to protest. Shake his head and tell her she had it all wrong. Instead, he was sitting there nodding at her.

Imogen had the urge to punch him in the face but she was distracted by Ruby walking over to sit down at the table next to Charlie, reaching for his hand.

"You don't have to do this.." Ruby said quietly, clasping his hand in hers.

"What are you talking about?" Imogen interrupted, staring at Ruby. "Do you realise what this means?" She gestured to her phone still turned upright on the counter, the screen just beginning to dim.

"It's not what you think it is." Ruby sighed back, looking up at her.

Imogen frowned. "What do you mean? Did you see how angry he was?" She turned back to Charlie. "What were you arguing with her about?" This hadn't exactly been the plan; going so hard on Charlie out of nowhere like this but it had sort of just taken her over. "What did you do?"

Charlie's gaze snapped up to meet hers. "I didn't *do* anything."

"I don't believe you." She stated.

"Imogen!" Ruby's voice held a warning in it and Imogen shifted her gaze to the brunette, frowning. It felt like she wasn't saying something and in a situation this important, that was frustrating Imogen further.

Charlie placed his hand carefully over Ruby's, shaking his head a little. "It's okay." He glanced through to the other room, where the children were still happily playing, and then he looked back at Imogen. "Look, I don't know where you got that picture but... it's not what you think."

"Then explain it to me." Imogen said, eyeing him suspiciously. She wasn't sure she was buying it. What else could it be, after all?

Charlie sighed, glancing at Ruby again which only irritated Imogen. "I *was* there. That night." He confirmed, causing a rush of satisfaction to course through Imogen's body.

She felt like she was literally about to crack this whole thing. She just felt sorry for Ruby.

"I did not hurt her." Charlie stated, looking Imogen in the eye.

Ruby shifted in her chair, shaking her head as if she was annoyed at the very thought that anyone could think such a thing.

Imogen didn't understand what was happening here. She had expected Ruby to be appalled, shocked, angry, upset. Not holding Charlie's hand like she had to comfort him.

"Annie found out that..." He stopped, glancing towards Ruby as if for permission, and turned back to Imogen when she nodded.

"Annie found out that Ruby and I were seeing each other."

Imogen blinked at him.

They had been eighteen that summer, just finished their final year of high school.

Charlie and Ruby didn't get together until after Sophie's death, three years later.

"Wait... what do you mean?" Imogen frowned, trying to make sense of what he was saying to her. Was he telling her that he and Ruby were already a thing and Annie found out?

So he killed her because she found out about some sordid affair he had with a student?

"Charlie and I were already together." Ruby spoke this time, shrugging. "Kind of, anyway. He didn't *do* anything, Imogen."

Well, it sounded like he sure did do *something* but Imogen did her best not to jump right into judgy mode.

"I confided in Annie because I trusted her. As a friend. I shouldn't have, it was a mistake, she… she went straight to blackmail."

Imogen watched Charlie squeeze Ruby's hand, offering her whatever comfort he could.

"That doesn't explain why he was in the woods that night." She frowned. "He was still married, Sophie could have found out, are you telling me that with that huge motive, showing up in the woods was a coincidence?"

Imogen did feel quite horrible because she saw the pained look that passed across Charlie's face when she mentioned Sophie. She knew it was still, and probably always would be, painfully raw.

"No, you don't understand… it was like a game. To Annie. Everything was a game." Charlie said, frowning at Imogen as though she should have been able to see that. "She was winning and she relished in it. So I went to the party because I knew she would be there, I knew it would surprise her if I showed up." He had been desperate back then, very desperate. For her to stop and for the secret to not get out. "I wasn't going to pay her anymore."

Charlie's eyes were dark as he stared back at her, the frustration and desperation evident. "*Fine.*"

Annie Pierce couldn't understand how one single word could send such an excited chill up her spine. Whatever the reason, she absolutely loved it. Next time she would ask for something bigger.

She had just found out about Charlie and Ruby the day before, and she already knew she could use this to her own advantage.

The possibilities were excitingly endless and Annie was already on the edge of her seat. She had been looking for something new to play around with. Her best friend's weird teacher fetish was perfect.

"I knew you would see things my way." Annie trilled, batting her eyelashes as Mr. Baker, English teacher and her best friend's secret love affair, glared back at her.

The smirk never left her face, her eyes gleaming with triumph as she stared him down.

Maybe he was attractive in that 'hot dad' kind of a way but what did that matter? Annie was furious that Ruby had kept such a big secret from her. Weren't they supposed to be best friends and tell each other everything.

Not that she told her friends everything… but they weren't exactly *mature* enough to deal with some of the things she kept to herself, like her little fling with Thomas. Though she was waiting for the right time to rub that in Sophie's face just because she knew Sophie liked him.

"This is it, though. Right? No more." Charlie's voice weaved its way back into the forefront of her thoughts and Annie raised an eyebrow.

Her laugh was like a rusty bell as she shook her head at him. "For now."

As his expression darkened, she smiled again, unable to shake the feeling of power that was coursing through her entire being. She felt like she was on fire.

"Oh, come on, Mr Baker. What would you prefer? Do a few *harmless* favours for me or end up in a jail cell? I think we both know which one you're going to choose." She paused, scanning his face carefully for any sign that he was about to refuse.

Instead, he only looked more resigned and his shoulders slumped slightly. She had won. As usual.

"Careful, *Charlie.*" Annie murmured as she slid around him and made for the stairs. "I know how they treat people like you in prison."

And with that she was gone, gliding down the staircase like a princess.

Everything around her felt heightened and she was giddy with the addictive excitement she always felt after she confronted somebody about something they wanted to stay hidden.

Of course, she knew that Charlie hadn't actually forced her friend into anything and he wasn't some weirdo who preyed on kids. Ruby was technically an adult and school had already ended. Besides, Annie really didn't care about that sort of thing, she had done much worse in her time.

Still, Charlie didn't need to know that did he? She wanted him running scared. Fear was a powerful thing and she knew that very well.

Annie couldn't resist one look back as she reached the bottom of the staircase and the sight of Charlie Baker's frustrated and worried face was enough to send another shiver of delight rushing through her veins.

She shot him her best angelic smile before turning and pushing open the door to walk out into the street.

Present

Charlie ran his hands over his face, slumping in the chair. "She wanted money, she wanted me to fake her grades, she wanted to get out of classes… She kept wanting more."

Imogen stared at him, not sure what to say, glancing at Ruby but she didn't seem surprised. She must have already known all of this. He must have already told her.

Some part of Imogen kind of felt like that made him seem more innocent to her. The fact that Ruby already knew. The fact they had clearly already discussed it at some point.

"I did go to the woods that night… I did." Charlie repeated, sounding resigned.

"I *was* there. I told her I was done. We argued and then I went home. That's it. I didn't hurt her." He looked up again, meeting Imogen's gaze. "She was *alive* when I left."

The silence in the room was deafening. Apart from the squealing of the kids drifting through from the other room but it barely registered with her. Imogen was staring down at her hand, tracing the shape of her wedding ring as she tried to process all of this new information.

Imogen knew that Annie had always had some weird power to glean secrets from people, or to use things she found out to her own advantage, but she felt suddenly deflated.

She had been so sure that she had cracked it. That she had figured out what happened to her best friend and she could help her rest in peace with the killer behind bars.

Now she was unsure. Charlie sounded so convincing and Ruby clearly believed it, and... well, it was Ruby's story too, wasn't it? She had been there at the time, witnessed most of this, and she confirmed that Annie had blackmailed Charlie.

Unless Ruby was just another victim of Charlie Baker's sick game.

"Why didn't you ever tell the police you were there? You could have seen something that would have helped." Imogen lifted her gaze again but Charlie shook his head.

It was Ruby who spoke though. "Immy, you just said it yourself. It looks like the biggest freaking motive in the world. Do you really think they would have looked anywhere else? The real killer would have gotten away."

"They *have* gotten away." Imogen snapped slightly, distressed once again at the thought of Annie lying under the dirt for all these years, while whoever did it to her got away scot free.

"Yes, but at least they can still *look* for them and not focus on a false lead." Ruby sighed. "Look, I loved Annie too."

Imogen lowered her gaze again, feeling slightly ashamed. She knew that, she did, but she was like a dog with a bone sometimes.

"I loved Annie. But she was a bitch."

Imogen looked up. "How can you say that?"

"Are you kidding, Immy? Do you not remember what she did to Sarah Clarke?"

"She didn't pour the pills down her throat, Ruby..."

"No. She didn't. She just deliberately slipped the need for them in her already fucked up, fragile mind." Ruby blinked. "She was our best friend. But we're not kids anymore. Annie thrived off blackmail and *bullying*. You know it. I know it. Kelly knows it. Sophie knew it." She squeezed Charlie's hand as she said his daughter's name. "I'm sorry, but I *know* that Charlie has nothing to do with this and if you try and insinuate otherwise, I will *never* speak to you again."

Ruby stood up, letting go of Charlie's hand and moving through to the other room. "I think play time's over. We'll reschedule."

eighteen

Imogen felt deflated as she pushed Brooklyn's buggy back in the direction of home.

The toddler had no idea that anything was wrong, happily talking away to herself.

She didn't really know what to believe. It was so convincing and she couldn't really see Charlie Baker of all people fatally hurting his daughter's best friend, burying her, and then continuing on a relationship with another of her best friends.

Still, didn't they always say that killers were always so charming and the person they'd least suspect?

God, she was so confused.

Imogen had been so sure after seeing that picture, she'd gone in guns blazing, and now she was no closer to knowing what happened to Annie. No closer to solving her friend's murder.

Imogen knew it was something best left to the police but these texts had really gotten to her and she couldn't let it go. It was wriggling away under her skin, burrowing deeper and deeper, and she had to keep scratching at it or she'd never get it out.

One good thing about today was that it confirmed to her that the texts were real and not just in her head, the product of a paranoid mind. Charlie and Ruby had seen it too. She wasn't going crazy. She wasn't losing it again. She wasn't having an episode. This was really happening.

Turning the corner, she strolled up the driveway of their house, talking away to Brooklyn. Imogen told herself she needed to just take the night off, distract her busy brain and forget about all this Annie stuff, at least for tonight.

She was reaching into her handbag for her keys when the figure moving to her right made her jump out of her skin.

"Shit!" Imogen dropped the keys on the ground, watching them skitter over the stones, landing at the feet of the person who had been lurking in her front garden by the bench.

"Kelly?" Imogen was surprised to see her. Surprised was a bit of an understatement, though. She was *shocked*. "What are you doing here?"

Kelly leaned down and scooped the keys up from the ground, taking a small step and holding them out for Imogen to take.

"Hey... we should talk."

* * *

"Tea? Coffee?" Imogen poked her head around the corner, peering into the living room where Kelly was sitting with Brooklyn. "Hot chocolate?"

Kelly looked over the back of the couch she'd sprawled herself across, shrugging. "Got any wine?"

Imogen wasn't totally sure that was a good idea but she was also too stunned to do anything but nod and reach for the wine glasses and the bottle of red sitting on the dining room table.

She swept back into the living room, sitting on a chair opposite the couch. She felt better now that she could keep a close eye on Brooklyn. Not that she thought Kelly would *do* anything, but… she wasn't exactly entirely *responsible* now, was she?

She felt guilty thinking it.

Just like she felt guilty about Charlie and Ruby.

"Perfect, thanks." Kelly muttered, pouring wine practically to the rim of her glass and throwing back a large gulp.

Imogen eyed her carefully. Kelly had always liked a good drink, she was the one who would get drunkest at parties, behind Annie of course.

Since that summer, though, Kelly's drinking had reached astronomical levels. Imogen wasn't even sure Kelly had sober days anymore. She was well on her way to becoming the town drunk.

And the town bike… but Imogen pushed that thought out quickly. She wasn't one to slut-shame and felt awful she'd even thought it. It was just so hard to be positive about Kelly anymore.

Kelly looked a lot different from their younger years. Her raven hair had deep purple streaks through it now. She had a nose ring. She also had an eyebrow and lip piercing. Her upper arms boasted tattoos of flames and skulls, likely done by Frances Kirk, Jamie's little sister, who owned Black Lotus Tattoo Parlour in town.

Kelly had gone off the rails after Annie disappeared and, once more, the picture where Kelly had been glaring at Annie floated across Imogen's thoughts. Her obsession with their best friend.

"So… to what do I owe this visit then?" Imogen asked, looking at Kelly curiously. She took a delicate sip of wine.

Kelly stared quietly back at her for a few moments before she took another gulp of her own wine and reached into her pocket.

When she pulled out her phone, Imogen was surprised.

"This."

Imogen blinked at Kelly for a moment before she held out her hand to take the phone that had been thrust towards her. She looked down at the screen.

"I know who killed Annie. Soon, Imogen will too."

Imogen looked back up at Kelly, stunned. It was the same number that had been texting her since Annie's funeral.

They had named her in this. They were leading her to the killer and now Kelly knew it too.

Why?

Why had this person decided to text this to Kelly? Why had they gotten her involved? Why would it matter to her if Imogen was being led to the killer?

Unless this was all a part of the game this weirdo was playing with her.

Maybe Imogen had been way, way off with Charlie Baker but maybe she had been closer to the mark with her old best friend.

Maybe Kelly had wanted to be Annie so badly that her obsession had gotten out of control. Gotten the best of her.

Maybe this person sending these texts knew Kelly had done something that night and had sent her Imogen's way to mess with them both.

Is it possible that *Kelly Sharpe* was the one who hurt Annie all those years ago?

Had an obsession turned deadly?

Imogen suddenly realised she hadn't said anything for the last five minutes. She had been sitting there, staring at Kelly's phone screen, which had gone dark already, not knowing what the hell to say.

"I mean, I didn't think you'd be jumping for joy but I expected *something*." Kelly muttered, pulling out a packet of cigarettes and a lighter.

"You can't smoke in here." Imogen finally spoke, frowning at Kelly.

Kelly looked confused but then she remembered the baby and rolled her eyes. "Right. Yeah. Sure." She shrugged and shoved the cigarettes and lighter back into the pocket of her leather jacket.

Imogen couldn't believe just how far removed she felt from this other woman. This person she used to feel so close to, who she spent practically every single day with.

Back then, Imogen felt like they were the closest group of people in the world and nobody would ever be able to break them up, no matter what.

Turns out murder is a pretty good incentive.

"I don't know what you want, Kelly." Imogen sighed, shrugging loosely.

She didn't understand any of this.

Who was texting her? Why had they text Kelly? Why not Ruby? *Had* they text Ruby and she hadn't said anything? Did Kelly send the message to herself to throw off suspicion?

The moment the thought crossed her mind, Imogen felt sick. What if that was it? What if Kelly was the one behind these texts *and* the one who killed Annie and she was messing with Imogen, trying to throw the suspicion on a bunch of other people?

God, she was *so* paranoid.

But it *was* possible... wasn't it?

Kelly was frowning as she stared back at Imogen. "Are you serious? Someone texts that you're going to find out who killed Annie and you expect me to sit back and chill?"

"I'm not going to--" Imogen sighed heavily, trailing off. "Look, I got a text after the funeral, okay? Someone says they know what happened... but they're only giving me little bits and pieces. I can't *do* anything."

Honestly, she felt like a pawn in some sick game and she couldn't decide what to do about it.

"Well, I want in." Kelly stated, crossing one leg over the other as she leaned back on the couch, looking like she owned the place.

"In?" Imogen shook her head, confused. "In on what?"

"Duh. In on this secret fuckin' mission." She said, as if it was obvious. "You're gonna find out who topped Annie and I want in."

"I'm not, like, going undercover and playing detective here, Kelly, I'm being sent creepy texts that really don't ever add up to anything."

Kelly shrugged. "Texts that will apparently lead us to a murderer."

Us. She had pushed her way in here already. Imogen couldn't read her expression.

"Aren't you curious?" Kelly continued.

Imogen frowned, looking away and down at Brooklyn, who at least didn't seem too fazed by this strange woman who had barged in.

"Yeah. Of course I am." Imogen said. "But I think I should take it to the police."

"Are you fuckin' mental?" Kelly snapped, frowning as she sat forward.

Imogen looked up in surprise. "Excuse me?" She didn't appreciate the tone or the word choice.

"The cops didn't do shit when she went missing, they're not gonna do shit now." Kelly rolled her eyes.

Imogen sighed. She had thought the same sorts of things in the past, frustrated that the police hadn't been able to track down her missing friend.

Kelly's father was the chief of police and she had always had a rebellious streak, going against the rules and causing issues for her family. Though the issues she would be causing now were a far cry from her teenage rebellions.

"If you don't think a police force with resources can do anything, what can two random girls do?" Imogen asked with a slight eye roll.

Kelly rolled her eyes back at her, shrugging. "I dunno. Don't you think it would be fun?"

That rubbed Imogen the wrong way. Fun. *Fun?* "Nothing about any of this is fun, Kel."

Kelly was quiet. She knew she'd fucked up. "I didn't mean…"

Imogen stood up, turning to gesture towards the front door. "I have to feed Brooklyn and get her down for a nap. You should probably go."

Kelly stared at her for a moment before she nodded, standing up from the couch. "Sure."

Imogen watched as Kelly drifted towards the front door.

She reached for the handle but turned back to Imogen just before she pulled the door open. "Think about it, okay?" Kelly gave her a look. "We owe it to Annie."

nineteen

Imogen was scrubbing away at the kitchen counters when Eric arrived home that night.

She had fed Brooklyn, put her down to sleep, then she had started cleaning and just never stopped.

"Oh, no." Eric said teasingly as he moved into the kitchen, putting his bag down on the table. "The anxious cleans are happening."

Imogen turned and gave him a withering look. She'd had this habit since she was a teenager. When she got in a complete frenzy and needed to clear her muddled thoughts, Imogen would clean and clean and clean. It helped to get out pent up emotions, letting her pour her anxious or annoyed energy somewhere that was outside of her own mind. It was probably one of her healthiest coping mechanisms.

Eric chuckled at the look she gave him, holding up his hands in front of him. "Hey, hey, I come in peace."

Imogen couldn't help but smile, rolling her eyes at him in a way that betrayed her amusement. "You're an idiot."

Eric moved over to the bunker, grabbing a banana off the counter. "I absolutely am." He joked, peeling the skin off and taking a bite as he watched her. "Stressful day?"

"Kelly came by." Imogen shrugged.

Eric's face showed his surprise. He stared at her with a frown for a moment or two. "Are you serious?"

Imogen nodded, turning to lean against the counter, chucking the tea towel down with a sigh. "Yeah." She could understand his shock. She was still reeling, herself.

"What did she want? Are you alright?" Eric moved to sit down at the table, banana forgotten as he stared back at his wife.

Imogen shrugged, moving to sit opposite him. "It's complicated." How did she even begin to explain? Could she? "I'm fine. I'm just... actually, I don't know, it was weird. You know? I don't even remember the last time I spoke to her."

Eric nodded. "Yeah. Of course. Did she just want to... check in after the Annie thing?" He wondered.

Imogen knew it was harmless but the question made her tense up just a little bit.

The Annie Thing.
That Night.

Imogen felt like her whole world had revolved around those phrases for years. She felt like maybe it always would.

"I guess so." Imogen nodded, shrugging again. "It's brought... a lot of people out of the woodwork."

Eric nodded, looking at her for a minute. "I can imagine. Are you alright?"

Imogen shook her head, deciding to just be honest. "I don't really know."

Eric nodded sympathetically. As if he understood. He couldn't possibly but Imogen was glad she had him anyway.

She opened her mouth, considering whether or not to just come right out and tell him everything but she closed her mouth again a few seconds later, pushing it away.

She would tell him another day. Imogen really didn't want to think about it anymore.

"Should we order a takeaway?" Eric asked, not having noticed Imogen's hesitation.

She grinned at him. "Hell yes."

Eric chuckled, loosening his tie. "Perfect. I'm gonna go get changed real quick. When I get back, we'll order and pop in a movie. Yeah?"

Imogen nodded, leaning forward and kissing him. "Yeah. Sounds great."

She watched him go, the ghost of a smile still dancing across her lips. He always knew how to distract her and make her feel better.

This was just what she needed. No thoughts about Annie or Kelly or *That Night*. Just a nice cosy night in with her husband.

twenty

Brooklyn had been screaming the house down for the past three hours and she showed no sign of stopping any time soon.

Imogen couldn't figure out what was wrong. She had never cried like this before.

She had been sick a few times that morning, and she was all sweaty and shaky.

"What's wrong?" She gently bounced the baby, frowning to herself as she tried to calm her down. "Are you hungry? You don't need a new nappy…" Imogen muttered away to herself, trying to figure out the problem.

Brooklyn just kept screaming and screaming. By the time Sasha stopped by, Imogen was beside herself.

"I'm taking her to the hospital."

Sasha reached out, frowning worriedly. "What's going on?"

Imogen shook her head, grabbing her bag, feeling like a madwoman. "I don't know. She just… she won't stop crying. Screaming. Something's wrong, Sash."

"Okay." Sasha nodded, turning to open the front door again. "Let's go, I'll drive."

Imogen's foot was tapping against the hard, dirty floor. The waiting room was dull, the lights dim, and it had a weird smell that she couldn't quite put her finger on.

She was impatient, frustrated. Brooklyn was still crying and people kept shooting her these little looks.

She returned the looks, wanting to shout at the judgemental idiots. Ask if they could magically fix whatever was wrong if it was that bothersome for them.

"Brooklyn Matthews?" A voice from across the room called her daughter's name and Imogen was up in a flash, rushing over to the doctor, Sasha following right behind her.

"What seems to be the problem?" The doctor asked, giving Imogen a friendly smile before turning her attention to Brooklyn, looking sympathetic.

"She hasn't stopped for hours… something's wrong, I don't know but… she *never* does this, I think she's sick."

The doctor nodded, reaching out to Brooklyn curiously, the cogs in her mind already whirring. "Has she thrown up at all?"

"No." Imogen shook her head but then she nodded. "Wait, yeah… yeah, this morning, she did a couple of times. I thought I fed her too quick."

The doctor took a couple of notes, nodding, and then proceeded to run off another string of questions, which Imogen answered best she could while not having a clue what was going on.

"Okay." The doctor nodded when she was done. "Well, she's clearly distressed. I think we should do a few tests, and get to the bottom of this. We'll need to take some blood…" Imogen winced. "I know, I know…" The doctor continued, looking sympathetic. "Best to rule everything out though."

Imogen felt slightly patronised because *duh,* she *knew that.* She also knew her emotions were heightened with worry right now and she needed to take a few breaths and wait - something she had never been very good at doing.

"What if it's something serious? What if they keep her in? What if--?"
"Hey, hey…" Sasha reached over, clasping Imogen's hand reassuringly, giving it a squeeze. "It's going to be fine, it's probably just the flu or something and she doesn't know what's going on because she's never had it before."
Imogen nodded. She felt in her gut that it was something serious but maybe Sasha was right. Imogen knew she had been on edge recently, to put it lightly. Maybe it was all getting to her, making her paranoid.
Her phone buzzed and she pulled it out of her pocket to check it. Eric was texting. He hadn't been able to get away from work, which she didn't mind because there was no point in them both sitting around here for hours waiting, right? Still, part of her wished he was here since his presence might comfort her some.
Imogen replied, letting him know there was no news yet, and then she wriggled uncomfortably in the hard waiting room chair.
They had taken Brooklyn through to a testing room where Imogen wasn't allowed to go for some reason. She hadn't been happy with that but the doctors and nurses had assured her everything would be fine.

She was pretty sure she could still hear her cry drifting down the hall and she wanted to run down there, scoop her up and take her home.

Eventually, they were called back into the room and Imogen had Brooklyn in her arms again, blinking impatiently at the doctor as she looked over the notes on her clipboard.

"Okay." She finally spoke, causing Imogen to release a breath she hadn't realised she was holding.

"So. We've given her some medicine and she's definitely feeling a little better - aren't ya?" She smiled at the baby, who had thankfully stopped crying.

"It is bad news though. I'm afraid that little Brooklyn here must have gotten into your cigarettes at home."

Imogen blinked at her, the words not really computing. "Sorry, what do you mean?"

"Her symptoms line up with nicotine poisoning." The doctor continued, not really helping with Imogen's confusion.

"No, but I don't…. understand, how can that be?" Imogen asked again, shaking her head.

The doctor gave her a little look and Imogen didn't like what she saw in the expression. "Mrs. Matthews-"

"Ford-Matthews." Imogen corrected, though it was really unnecessary and she barely even knew she was saying it. She usually still just went by Ford anyway.

"Mrs. Ford-Matthews." The doctor tried again, talking in a very overly patient manner as if she was talking to a three year old. "Brooklyn must have ingested a fair amount of nicotine." The doctor blinked. "Cigarettes."

As if Imogen didn't know what the fuck nicotine was. She flushed, feeling angry.

"She was suffering the symptoms of nicotine poisoning but we--"

That was all Imogen heard before her brain felt like it had grown to five times the size and the ringing in her ears was all she could focus on.

Cigarettes? Nicotine *poisoning?* Imogen didn't understand a thing this woman was saying to her because she didn't smoke. She hadn't smoked since she was eighteen years old. Eric didn't smoke, he never had. They did not have cigarettes in their house at all, let alone lying around all over the place. Nothing the doctor was saying to her made any sense.

"I don't smoke." She murmured, the words feeling thick and gummy in her mouth.

"I'm sorry?" The doctor eyed her patiently. Clearly she dealt with idiotic parents all the time and this was how she was viewing Imogen.

"I don't smoke." She said again, a little louder and more firm.

"Your husband then." The doctor waved a dismissive hand, as if the technicalities didn't matter one bit, but Imogen shook her head, standing up quickly.

"No. Listen. I don't smoke. My husband doesn't smoke. We do not smoke." She was frowning at the doctor, trying to figure out what the hell was going on here. They had to have gotten it wrong, didn't they?

"It must be something else, you have to check again." She said, but the doctor shook her head.

"Mrs. Matthews, we're very sure."

She didn't bother to correct her this time, the room starting to feel too cramped. Imogen shouldered her handbag and glanced at Sasha as she suddenly remembered she was there. "We're leaving."

The doctor jumped up from her chair as Imogen reached for the door handle. "Wait! Due to the severity of the situation, we have no choice but to call child services."

Imogen turned and stared at her like she had suddenly sprouted five extra heads.

"Wait, is that really necessary?" Sasha's voice.

"It's routine." The doctor explained, looking between the two women. "We don't have any choice. They need to check your house for potential hazards."

Imogen shook her head, feeling too stunned to argue as she turned away again and stepped out of the room.

She rushed off down the hall, Sasha hurrying behind her, heading towards the car park, feeling like she wasn't getting enough air into her lungs.

Her thoughts were scrambled and she couldn't put all the information together in her mind to make it make one bit of sense.

Imogen was aware that Sasha was talking to her as she moved to ease Brooklyn into the car, shoving the medicine the doctor had given her into her handbag so she wouldn't lose it, however she could barely hear anything she was saying.

A horrible thought had twisted its way into the forefront of her mind.

She and Eric didn't smoke. There were no cigarettes in their house. Not one. None of their friends really smoked and if they did, only on nights out or in the car. Never in their house. Imogen didn't allow it and she knew for a fact nobody had ever *left* their cigarettes at their place and certainly not in reach of their sixteen month old daughter.

There was only one person who she knew who smoked who had been in her house recently.

Kelly.

twenty-one

Imogen had been cleaning again. Scrubbing away at the counters and shoving the hoover into every tight corner of the room.

Now she was sitting on the sofa, watching Brooklyn as she crawled around on the floor, playing with her toys.

She seemed to be feeling a lot better now, which was a relief but Imogen couldn't really relax.

The lady from social services was stopping by in a couple of hours and, while she knew they weren't going to find anything, she couldn't help panicking anyway.

Her thoughts kept drifting back to Kelly. Her strange appearance. All her questions about Annie. The fact she'd gotten a text like Imogen had. The cigarettes.

She kept trying to remember if she had left Kelly alone with Brooklyn at any point. Did she leave the room to get a drink? She couldn't remember.

Imogen couldn't stop thinking about how strange it was that Kelly would show up the way she had, after Annie's body had been found, with a similar text message to Imogen.

She kept wondering if Kelly had sent herself the text to throw Imogen off, as a way to gain access to her house. To her child.

Was she behind the texts? Was she Annie's killer? It was still distressing to Imogen to even consider that but wasn't it possible?

Imogen had done some reading online. She knew you shouldn't google or you'd end up going down a rabbit hole and making your paranoia worse, but she hadn't been able to help herself.

Her mind was already running away with itself and she felt helpless to stop her thoughts snowballing.

Kelly had been *obsessed* with Annie, it was clear even back then.

Imogen had read all about how obsession could so easily turn deadly. The object of the obsession falling victim to the obsess-ee. It happened all the time.

Maybe Kelly had snapped. Maybe that's why she was so messed up now, why she drowned herself in alcohol. Maybe it was the guilt of what she had done to their best friend.

Even if this was all true, though, *why* would she send Imogen weird texts? *Why* would she want to hurt her child?

Maybe she was trying to throw Imogen off with the texts. Make her look at everyone *except* Kelly. Make her think they were both on the same team.

Maybe Kelly wasn't the one sending the messages at all. Maybe the same person who text Imogen really did text Kelly too, knowing that Kelly was Annie's killer and made her believe Imogen was going to get to the truth, prompting Kelly to rush round to Imogen's to find out what she knew. To get her back on side so she could keep what she'd done a secret.

Maybe poisoning Brooklyn was a distraction. Maybe she hadn't meant to give her so much. Maybe she just wanted to keep Imogen occupied with something that wasn't Annie's murder.

Or maybe Imogen needed to cool it with the damn conspiracy theories and focus on the problem at hand.

Just as she had thought this, there was a knock at the front door.

Imogen sucked in a deep breath, telling herself to stay steady, to calm down.

This was just a routine visit and there was nothing to worry about. They weren't going to snatch Brooklyn up and walk straight out with her.

She hoped.

Imogen opened the door with a polite smile. "Hi." She stepped aside for the lady to come in.

"Hello." She smiled back, fingers clutching her bag strap as she stepped into the house and had a cursory look around before her gaze fell on the baby. "This must be Brooklyn."

Imogen smiled, nodding. "Yep… our little trooper."

"Do you always leave her on the floor there when you go to answer the door?" The question was unexpected and seemed pretty judgemental.

Imogen frowned lightly, unable to help herself. It was five steps away. "It's not far, I can see her." She stated, though suddenly felt very unsure.

The woman nodded. "Of course. It's not far. Mind if I have a little look around and then I'll come ask you some questions?"

She was smiling but Imogen didn't feel put at ease by it. It looked fake.

Imogen felt like the woman's teeth almost looked like they were about to pop themselves out of her mouth and jump across the room at her. It was a disgusting, nonsensical image that she did her best to banish as soon as it appeared.

She nodded, gesturing for the woman to go ahead as she moved over and scooped up her daughter. "Sure. Knock yourself out."

* * *

That had *not* gone well. Imogen was panicking again, telling herself to remember her breathing exercises to calm down, but nothing was working.

That woman didn't believe a thing she had said. It was obvious she had made up her mind before she even set foot inside.

There weren't any cigarettes anywhere in their house.

The medicines were all out of reach of the baby, tucked away in kitchen cupboards and bedside drawers.

The bleach was safe under the kitchen sink with the other cleaners, and Brooklyn couldn't open the door.

They didn't have rat poison in the house.

They barely even had anything toxic at all.

It's not like Imogen sprayed deodorant and shoved cigarette butts down Brooklyn's throat on a daily basis but that's what the woman had made her feel like.

Like some terrible mother. Like she was unfit.

It had always been one of Imogen's biggest fears, after she had her big episode triggered by Sophie's death and her schizophrenia was diagnosed, then later found out she was pregnant.

She had worried that she would do something to hurt her unborn baby, that she would snap again and do something when they were born.

She had been scared she would end up like her mother, trying to drown her baby girl in the bathtub.

But Imogen had done everything in her power to make sure Brooklyn was safe and sound. That nothing would ever hurt her, especially her tragic, mentally ill mother.

Imogen was a *good mother*. She knew she was. Brooklyn loved her and she adored Brooklyn in return.

Eric was a good father. He was a fantastic father, even. Brooklyn was as happy and safe as she could possibly be.

So why was this happening?

twenty-two

"I'm sure it wasn't as bad as you think." Eric said as he bounced Brooklyn on his knee, causing her to giggle.

Imogen rolled her eyes in response, crossing her arms as she leaned back on the couch.

"You weren't there." She muttered glumly, reaching for the TV remote and turning the news off. She was sick of the background noise of death and war and destruction. The world was fucked but she had learned that years ago.

"I know, I'm sorry." Eric sighed, looking over at her. "This Annie thing has taken over the whole paper. We got this anonymous tip last night."

Imogen was distracted from her annoyance at the phrase *the Annie thing* by his next admission. She sat up a little, looking over at him. "What do you mean?"

Eric shrugged. "There was a message taped to the front door of the offices last night. Nikki was working late and found it."

"What kind of message? From who?" Imogen pushed, aware she should probably reign it in a little but the words *anonymous* and *message* were spinning around in her head. Still, the second question came out as if he would magically be able to give her a name.

"No idea." He shrugged, seeming a bit too calm for her liking but she knew he didn't have the same knowledge she did. "It was just something about knowing who killed Annie."

Imogen frowned. So whoever was texting her was spilling out into the rest of her world now? Spreading around town like an infectious disease.

"I'm getting those messages too." Imogen found herself saying, without even really meaning to.

"What?" Eric's gaze snapped to her face, frowning. "What do you mean?"

Well, there was no going back now, was there? Imogen sighed, shaking her head. "After… the funeral." She watched Eric's expression, trying to read him. "I started getting texts from some number telling me they knew who hurt Annie."

Eric was staring at her like she'd just punched his mother in the face which, honestly, she wouldn't mind doing sometimes. "Are… are you serious? Imogen…" He was sort of speechless. "Can I see?"

Imogen shrugged. There was no point in hiding it now, was there? She reached for her phone and opened the message thread.

Eric took the phone from her and read the messages, letting Brooklyn slide into the space between the two of them on the couch.

Imogen watched him, feeling like she was going to throw up.

"You need to go to the police." Eric said, looking up at her.

She shook her head. "No, it's… look, they'll just say it's a prank." She said, "and if it's not, whoever is sending me these, whoever *knows* something, might get spooked if I go to the cops… then I'll *never* know."

Eric stared at her and she could tell he thought she was insane. That she was being ridiculous. Eric had always been a straight-laced, follow-the-rules kind of guy. Imogen was flighty and impulsive and a little bizarre. They sort of tamed each other in different ways but sometimes she knew he thought she was immature or just plain wrong.

Now was most likely one of those times.

Eric shook his head. "I don't like it. This person could be dangerous."

"I don't think so." Imogen found herself saying. She didn't really know where it came from because hadn't she recently been wondering if this person was the same one who killed Annie?

Imogen just didn't think so anymore. Not after Kelly showed up after getting a text. She had decided that it was all a little too convenient.

It was a shitty thing to think but Imogen didn't believe Kelly was smart enough in her current state of mind to be a double agent sending herself messages.

She was starting to really believe that Kelly had been prompted by the text from this anonymous person to pop back into Imogen's life to make sure she didn't find out about That Night.

Imogen was genuinely leaning towards the idea that Kelly felt guilty about something and that's why she had shown up.

She also thought she was the one who had poisoned her child. It was all too suspicious and convenient.

Imogen was angry and she was determined to get to the bottom of this now.

"I've wondered what happened to Annie for years, Eric. I *need* to know what happened. I'll never be able to move on if I don't."

Eric sighed, glancing down at Brooklyn. He knew that that summer had affected Imogen a lot and he wanted the truth for her, he wanted her to move on, but he was concerned that this was only going to end badly.

The thought that some random weirdo was messaging his wife put him on edge.

"Alright, look… I won't get the police involved." Eric said, reaching out for her hand as he glanced back up to her face. "Yet." If things got out of control, he would, no question, but he always respected Imogen's wishes first and foremost. "But you have to keep me in the loop. You don't go anywhere without telling me. You don't go alone, if you can help it. I need you to be careful… I need you safe."

Imogen couldn't help but smile softly. She was glad he wasn't pushing the whole thing. She didn't think she was in any danger and the police most likely wouldn't even believe it was anything serious. Maybe she was being naive but she felt like this is the way she had to go about it, at least for now.

"Kelly said she wanted to help." She told him, watching him nod because at least that meant she wouldn't be alone.

Imogen decided not to tell him that she thought it was possible that Kelly was the one who'd hurt Annie. Not until she was sure.

She didn't want to send Kelly running before she could find out more.

twenty-three

Imogen checked her phone for the hundredth time that afternoon. She had text Ruby to apologise about the Charlie situation but she hadn't gotten anything back yet. She did feel really bad about the whole thing.

Imogen also wanted to talk to Ruby about everything that was going on. The texts. Kelly. She didn't know what Ruby would think about the Kelly part of it but she wasn't sure who else she could talk it over with.

Other than Sasha, of course. Whose presence was announced with the ring of the doorbell.

Imogen moved to answer it, smiling as she stepped aside for her friend to come in. "Hey. Wine's on the table." She chuckled, closing the door.

Sasha grinned as she moved inside and over to the couch. "You're an angel." She teased as she turned her attention to Brooklyn, who was sitting on a playmat on the floor. "And how's *this* little angel doing?"

Imogen sat down beside her, reaching for one of the glasses of wine. "Much better, thankfully." She sighed, her thoughts drifting back to the visit from that woman. "I just hope that's the end of it."

"Have you heard anything else?" Sasha wondered, reaching for the other glass.

Imogen shook her head. "No one's called or anything yet. I keep waiting for them to descend on me and snatch Brooklyn away." She rolled her eyes, having a gulp of wine. She knew she was just being paranoid but still.

"Sorry." Sasha sighed, shaking her head as she looked back over to Brooklyn, playing obliviously with her toys. "I'm sure it's going to be fine, though. It was obviously an accident."

Imogen nodded, though she couldn't help but wonder in the back of her mind; *was it?*

Was it a horrible accident or had Kelly Sharpe deliberately hurt her daughter? Would she try again?

Did she do something to Annie and was now scared that Imogen would figure her out?

"What is it?" Sasha frowned softly.

Imogen couldn't help a tiny smile. Sasha always seemed to know when something was up. She sighed. "I don't know, it's probably nothing."

Sasha gave her a look that said even if it was nothing it still mattered.

So, sighing again, Imogen just let it all out. She told Sasha everything. The text messages, Kelly's weird visit and the suspicious circumstances surrounding it. She didn't say anything about Ruby and Charlie. That wasn't her place.

When she was finished, Sasha was staring at her, obviously stunned. "Shit..." She covered her mouth as soon as she'd said it, glancing guiltily at Brooklyn, but Imogen just shrugged. She felt the same way.

"Yeah... it's... a lot."

"Too right it is." Sasha frowned at her, shaking her head. "I don't even know what to say."

"It's crazy, huh?" Imogen made a face.

"That's an understatement." Sasha agreed, still looking pretty flabbergasted as she processed all the information Imogen had just dumped on her.

"So... you think *Kelly* is involved?" She asked, frowning.

Imogen shrugged. "I don't know, really. I just... it's all too convenient. The way she just showed up, it was weird." She explained. "It kind of felt like... like she was trying to suss out what I knew."

Sasha made a face. "Well, that's kinda creepy."

"Yeah." Imogen threw back the rest of her wine, set the glass on the table and then turned her focus back to Brooklyn. "I'm not really sure what to do but... I think I have to keep her close. Keep my eye on her, you know? Make her think I don't suspect a thing just in case."

Sasha nodded. "I think that's a good idea but, Imogen, what if she hurts you?"

Imogen shook her head. "She wouldn't."

"That's what you would have said about her hurting Annie a week ago."

Imogen didn't know what to say to that because she was right. It was true but, at the end of the day, she didn't really know what was true and what wasn't.

It felt like she was playing a game but she didn't know any of the rules.

"Have you said anything to Ruby about this?" Sasha wondered.

Imogen shook her head. "No. Not yet. I don't really know if I should."

"Why not?"

Imogen shrugged. "If I'm wrong, I don't want to put that image in her head."

"But if you're right." Sasha said quietly. "She probably needs to be prepared."

Imogen knew she was right, scrunching her nose up at the thought of having to talk about this with Ruby. It was bad enough admitting it to Eric and Sasha and they were the closest people in the world to her.

"Yeah, I know." She groaned, tipping to the side slightly and resting her head on Sasha's shoulder. "This is a mess."

"It really is." Sasha chuckled, resting her own head against Imogen's, lifting her arm and combing her fingers through Imogen's hair. "You'll figure it out."

Imogen hoped that Sasha was right, but she was beginning to feel like she was treading water and only just keeping her head above the waves.

twenty-four

The door opened and Imogen held up a bottle of red wine in front of her as a greeting.

"I come in peace." She teased lightly, feeling a little anxious as Ruby looked back at her from the doorway.

There was a moment as Ruby looked back at her and Imogen thought she was going to have the door shut in her face, which she might have felt she deserved.

A moment later though, Ruby had moved aside to let her in. "Come on then."

Imogen smiled slightly, stepping inside and wandering through to the living room. "Is Charlie around?"

Ruby shook her head. "No, he took Hope to see his cousin." She said.

Imogen nodded, feeling both relieved and let down. Half of her wanted to apologise, half of her was glad not to have to face him. "Look, I wanted to say I was sorry."

Ruby shook her head, taking the wine and moving through to the next room. "It's alright. We know what it looks like. Charlie gets it."

Imogen had to admit that hearing this gave her an instant sense of relief. "Yeah?"

Ruby nodded, grabbing a couple of glasses out of the cupboard. "Yeah."

Imogen smiled lightly. "Cool."

She watched Ruby filling up two glasses, one for each of them, with the wine she had brought. Imogen was mildly concerned that she had been drinking a little too much wine lately but she pushed it away. It's not like things could get any worse.

"So… there was something I wanted to talk about." She said after a few moments of silence in which she went back and forth over whether she could actually do this.

"What's up?" Ruby gave her a look, wondering what she could want to talk about.

Imogen hesitated. How did she start? What did she say? Would this end up in another argument?

"It's about Kelly."

She watched Ruby frown, saw the surprise at Kelly's name being mentioned at all.

"What about her?"

Imogen supposed she couldn't really go back now. Could she? She had brought Kelly up and now she had to just go with it. Tell Ruby everything.

She wanted to, parts of her had found relief at telling people about all of this, but she was also scared of Ruby's reaction.

She worried that Ruby wouldn't believe her, would think she was crazy or causing problems, or that she would tell Kelly that Imogen was poking around.

"Well, I've been getting these texts lately-" Imogen began, going on to explain the whole situation to Ruby much like she had done with Eric and with Sasha.

She kept an eye on Ruby's face, watching her expressions shift from confusion to something that she couldn't really place. Annoyance? Fear? Pity?

Did she think that Imogen was crazy?

"So she just showed up? Out of the blue?" Ruby asked, frowning as she thoughtfully sipped the wine.

Imogen nodded, fidgeting anxiously, her fingers worrying at the sleeve of her jumper. "Yeah. It was really weird. It kind of felt like she was trying to see if I knew something."

"About what, though?" Ruby asked, eyeing Imogen carefully. "Do you really think she would do anything to Annie? Imogen, Kelly *loved* Annie."

"Maybe it was an accident. Maybe they argued. You know what she could get like when she was drinking."

Ruby sighed, nodding because she couldn't deny that.

They could both remember one time, years ago now, when they had all been drinking in Sophie Baker's treehouse. Annie and Kelly had had about the same amount - a fuck load - and a huge fight had erupted.

Annie had been frustrated with Kelly's copy-cat adoration and the two had just gone at each other. The snide remarks had gone on and on and on until, finally, Kelly nearly shoved Annie right out of the treehouse.

"I'd almost forgotten about that." Ruby sighed softly, knowing that she and Imogen were both thinking about the same thing.

Imogen nodded. "Yeah... me too." It had come back to her clearly now, though. She could see the moment Kelly shoved Annie, clear as day.

"We can't tell anyone else." Ruby said, looking up from the wine glass in front of her. "About Kelly. Not until you know for sure."

Imogen nodded in agreement. "Yeah, I know." She wouldn't want to anyway. "I just wanted you to know."

"Thanks." Ruby did seem grateful and Imogen was glad about that. It was nice to feel like they were on the same team again.

The front door opened and the sound of Charlie coming in with Hope filled the house.

Imogen jumped a little in fright as Ruby sat up and slipped off the dining chair and through to the next room. "Hey, you two." There was a smile in her voice as she leaned in to give Charlie a kiss and then took Hope.

Charlie was smiling too when he walked into the kitchen after her, though Imogen was sure she saw it fall just slightly as he saw that she was there.

Still, he covered it pretty well, if it had even happened. Maybe Imogen had just been imagining things.

"Hey." He said as moved over to fill the kettle and make himself some tea. Charlie sure loved his tea.

"Hi." Imogen smiled lightly, glad that he wasn't telling her to get the hell out or glaring at her.

"No Brooklyn today?" He continued the conversation, though he was focusing on his mug and not on her.

"No, she's with Molly today." Imogen told him, glancing at Hope with a little smile as Ruby was moving to get her some food.

She felt more comfortable as she sat there and watched them, feeling the comfort and the familiarity as they both danced around the kitchen together carrying out their tasks.

"I better get going though. I actually have to pick her up soon." She said, gaining a small smile and nod from Charlie. Imogen was just glad that he didn't seem to still be angry with her.

"I'll walk you out." Ruby said, still balancing Hope on her hip as she moved with Imogen over to the front door.

twenty-five

Kelly was frowning as she looked back at Imogen, as if she couldn't quite believe what she had said to her. "Are you kidding?"

"No?" Imogen frowned back, confused. "Why would I be?"

Kelly shrugged, flicking her lighter and sparking up a cigarette. "Dunno. You didn't seem keen the other day."

"I changed my mind." Imogen said. "Don't you want to find out who hurt Annie?"

She studied Kelly's face as the dark-haired girl turned to look at her, trying to see if there was anything hidden in her expression.

Kelly blinked calmly, but there was something in her eyes. Some thought that Imogen wished she could hear. Some secret she wanted to decipher.

"Yeah. 'Course I do." Kelly said after a moment, nodding as she reached for her cigarette pack.

Imogen's gaze moved to the cigarettes, a flash of anger surging through her, but she did her best to push it back down. She still had her suspicions about Kelly giving Brooklyn the nicotine but she had to keep it hidden for now.

Do you really? She wanted to ask, but of course she kept her mouth shut and just nodded. "Okay. Good."

"So what do we do?" Kelly's question stumped Imogen for a few moments. She had really wanted to do all of this alone but now she wanted to keep a close eye on Kelly.

"Well, the last texts I got sent me in the direction of Dakota Pike and Kyle Flynn." She shrugged, deciding to keep Nina's name out of it for just now.

Kelly frowned at that. Imogen had to admit, she looked genuinely surprised. "What? How come?"

Imogen was still having trouble wrapping her head around it herself. "Apparently Kyle was cheating on Annie." She said, looking back at Kelly. Despite the fact her face had changed over the years and she looked very run down, it was difficult not to feel like old times, sitting here with Kelly.

"Dakota's son is Kyle's. Apparently, anyway."

"No way." Kelly blew smoke, shaking her head.

Imogen shrugged. "That's what they said."

"They're bullshitting." Kelly stated confidently, rolling her eyes. "It's a joke, they're messing with us."

Imogen resisted the urge to tell Kelly there was no '*us*'.

"Can you imagine Kyle screwing around on Annie?"

"I mean… no…" Imogen shrugged. She hadn't been able to imagine one of her friends killing the other one either. Or Annie cheating on Kyle with Thomas Playfair.

"Right." Kelly had interrupted her, shaking her head in annoyance. "Ridiculous. I kinda thought this was legit, turns out it's a wild fuckin' goose chase."

Imogen was a little taken aback by the sudden turnaround. Kelly had made her mind up very quickly, basing it off what? Her own feelings. If the truth about That Night was so obvious, the cops would have solved it by now.

Imogen was growing more and more curious about Annie's supposed secret summer that she'd known nothing about. It seemed like she'd been getting up to an awful lot when she wasn't with her friends.

She looked at Kelly quietly for a minute. Did she look relieved? Relieved she thought this was apparently a big joke and she could go on with her life and get away with it?

Imogen knew she was jumping the gun a bit there, thinking as if Kelly had already been found guilty, but she couldn't shake the thought now that it had taken hold.

"Fuck sake, Kelly." Imogen found herself frustrated by Kelly's disregard after she'd swept in the other day and done this big song and dance.

Kelly seemed surprised that Imogen was being so blunt. Imogen knew she wasn't entirely the same girl she'd been back in high school. Back before she and Kelly lost touch. Imogen spoke her mind more, she was a little rougher around the edges but in a good way.

"I've already spoken to them. It's all true, they admitted it." She finally managed to spit the words out now that Kelly had shut her mouth. "So, either you're in or you're out, but stop wasting my time."

She watched Kelly staring back at her, blowing smoke into the air between them, before the dark haired girl finally shrugged. "I'm in."

Imogen nodded. "Right. Good."

"So, what? We start with Kyle?" Kelly wondered, stubbing out her cigarette.

Imogen shook her head. "No, I've been there already, he's got nothing." Beating that dead horse wasn't going to get them anything, not right now anyway.

"Hannah Clarkson." She said after a moment.

Kelly looked confused so she quickly explained about Thomas and Annie's affair and Hannah seeing the two of them together.

"Come on then." Kelly stood up, taking another puff of her cigarette as she did, and stomping towards the front door in her big heavy boots.

Imogen rolled her eyes and moved to follow. This was going to be hell on earth.

* * *

"We already know you saw it happen, just admit you went into the woods and did her in." Kelly snapped at Hannah, who was glaring back at her.

"Kelly!" Imogen's stomach twisted anxiously. This wasn't going well in the slightest.

Hannah was defensive the second she opened the door, Kelly was defensive the moment she got in the car, and Imogen was just along for the uncomfortable ride.

"How dare you bitches come into *my* house and accuse me of *murder!*" Hannah snapped, practically screaming at this point. Her voice was all nails on a chalkboard.

"No, we're..." Imogen started but Kelly was already talking over her before she could get much out.

"The only bitch here is *you*." Kelly prodded Hannah's chest with her finger. Was she drunk? "Admit it. She screwed your boyfriend and you killed her for it."

Imogen had definitely not wanted it to go like this. She was mortified as she stood there, watching Kelly.

"You're way out of line, little girl." Hannah shouted, pushing Kelly's hand away from her.

Kelly laughed loudly and Imogen stared at her like she'd lost her mind. "Your boyfriend screwed Annie. He screwed *me!* You gonna kill me next too ?"

Imogen was stunned by the revelation and before she could do anything about it, Hannah had slapped Kelly across the face.

"Get out of my house!" The redheaded woman screeched at them.

"Screw! You!" Kelly screamed back, lunging for Hannah and shoving her to the ground, her head hitting hard off the tiles.

"Kelly!" Imogen lurched forward, reaching out to grab Kelly's arm and attempting to haul her onto her feet.

Kelly shoved her away and Imogen lost balance, tumbling to the ground, landing right on her ass. She crawled back over to where Kelly was now punching Hannah in the face.

"Stop it!" This time, she managed to pull Kelly back, Hannah's legs kicking out all over the place, and she dragged her old friend off the other woman and over towards the front door.

Imogen shoved her outside. "Get the hell in the car."

"You are not the boss of me, *Immy.*" Kelly's voice was sarcastic and it annoyed Imogen.

"Fine, you can walk." She stalked off towards her car and got in the driver's seat, starting the engine up.

A second later, Kelly got in the backseat.

Neither of them said anything as Imogen pulled away from the curb and drove back in the direction of the part of town Kelly lived.

She tried to figure out what the hell had happened to make the situation spin so out of control but she couldn't.

"Did you actually sleep with Thomas?" She couldn't help asking, her voice tight. She thought it was cruel to spit that at Hannah when it was obvious to everyone but her that her relationship was simply a habit.

"So what if I did? He'll screw anything with legs." Kelly rolled her eyes and Imogen's fingers gripped the steering wheel.

"You're unbelievable." Imogen muttered.

Kelly had never liked Hannah. Even back in school, she was always bad mouthing the redhead, always looking down on her.

Yes, Hannah was a spoiled brat. Yes, she could be a bitch. Imogen had always thought it was better to just ignore people you didn't like or get on with.

"What are you so worked up about?" Kelly shook her head as she stared at the back of Imogen's head.

Imogen rolled her eyes, glancing as briefly as she could over her shoulder at the other woman. "Are you serious?"

Kelly's face said that she was.

Imogen gripped the steering wheel a little harder, staring at the road through the windscreen. "You *attacked* her."

Kelly scoffed. "Oh, hardly. Anyway, she was asking for it."

Imogen started to feel more horrified with every passing second she spent in the car with Kelly.

"Are you-?" She was about to say something like *fucking serious?* but she was sure she would have only gotten the same reply.

It didn't seem like Kelly had any sense of right or wrong, she didn't feel bad, she thought practically tackling and punching somebody for no good reason was a perfectly reasonable thing to do.

It was looking to Imogen more and more likely that her suspicions about Kelly hurting Annie had been right. That thought terrified her.

She drove in silence until she reached Kelly's building and she stopped the car.

They sat there for a few moments, silent and unmoving until eventually Imogen had to turn around. "Get out of the car."

Kelly was staring at her like she was mental. "We should be going to Thomas next and-"

Imogen shook her head. "No. This was a bad idea. I'm done, just get out." Kelly was scaring her, quite frankly. She was clearly capable of snapping at very little.

Kelly rolled her eyes and made a face before reaching for the door handle, throwing it open. "Whatever. You don't give a shit about Annie."

Imogen took off from the curb before Kelly was even out of the car properly, angered by that. She looked in her mirror, watching Kelly stagger across the pavement before lifting her hand and sending a big middle finger after her.

"Nice." Imogen muttered to herself.

When she finally got home, she slammed the front door and stalked through to the kitchen.

Eric was sitting in the living room with Brooklyn and watched her go. "Everything okay?"

"Obviously not." Imogen muttered, frustrated, before she reminded herself that it wasn't his fault. "Sorry. I'm fine."

Eric didn't say anything for a moment, letting her calm down some more. She eventually walked back through from the kitchen with a glass of wine and sat beside him, looking down at Brooklyn playing.

"Kelly is insane." She said after a beat.

Eric glanced at her, though she saw him eyeing the wine as well, as if it was a bad idea but she ignored him. "What happened?"

Imogen spent the next few minutes filling Eric in on everything that had happened. The way Kelly had just flown for Hannah, like she was completely out of control.

Eric frowned, shaking his head in shock. "Seriously? What a… I don't even know what to say."

Imogen shook her head. "It was awful. Now all I can see in my head is…" She had a sip of wine. "Is her doing the exact same thing to Annie in the woods."

Eric moved his arm around her shoulders and pulled her close. "I'm sorry, honey."

Imogen sighed. "I don't know what to do."

Eric was quiet for a few moments. "Maybe you should go to the police now."

Imogen sniffed. She still wasn't sure she liked the idea in the slightest but maybe he was right. She was just one person, she wasn't qualified to hunt down killers, and this anonymous game was wearing her down.

"Maybe."

Eric seemed satisfied enough with that and they eventually changed the subject and Imogen managed to relax somewhat as the time ticked by and the wine took hold.

twenty-six

The next day, Imogen found herself standing outside the police station.

She hovered by the front doors for what felt like forever, swithering between marching in and running back to her car and pretending she'd never thought about going to the police at all.

Eventually, Imogen told herself to stop being so ridiculous and marched into the building before she could change her mind. The cool air flowing from the vents didn't make her feel any less uncomfortable and hot.

She moved up to the reception desk but just as she was about to open her mouth to ask to see somebody, Lauren Hayes walked out of her office.

"Oh, hey!" She seemed surprised to see Imogen and Imogen didn't blame her. It's not like she made a point of dropping in very often.

"Hey." Imogen worked up a smile.

"What's up? Lauren asked, moving to hand a folder to the receptionist. "You need something?"

Imogen could tell Lauren thought she wanted to talk about the fact Annie's body had been found and she supposed that technically that was true.

"Um, yeah." She said carefully, nodding. Imogen was having second thoughts about this but she'd been having them all morning. "I needed to talk to you about something."

Lauren must have seen the seriousness in Imogen's eyes because she frowned, nodding as she gestured for Imogen to follow her. "Sure. Yeah. Come on."

Imogen trailed behind Lauren towards an empty room, sitting at the table as the older woman closed the door.

"What's going on?" Lauren asked once she had taken a seat at the other side of the table.

Imogen didn't even know where to start so she decided to just jump in and info-dump all over Lauren and let her figure out how to sift through it.

So she told her all about the funeral and the texts she had been receiving since. She also told Lauren about her suspicions of Kelly, and her altercation with Hannah, which earned an eyebrow raise.

"I know it sounds crazy but…" Imogen cut herself off, shrugging. She didn't know what else to say.

Lauren was quiet for a few moments, looking back at her with a thoughtful expression on her face.

"Well." She started, looking up and meeting Imogen's gaze. "First of all, I don't think you're crazy."

Imogen still felt tense but she relaxed somewhat as she gazed steadily back at Lauren.

"Second." Lauren continued. "I'd really like to see these messages if that's okay."

Imogen nodded. She didn't feel so good about it but she felt like she'd gone too far now to turn back.

She also felt a flicker of hope. All the police had needed was a lead, right? A break in the case to push it all forward. Ever since Annie disappeared, there had never been many clues to lead the way, to tell them what happened. Maybe this would lead somewhere. Maybe they could track the number or something.

Lauren nodded. "Thanks." She scribbled something onto the paper in front of her and then reached over to take Imogen's phone. "Be right back."

Imogen watched her stand and leave the room, assuming she was going to copy the messages or run a trace or something. She didn't really know how policing worked.

She sat there for what felt like ages, fidgeting as her anxiety built. What if she *was* being watched? What if this was a huge mistake?

When Lauren came back into the room, she was frowning. She handed Imogen her phone back and nodded. "Thanks, we've taken copies and we're trying to trace the number but there's no promises that we'll get any hits at this point. They could be using an app."

Imogen looked back at her dumbly. "An app?"

Lauren nodded as she went on to explain. "There's mobile apps that you download that give you a fake number that you can text from without giving anybody your real number."

Imogen bit her lip at that, frowning. She hadn't thought that the number could be a fake. Did that mean they couldn't trace it? Imogen didn't ask but she started to feel a little less positive.

Lauren was quiet for a few moments, scribbling something down onto the paper in front of her.

Imogen stayed quiet but her anxiety was rising as the silence stretched between them.

"Okay." Lauren finally said, putting her pen down and looking across at Imogen. She smiled just slightly. "Thanks. I'll get in touch with you if we find anything."

Imogen blinked a little. "That's it?"

Lauren nodded, standing up to let her know the meeting was essentially over. "Yeah. I'm sure it's nothing, you should try not to worry."

Imogen followed suit, still frowning a little. "When you say nothing..."

Lauren moved to open the door, looking back over at Imogen. "Look, it's probably just a prank. You know? Like you said." She told her, walking her back through to the reception area. "I *will* look into this." She promised. "And I'll be speaking to Kelly. And Hannah. I just don't want you to stress yourself out over it. I'm sure it's just somebody screwing with you. And I'll find out who."

Imogen nodded, turning to look towards the exit. "Yeah, okay."

She wasn't sure what she believed or thought anymore but she did kind of feel a little let down. Maybe she had gotten her hopes up too much. She had kind of expected everyone to jump up like in the movies and throw everything they had at this.

But realistically all she had was a few texts and a bunch of random nonsense about her suspicions.

"Thanks." Imogen nodded, gripping her phone as she turned to leave. "Tell mum I'll call her tomorrow." She said over her shoulder, pushing through the doors and into the street.

Around the corner, Imogen came to a stop, leaning against the wall.

What was she going to do now?

Imogen knew that she should go home.

She should go and play with Brooklyn and watch crappy afternoon TV.

She should wait for a call from Lauren, which would no doubt tell her that it was all a big joke at her expense and then she would go on with her life and the police would continue to look into Annie's death without her running around playing detective.

But she knew that she wasn't likely to listen to that rational part of herself. Even before the next message popped up on her phone screen, Imogen knew she wasn't going to be giving up.

"It's not ME you need them to find."

Imogen looked around, nerves ablaze. She really was being watched, wasn't she?

As she scanned the street, she couldn't see anybody familiar, let alone anyone standing on their phone or staring at her.

She looked back down at her phone, reading the message over and over again. As she stared at the screen, another one popped in.

"Ready to keep playing?"

Imogen didn't like that. It made this whole thing sound like a game, but it wasn't anything close to a game for her. This was her real life. This was her best friend, dead and buried. This was a killer running loose around town.

Still. If the police weren't going to help her, Imogen didn't feel like she had much of a choice. She gripped her phone and typed out a response.

"Yes."

She turned and walked around the next corner, just needing to keep moving due to the nerves. Imogen wished she'd brought the car but she'd walked today so she could walk off all of her anxious energy.

Every second that her phone didn't go off with another message notification made her more jittery.

Eventually, Imogen got what she was waiting for, but she wasn't sure it was what she wanted.

"Time to pay Chloe a visit."

Annie's twin sister was someone that Imogen tended to avoid as much as possible these days. It was just a little too difficult to look at her and see Annie's doll-like features staring back.

Chloe had never really hung out with them all back in the day. Imogen couldn't really remember Annie and Chloe being that close, even though they were twins.

Maybe when they were little kids, but Annie was always complaining about Chloe when Imogen was younger. She remembered her bitching about Chloe following her around and reading her diaries, and wanting to be her. Once or twice, she'd said she was pretty sure that Chloe wanted to get her out of the picture so she could take her place, but Imogen had put it down to her being her usual overdramatic self. Which is probably all it was considering Chloe hadn't done anything like that. Chloe was still Chloe and Annie was still dead.

As she turned it over in her mind, the memory of what Sasha had said about the fire at the shop the other day popped back in. The fact that Chloe had been hanging around out the back, looking suspicious.

Why would anybody have set fire to the shop?

Imogen turned and hurried on her way, turning everything over in her mind as she went.

twenty-seven

When Chloe opened the door, Imogen watched the confusion flash across her face. It wasn't in the least bit unexpected, considering.

"Hi." Imogen worked up a smile, though she could see suspicion etching itself all over Chloe's features.

"Hey." The other girl returned the greeting cautiously, glancing past Imogen to look down the street before turning back to her. "What's up?"

Imogen felt like she was on the verge of getting a door slammed in her face so she decided to play it safe to begin with.

"I heard about the fire at your mum's shop." She said sympathetically, but she was studying Chloe's face.

Did she look guilty?

"I just wanted to check in, see if you needed anything… or your parents." Imogen continued.

Chloe was quiet for a moment longer than she would have liked but she had always seemed quite awkward so it wasn't too unusual. Then, she seemed to relax somewhat and her grip on the door loosened.

"Right. I… that's nice of you." Chloe said, nodding, giving Imogen her best imitation of a smile.

Imogen smiled back. "Yeah. So. Uh. Is there?"

Chloe shook her head. "I don't think so."

This was a bit like pulling teeth and Imogen held back a sigh. "Do you mind if I come in for a bit?"

Chloe looked a little unsure or hesitant but she nodded and moved aside, pulling the door open a little wider for Imogen to enter.

"Thanks." Imogen flashed Chloe another smile as she slipped past her and into the apartment. She glanced around as Chloe closed the door. "Nice place."

"Yeah." Chloe walked out in front of her and shrugged. "Um. Want anything to drink?"

"Sure. Just water would be great. Thanks." Imogen nodded, following Chloe as she turned for the kitchen. "So... the fire, huh? It's a good thing they caught it quickly."

Chloe nodded, but she didn't seem too glad about it. "Don't think that gives my mum much comfort."

"Yeah. I can imagine she's anxious not knowing who started it." Imogen blinked. *Was it you?*

Chloe shrugged. "Yeah. But it still torched the diaries. That's what's upset her most."

Imogen frowned lightly. "Diaries?"

Chloe turned to her in surprise, handing her a glass of water. "Oh. I figured it would be everywhere by now." She shrugged, leaning against the kitchen counter. "Mum's been clearing out the attic at the old house." The one she'd grown up in. "She was keeping a box of Annie's diaries at the shop." Chloe shrugged. "Now they're just... ruined."

Imogen hadn't been expecting that. She was quiet for a moment, something bugging her that she couldn't quite put her finger on.

Then it hit her.

The fire was thought to be intentional, right? Did whoever set the fire *know* that Annie's diaries were in there? Was there something in Annie's diary that could maybe point to her killer?

"Are they all totally gone?" She wondered, trying to sound more casual.

Chloe shrugged. "I dunno. Mostly. I think some bits survived. The fire seemed to start near the box. Pretty bad luck that whoever did it decided to pick there."

Imogen nodded but the cogs in her mind were turning. Bad luck or a well calculated move?

"You were there that day, right?" She asked, keeping her tone light.

Chloe looked up from the counter and frowned a little. "I mean, yeah. I was meeting mum for lunch."

Imogen nodded. "Yeah, Sasha mentioned she saw you waiting out the back." She did her best not to look like she was studying Chloe's expression too hard but it wasn't easy. Imogen was eager for any subtle clue she could get.

"Right." Chloe seemed to almost roll her eyes and then think better of it, turning her face away.

Imogen frowned, a little irritated. "What?"

"Nothing." Chloe shrugged, turning back to look at Imogen with a shake of her head. "Absolutely nothing."

"It definitely seems like something." Imogen pressed, not liking that Chloe seemed to be thinking negatively in regards to Sasha.

Chloe shook her head again. "I dunno what you mean. Look, I've got a lot to do. Thanks for stopping by. I'll tell mum and dad you were thinking about them."

Clearly Imogen was being pushed out but she felt like she hadn't gotten much yet and was frustrated by it. It's not like she could keep coming back and poking around for information. It would just look weird.

"Right." Imogen put her glass down on the counter and turned, hiking her bag up on her shoulder. She turned. "Just… one more thing. The night of the party."

She saw Chloe's eyes flash with something. It could be that she didn't want to think or talk about the night her sister was killed or it could be that she herself was hiding something about That Night.

"What about it?"

Imogen shrugged. "I just can't remember. Were you there?"

"Nope."

"Are you sure?" Imogen put on a thoughtful expression. "I think I remember seeing you, that's all." This was a lie but it's not like Chloe would know that.

"Well, you didn't. Must have been Annie." Chloe stated, though Imogen had always, *always* been able to tell the twins apart.

"I stayed in. That whole night." Chloe continued, but Imogen already knew that this was a lie because she remembered very clearly Annie seeing Chloe leave the Pierce home and ushering the girls on, worried that Chloe would try to follow them and invite herself along.

Why was she lying about being inside all night? Unless she needed an alibi.

Imogen blinked, letting too many seconds of silence spread out between them. Eventually, she turned and opened the front door without a word. She didn't know what to say and she was worried she would say the wrong thing and it would clue Chloe in that she was on to her.

"I'll see you later, Chloe."

"Yeah. Bye." The door shut swiftly behind her.

twenty-eight

Later that night, Imogen was standing around the back of Lace Boutique.

She had been lurking by the back door for the past ten minutes, anxious that someone was going to stumble across her.

Eric was looking after Brooklyn back at home and Imogen had told him that she was having a catch up with Sasha. Hopefully he wouldn't end up checking in with her because she hadn't told Sasha she was planning to do this either.

Deciding that lurking suspiciously for too much longer would probably just make things worse, she finally moved into action.

Imogen's father had been a bit of a rebel in his youth, to put it very lightly, and one of the birthday presents he'd given her growing up was to teach her one of his favourite skills. Lock picking.

Her grandparents would not have been amused but luckily this particular skill had stayed between her and her dad. Imogen had the feeling that her mother would have found it amusing but she hadn't told the other woman either. It had been nice to have something just her and her dad could share.

Imogen pulled her little kit out of her jacket pocket, grasping the tension wrench between her fingers. She was around the back of the shop by the bins, where nobody could see her unless they ventured around here too, but she still felt exposed, like she could be caught at any moment.

Crouching down, Imogen squinted through the dark and began working away at the lock, her heart thundering away in her ears.

This was beyond just entertaining a few texts from a random weirdo. This was literal breaking and entering.

"Oh, and let's just add burglary to that list, shall we?" Imogen muttered to herself as she continued to work on the lock. Of course the only reason she was here was for those diaries. She just hoped that at least one of them would prove even semi useful.

The longer it took Imogen to get into the lock, the more anxious she got. It felt like it took a long time to figure out but Imogen didn't know if it was because she was already a bundle of nerves and expecting police to jump out from the corner and haul her off to prison, or if it was just a tough lock to crack.

Eventually, after a fair bit of struggling, she felt it catch and straightened up again, inching the door open.

She froze, waiting for an alarm to go off, but nothing happened.

Imogen glanced over her shoulder and then stepped inside, walking slowly, like she was waiting to be swarmed by a pile of cops or something. Part of her probably was.

Grabbing her phone, Imogen turned on the flashlight, and carefully looked around. She was in the back staff room. Her attention was immediately drawn to the scorch marks on the wall by the back door, the floor. It looked like it had started on or near the desk.

It looked worse than she had been led to believe and Imogen bit her lip as she turned herself around.

She had to focus on finding the diaries.

They weren't by the desk, which she supposed made sense since after the fire got to them, Annie's mother would most likely have moved them, right?

She tiptoed around, searching high and low, though the thought suddenly occurred to her that the diaries might not even still be in here. What if they'd been removed after the fire? What if they'd been so damaged they had been thrown away?

Imogen was frustrated with herself for not thinking of these possibilities before she'd decided to do this.

She did one last mini sweep of the back room before she walked out onto the main shop floor.

Immediately, Imogen realised that her phone flashlight had caught the attention of somebody outside on the street. She could see through the window as they were walking past, watched them do a double take and then take a few steps backwards to peer in through the window.

Imogen made a short dive behind the counter, curling her legs up to make herself as small as possible.

She panicked as she had a problem concealing the phone light for a few heart stopping moments. Eventually, she just shoved the whole thing into her coat pocket.

Imogen sat there in silence, hardly even daring to breathe. She could feel her heart hammering away in her chest and she wanted to peek up over the counter to see if the person had gone yet but she was scared they'd still be there and would see her.

Eventually, Imogen knew she couldn't sit there any longer. Her legs were beginning to feel heavy and she felt even more breathless with each painful second that passed.

She forced herself to move, crawling back around the corner of the counter and peeking around very cautiously. Her gaze scanned every inch of the windows at the front of the shop, worried whoever it was was still lurking out there on the high street.

The window was empty.

Imogen breathed a sigh of relief, her whole body relaxing as the tension flooded out of her limbs.

As her breathing slowed to a more normal pace, her focus started to come back to her. She looked around, squinting through the dark, a little too nervous to put the flashlight back on yet.

Turning back to look down the length of the counter, Imogen caught sight of what looked like part of a cardboard lid sticking out from a hiding spot underneath.

She crawled back across the floor towards it, reaching out and tugging the box out of its hiding place and opening the top of it up.

Bingo.

Imogen could see that this box was full of little notebooks of various different sizes.

Annie's diaries.

She turned the phone flashlight back on to get a better view of the contents.

It was clear that a lot of the diaries were burned and scorched, the pages tattered and blackened.

Imogen reached into the box and rummaged around, trying to find the least ruined diaries, if there even were any.

As a rule, it seemed that childhood diaries were colourful, adorned with pretty patterns. At least Imogen's were, and the type of personality Annie had had, she knew that hers would have been too. Bright and colourful and in your face, just like her.

Now they were all charred and crumbling to pieces. Most of them, anyway. You could see some of the patterns through the ash. Butterflies. Rainbows. But they were faded, not as vibrant as they would have been before the fire.

It was sort of like a metaphor for childhood fading away into nothingness.

As she pulled one out of the box, something fell from between the pages. Imogen picked it up and turned the light onto it. It was a photograph. One of Annie with the rest of the group. The edges were scorched.

She scanned the faces. Her younger self smiled back at her, clinging to Annie's hand like she was a liferaft.

Kelly and Ruby were next, Sophie standing on the end. God, it was all so long ago. How could so much have changed? Annie and Sophie were gone and Kelly could be a monster.

Imogen shoved the photograph away between the tattered pages again, continuing her search through the cardboard box.

Gathering a few that looked promising and shoving them into her own bag, Imogen suddenly froze as she heard a noise from out the front.

She clutched her bag, listening tensely.

There it was again.

A clinking.

A key in a lock!

"Fuck." Imogen muttered, shoving her phone deep into her bag with the diaries and crawling at speed across the floor, back towards the other room.

Just as the front door of the shop opened and footsteps echoed through the store.

There was a long silence and then a light came on, just as Imogen dragged her legs through the back and jumped to her feet as quietly as she could.

"Hello?" A voice from the other room called. "Is someone in here?"

Imogen was at the back door now, but she knew she didn't have time to fix the lock or even clear anything away. She hadn't made much mess but she had moved things when looking for the diaries and she was sure it was obvious someone had at least been in here.

There was no time to worry about that, though, as the footsteps started moving across the room and Imogen darted out the still-open back door.

She didn't hesitate. Taking off over the ground, she made straight for the corner, fleeing down the street.

Once safely back at home, Imogen breathed a sigh of relief. That was close. Too close.

Maybe this had been too crazy of an idea but it was done now and she couldn't exactly take it back.

She walked up the stairs and peeked into Brooklyn's room, checking on her. She was fast asleep. No wonder since it was later than Imogen had intended to get home.

She quietly closed the door and padded down the hall towards the bedroom she shared with Eric, tiptoeing in. He was fast asleep too.

Imogen smiled softly, turned to quickly get changed, and then quietly made her way back down the stairs.

Moving into the kitchen, she poured herself a glass of wine and walked through to the living room, sitting cross-legged on the couch as she tugged her bag towards her.

Imogen knew she wouldn't be able to sleep tonight without at least skimming through these diaries. She would toss and turn all night. There was no way she could put it off.

Annie's diaries stared out at her from her bag. She could practically feel their invisible eyes boring into her.

She sucked in a breath, gulped down a swig of wine, and reached out to pull one of the books out.

twenty-nine
Annie's Diaries

9th February

Chloe was questioned by the police today!!! Oh my God, her face was a fucking picture. She kept trying to convince everybody that I'd framed her but who's going to believe that? She's right, obviously, but I only did it because she told dad I was sneaking alcohol from his cabinet.

She's just such an inconvenience. I wish she would disappear. -A ♥

8th March

I have a stalker. And I'm not talking about Gemma Harris. I got these really creepy text messages today. Basically telling me to watch my back and stuff. It's obviously just some jealous bitch who wishes their life was as fabulous as mine! It'll blow over soon. -A ♥

14th May

Got four texts today from that stalker freak. FOUR! Somebody clearly needs to get a life. If they're trying to scare me, they're going to have to try a lot harder.

When I find out who they are, *they're* the one who's going to need to watch their back... -A ♥

11th June

Just over a week until summer's over. Jason Wright's bonfire, here I come! This is going to be the best one ever. I can just feel it. The girls and I are going to have so much fun.

Now, I just have to get my stalker to buzz off and everything will be perfect…

I stole a necklace from that new shop, Carat, because I was feeling stressed out earlier… everyone will think it was Chloe because I put it under her mattress. I really hope they cart that bitch off to jail or something, she's always <u>right there</u>. Ugh. -A ♥

13th June

Ruby came over earlier. God, she's such a bore right now. I wanted to hit the shopping centre because they've just opened this new clothes shop that I'm dying to check out but she just wanted to stay in and watch a movie or something. As if I was going to stay here while Chloe shot me daggers all evening because of the necklace-under-the-mattress thing.

I convinced her in the end, though. Told her it would be a good way to take her mind off the whole "Mr Baker thing". The second I mentioned him, she got all weird and agreed to go. I probably could have asked her for a hundred quid and she'd have said yes just to get me to shut up about him.

This is going to be so much fun!

Gemma Harris was at the shopping centre when we got there, though. *Yawn!* It's nice to be admired and everything but can't she admire me from across the street or something? She came running over, excited as you like. It was kinda nice... like I was famous or something.

She left eventually when her mother came out of the book shop. She just about had a heart attack when she saw her talking to me! I don't think that bitch likes me very much. Feeling's mutual, thanks. I don't care if her husband did die, she doesn't have to act high and mighty. Anyway, it's not like I care.

I don't even know why I still keep this goddamn diary.

I'm going to go and see if Dad will give me money for the train tomorrow. I need to go into the city. I need to get away for a while. -A ♥

19th June

You'll never believe what happened today. I went ice skating with Imogen and she kissed me. As in, properly kissed me! I always knew she was playing for both teams. She pretended it was a joke but I could see it in her eyes. I laughed at her and she looked upset but she was just pretending that she wasn't. Like I care.

You can't just go around kissing anyone you feel like. What if somebody had seen?!! She's going to have to keep her stupid feelings to herself or I don't think I can be friends with her anymore. I don't care how easy she is to talk to… I can't have a *girl* kissing me in public places like that. It just can't happen.

If she wants a girlfriend, she's better off turning her attention to Lacey Dixon… because I know she's the same. You should have seen the way she was looking at this girl the other week. I mean, do what you want but do you have to be so obvious about it?

I don't really care who someone screws around with but it's always good to know that *they* care… -A ♥

20th June

Kelly keeps phoning me. She's become super clingy. I mean, does she not understand that I just want to be alone for a bit? I'm so sick of these four, I really am. It's as if they're obsessed with me… like too obsessed. Maybe I need to find some new friends to hang out with, friends that give me space. Besides, none of them ever want to know how I'm doing, they just want me to solve all their problems and act like some perfect goddess all the time.

Well, newsflash bitches. My sister is mental and wants me dead, my father clearly hates me, and my mother is smothering me. Then again, I can snap my fingers and make her do whatever the hell I want so maybe I can put up with a bit of smothering.

Still… does anybody want to know what's actually going on in my life? No. They just want to be seen with me and talk to me about themselves. Like they need to talk themselves up all the time to keep me interested in them… but they never really tell me anything.

I mean, aren't friends all supposed to care about each other? And aren't they supposed to *tell* me their secrets, not keep them from me?

Keeping secrets keeps us apart. Maybe if they told me some of their own shit instead of *making* me go digging, I'd feel like they were better friends.

God, she's texting me now. Where am I? In my house, avoiding you, because you're pissing me off!!

It's like she wants to be me, it gets creepy. She's addicted to me or some shit. I swear, she's going to go off and get addicted to drugs or something one day and I'm not going to be there for her when she does. Jesus. I'm going to go insane.

I'm going to go and hang out with Dakota and the others… they're so much cooler than the girls right now. It's always nice to get some space from your friends, right? -A ♥

1st July

Remember how I told you that Ruby was sneaking around with Mr. Baker? Well, she isn't any more! Looks like I'm winning. She came round today, practically in tears because he'd broken it off. As if they were an actual couple or something. She even said she couldn't ever go round to Sophie's again.

God, she's so fucking naive. I don't even know how to talk to her anymore, she's just so depressing and now she's going to be even worse because she'll be all upset about this 'break up' and... ugh. Imagine sleeping with a teacher, though? I mean, older men, fine, that can be kind of hot. Maybe even a young, cool, teacher... but he's Sophie's Dad. And he's always staring at me. He's just creepy.

Anyway, I saw the way he looked at her in class the other day. I think he loves her. How pathetic is that?! She's eighteen!

I'm so going to tell everyone, just you wait. Of course, not until I bleed him dry. I mean, where's the fun in turning him in without making him sweat it out a bit first? I could make him do anything I want. I even managed to convince him I thought he was some kind of kiddie lover. He's so freaked out, you should see him!

I'm going to be able to get whatever I want and nobody can stop me because he's so scared that I'm going to tell someone he tried it on with me too. He is so easy! Just like Ruby… is she that desperate for some attention that she'll happily screw anybody who tells her she's pretty? Idiot.

Ruby will thank me for this in the end. He doesn't deserve her and she can probably do way better if she just loosens up a bit and stops hiding behind that ridiculous hair. Who cheats on their wife with their daughter's friend anyway? God. Maybe he really is a proper creep after all.

Ugh, Ruby just texted me. She wants to meet up or something. As if I can be bothered… Guess I'll go, though. Beats sitting around here with the sister from hell… I swear to God, Chloe's out to get me. -A ♥

10th July

You'll never guess what's happened now. One of my old diaries has gone missing. I bet Chloe stole it… it's not in her room, though, I turned that place upside down looking for it. Bitch.

I've had enough of her trying to ruin my life - or trying to be me. It's creepy but if she wants a fight then she's going to get it.

I've been getting more texts from that weirdo too. They're honestly so creepy, I think they were following me around town today. They kept texting me pictures of myself in different shops. Way creepy. -A ♥

20th July

I dragged the girls to the shopping centre today. Sasha was there. I hate that girl. I don't even know why, she just really gets under my skin. Thing is, under all that attitude and crappy make-up she's probably pretty. Maybe we'd get along if she weren't such a moron and her family wasn't psycho. She was following Harvey around again - I saw him outside a shop with Clara. None of the others batted an eyelid, obviously, but Imogen was uncomfortable. She doesn't like lying but she does anything I ask her to do.

It's funny really. Everyone does whatever I ask them to. I keep trying to find the line. Ask them to do something for me. Do something myself to see if they tell me to stop. No one ever does. I can do whatever I want... but I can't tell people how that makes me feel. I'm Annie Pierce. I have a reputation to uphold.

I do really love my friends. You know when you just have a really great group of girls that you know are going to be there for you no matter what? That's what I've got and it sounds stupid but I really love them. They can get on my nerves sometimes (okay a lot of the time) but I suppose everyone gets on my nerves.

~~I get on my nerves...~~

I don't even really think Ruby's easy, I didn't mean that. Sometimes I say things to make myself feel better than everyone else. ~~Even though I kind of already am.~~ I wish it didn't feel like they were always dumping their problems on me. I have secrets too, you know, things I'd like to talk about. I can't because I'm Annie Pierce. Annie Pierce doesn't have problems, ~~she's everyone else's problem.~~

UGH. Do you know who REALLY gets on my nerves?? Chloe!! She just came in here and tried to take back 'her' favourite shirt. It's mine. Mum bought it for ME. She did nothing but pick on me all day today and she calls me horrible?! Aren't twins supposed to be all connected or some shit? Whatever. I'm over it. She doesn't like me, she obviously wants me dead. She wants our parents all to herself.

~~I kind of do hope I die young. Being old would suck.~~ -A ♥

23rd July

Yet another text from this stalker weirdo. Who is it? Who the hell is doing this? Whoever this is is going to seriously regret it. -A ♥

2nd August

Sasha is skating on thin ice right now. She better cough up the money soon or there'll be hell to pay. -A ♥

10th August

My stalker actually helped me out for once! They sent me a bunch of pictures of Sasha following Harvey around like the freak she is. Just the extra blackmail material I needed to give her another push and I didn't even have to lift a finger! -A ♥

15th August

I'm over these creepy texts. It's getting a bit scary now. -A ♥

17th August

How do I make this stop? -A ♥

18th August

Kelly is really testing my patience. I saw her lurking down the street today after I told her I couldn't hang out. Is she stalking me now?

What if she's the one texting? -A ♥

20th August

I'm so excited for Jason's party. I need to let loose!! Hopefully Kelly lets me enjoy myself and Ruby isn't such a drip.

I saw Sasha today. She gave me like a quarter of the money. Not good enough but she'll get what's coming to her. -A ♥

thirty

Imogen put the diary down. A lot of the pages were ruined and unreadable but some were still intact and, squinting, Imogen could just make out the words.

The diary she'd flipped through seemed to be the last one Annie had used before that night. It made Imogen want to cry.

What made her want to cry more was some of the things Annie had written about her and her friends. It seemed like they had been an inconvenience to Annie's perfect little life.

Why did she keep them around then?

There was one part where she backtracks and says that she did love them but Imogen was still hurt by what she'd written - especially the stuff about that day at the ice rink. She'd been unable to reign in her impulses and had kissed Annie. Maybe she shouldn't have but she also didn't think Annie needed to be so cruel about it.

She'd had a crush for such a long time and hadn't known how to deal with it or what it even meant.

She had just been a teenage girl trying to figure out her confusing feelings, it had been hard. Annie laughing made it harder and now seeing the way she'd written about it brought it all back.

What struck Imogen the most, however, were the various mentions throughout the diary entries to a mysterious stalker. Someone sending texts to Annie, someone Annie didn't know and couldn't see, but someone who was watching.

Someone like the person who was texting Imogen right now.

Were they the same person?

Was the person who had been stalking Annie now stalking Imogen? Had they witnessed her murder or had they carried out the act themselves?

Was Imogen in danger?

The parts of the diary that mentioned Kelly had really caught Imogen's attention. It seemed like Kelly was watching or following Annie judging by the entry where Annie details her lurking down the street.

It really confirmed Kelly's obsession more in Imogen's mind.

This was all so confusing. So there was Kelly, and there was this mystery stalker. Imogen was leaning more towards them being different people but she supposed the possibility that they could both be Kelly was still there.

Her thoughts drifted to Brooklyn. If Kelly had given her daughter cigarettes, what else would she do?

She looked through the other diaries she had taken but one was from when Annie was about ten and no help and the others were too ruined.

Imogen finished off her wine as she sat there for a few more moments before she realised how tired she was. Breaking and entering takes a lot out of you, apparently.

She trailed up the stairs, peeked in on Brooklyn one last time, took her medication (a few hours off schedule), and then crawled into bed next to Eric's sleeping figure.

Once she was there, however, her thoughts started swirling again. She couldn't shut her mind off and Imogen lay there going over and over everything in her head before finally drifting off into a fitful slumber.

* * *

The next afternoon, while Imogen was getting Brooklyn's lunch ready, a revelation hit her.

What had Annie meant in those diary entries about Sasha and money?

What money?

The thought niggled at her throughout the rest of the day and eventually she had to just call Sasha because she was too curious now to simply let it go.

"Hey, what's up?" She sat down on the couch, letting Brooklyn crawl around on the floor playing with the dogs.

Sasha sounded stressed as she replied. "God, it's been a long day."

"What happened?"

"The shop was broken into." She said, and Imogen suddenly remembered that she had this knowledge because she had broken into Isabel Pierce's shop and stolen her dead daughter's diaries.

"What?!" Imogen cringed at how fake she sounded but her friend didn't seem to notice.

"Yeah, last night. It's been crazy, the police were interviewing everyone, I guess I was a suspect because I work there."

Imogen bit her lip, suddenly feeling guilty. She hadn't thought about those kinds of consequences but in her defence she hadn't intended on someone catching her.

"Shit, Sash, that's mad." Imogen just felt like she sounded so insincere and now she was trying to figure out a way to bring up Annie and money without letting on that it was her who had done it.

Though, from the sounds of it, nobody had mentioned any missing diaries. They most likely thought it was just an attempted robbery.

"Yeah." Sasha sounded tired. "I think it'll be alright though. I was at my mum's last night and her boyfriend was there. Alibi and all that."

Imogen suddenly felt even worse. Sasha's mother was a drug addict and an alcoholic, not a very functioning or friendly one at that, and since her brother died it was down to Sasha to check in on and make sure the woman hadn't died from an overdose or alcohol poisoning or something.

Usually, she would just call and end up checking in with whichever man the woman was seeing at the time. Her actually going over there wasn't as common an occurrence as it used to be.

Imogen got the impression that if it hadn't been important to her brother, Sasha wouldn't bother. She couldn't really blame her.

"Was she alright?" Imogen asked, watching Brooklyn throw a ball and burst out giggling as Buddy took off after it across the living room carpet.

"Depends on your definition of alright. She's in the hospital now. It got pretty bad."

"I'm sorry." Imogen frowned, not wanting to push.

"It's fine. She'll live." Sasha sighed. "What are you up to?"

"Oh, you know. Mum life." Imogen said lightly, not blaming Sasha for wanting to change the subject. She never really liked talking about her mother.

"I miss Brooklyn's little face." Sasha chuckled, sounding a little bit more like herself.

Imogen smiled, looking over at her daughter and the dogs again. "You'll need to come and see her again soon."

"Oh, definitely. Hey, did you go to the police about the whole Kelly thing?"

"Yeah…" Imogen thought back to her trip to the police station, Lauren's unconvinced face floating into her mind.

"Uh oh."

Clearly Imogen hadn't done a great job of hiding her feelings and she smiled a little. Sasha could always see through her.

"I don't think they were that convinced, that's all." She explained, sighing as she switched the phone to her other ear.

"At least they'll probably be aware and keeping an eye on her now though, right?"

Imogen nodded even though Sasha couldn't see her. "I suppose so."

There was a brief silence and then Imogen continued. "Hey, I was thinking about something the other day."

"Oh, yeah?"

"Yeah, I remembered this weird thing Annie said." She tried her best to sound as casual as possible. "About you."

Sasha chuckled. "Oh, I'm sure whatever she said was just *lovely*."

Imogen forced a little laugh in return. "Yeah, yeah…." She paused. "She was going on about money. How you owed her money or… something, I don't really remember."

There was a silence and it went on so long that eventually Imogen thought the call had dropped. "Hello?"

"What are you talking about?" Her friend didn't sound so impressed.

"Just… I don't know, I just remembered it, I thought it was weird. I didn't know what money you could have owed her."

"I didn't owe her any fucking money." Sasha snapped before Imogen had even finished speaking. "Why would I owe *her* anything?"

Imogen bit her lip. "I don't know, that's why I brought it up. Because I thought it was weird."

"Well, obviously she lied to you." Was Sasha's very matter of fact response.

Imogen knew that wasn't the case though, however, because of course Annie hadn't spoken to her about it, she had written it in her diary, for only herself. Why would she lie about something like that in a diary nobody else would ever have been intended to read?

Imogen went quiet then, not sure what to say next. She wasn't entirely sure what she had expected but not a full blown argument.

"Sorry." She eventually sighed, figuring it was better to just drop it. Annie had always been a touchy subject but usually she was able to at least get Sasha to listen. Obviously this was too close to home.

Sasha breathed out on the other end of the line. "It's fine. Whatever."

Imogen opened her mouth to speak again but Sasha's voice came first. "I gotta go, okay? I'll see you later."

Then she hung up.

Imogen frowned a little, sighing as she put her own phone down. Well, she'd gone and fucked that up a little bit, hadn't she?

* * *

A few hours later, Imogen's mobile phone buzzed from the coffee table, and her heart practically sank into her knees.

What used to be a normal everyday sound had turned into something she dreaded. She used to like getting texts. They would usually be from Eric or her friends, her mum, or even her dad who was travelling around France right now.

Now, the sound immediately set her on edge.

Putting down the book she had been reading, Imogen leaned over and plucked her phone off the table, the screen lighting up almost immediately

"Head to the Coffee Bean cafe or you'll miss your chance."

Attached was a photograph taken from inside the cafe. It showed Oliver Brown sitting in the corner, reading the newspaper, a cup of coffee on the table in front of him.

Imogen thought back to the funeral. Seeing him there with Macey and finding it odd that the two of them would show up.

But she was pretty sure that Oliver had still been in Yorkshire at the time of Annie's murder, so why would this person want her to go and talk to him?

She set her phone back down with a soft frown and settled back against the sofa. Just as she was reaching to scoop her book back up and continue reading, the phone went again.

"Tick Tock."

So Imogen found herself pushing Brooklyn's buggy into the Coffee Bean cafe, hoping she wasn't too late since she had taken longer than expected to get the little girl to settle down.

She noticed that Oliver was still there and then Imogen did a quick sweep of the whole room. Nobody was looking her way. Nobody seemed suspicious.

Had they left? Were they still lurking? Could they see her and she just couldn't see them?

A chill ran through Imogen as she forced herself to move again, ordering a simple tea and scurrying over to sit at the table right next to Oliver.

She was silent at first and he didn't even seem to notice that she was there, fixated on the newspaper spread out in front of him.

"Can I borrow that sugar?" Imogen finally piped up, deciding that was the best way to strike up the conversation.

He didn't even look up and she hesitated before she tried again.

"Hey... Oliver."

Finally, he lifted his gaze, a soft frown dancing across his features. "Hm? Oh. Hey. Sorry. What's up?"

"I just asked if I could use that sugar." She pointed to the packets on the table, thankful that her own didn't seem to have anything on it.

"Yeah. Yeah, 'course." Oliver nodded, reaching out and grabbing up the sugar to hand over to Imogen.

"Thanks." She offered him a smile, which he returned, and then she focused on putting sugar in her tea, trying to decide how to continue the conversation.

"So, how you been?" Oliver's voice chimed up again, making the decision for her.

"Alright." Imogen nodded. "You know. There's a lot going on."

Oliver nodded. "Yeah. Yeah, I can imagine." There was a brief pause. "Sorry. To hear about Annie, y'know."

God, Imogen was so sick of hearing those words. Still, she nodded politely and offered him another tiny smile. "Thanks. Yeah, I... saw you at the funeral."

Oliver nodded again. "Figured it was the right thing to do."

"I didn't know you were close." Imogen continued, though she knew they hadn't been close at all, the two had barely interacted. To Annie, Oliver had been Macey Cross's boyfriend and that's it.

"Uh, we weren't really, I just..." He shrugged, trailing off and going quiet, much to Imogen's frustration.

"That night.." Imogen tried again, looking down at Brooklyn who was falling asleep in her pram. "You were still at your dads, weren't you?"

She knew for sure he hadn't been at the party. A few years before, he'd been moved to his father's place in North Yorkshire. His parents were divorced and he had regularly split his time between the two places.

To Imogen's surprise, Oliver shook his head. "No. I was here. I just got back that afternoon."

"You were?" She couldn't conceal her surprise. "Did you go to the party?" Imogen asked, though she couldn't remember seeing him there.

Why had the text messages sent her here?

Oliver shook his head once more. "No." That was all he said, but there was something written on his face. Something Imogen couldn't quite read.

"What?" She found herself prompting, unable to help it.

Oliver looked up at her in surprise, shifting uncomfortably in his chair. "Nothing, nothing." Then he sighed heavily and shrugged. "I wasn't at the party but I was cutting through the woods."

That surprised Imogen. First she thought he wasn't even in town and now he was placing himself in the woods the very night of Annie's murder. Annie, who was his girlfriend's biggest enemy.

"And...?" Imogen pushed again, feeling like there was more that Oliver wanted to say. "Did you see Annie?" She couldn't help but ask.

Oliver was quiet for a few more moments, his gaze fixed back upon the newspaper spread before him. Then, slowly, and much to Imogen's surprise, he nodded.

"Yeah. I saw her."

"Did you..." Imogen started but she trailed off because she could barely even say it. She was so sick of thinking it...

Did you kill my best friend?

Oliver seemed to understand what she was getting at because his gaze shot up and he frowned deeply. "What? No. *No.* I bumped into her, she was drunk as shit. She was talking all sorts of crazy stuff, telling me she had this stalker. She was *crying.*"

Annie had been crying? Imogen didn't think she had ever seen Annie cry, or at least not real tears. She could turn on the crocodile tears to get out of any situation but proper crying? No. Annie didn't cry.

"Stalker?" Imogen's stomach twisted uncomfortably, her thoughts immediately flashing to the texts she was receiving and then back over some of Annie's diary entries.

"Yeah, she was a mess. She was so drunk and just kept ranting about it. I think she was going to say something else but then she ran off..." Oliver looked uneasy as Imogen stared back at him. "I sort of always regretted not... y'know... going after her. Maybe she'd still..."

Be alive.

Imogen supposed that explained why he was at the funeral. Guilt was usually a pretty good motivator.

The conversation lapsed into silence, Oliver going back to his newspaper, though looking less relaxed than he had when she'd first walked in.

Imogen sat there quietly for a few more minutes, going over everything in her mind, wondering what Annie's stalker had sent her here for.

Was this the next piece of the puzzle?

Had Annie gone from Charlie to Oliver that night?

Where had she gone after?

Had her next move led straight to her death?

thirty-one

The doorbell went when Imogen was sitting at the dining table, hands clasped around a mug of hot chocolate.

She was planning to ignore it but whoever it was wouldn't give up as it rang again. Then again. And again.

"Jesus Christ, *alright*." She muttered as she stood up and marched towards the door. Brooklyn was napping and if this woke her up, whoever was at the door would not be getting a warm welcome.

Imogen wrenched the door open, coming face to face with Kelly Sharpe.

"Jesus Christ." She said again, frowning as she held the door just a little bit ajar. "What do you want?"

"You have to listen to me, okay?"

"I don't have to do anything." Imogen stated, shaking her head at the other woman.

Kelly put her hand out and stopped the door just as Imogen was beginning to close it in her face.

"Listen."

"What the hell do you *want*, Kelly?"

Kelly pushed her way past Imogen, into the house. Imogen, frustrated, slammed the door and turned around.

"What did you say to the cops?"

Imogen rolled her eyes and sighed. "God, is that really what you're here to talk about?" At least now she knew Lauren had spoken to Kelly like she said she would. "What do you think?"

Kelly turned around to look at her, quiet for a few moments as she just sort of stared at her. "I think you're looking in the wrong place."

"Oh, yeah? And where exactly should I be looking then?"

"A little closer to home would be a good start."

Imogen frowned, folding her arms defensively. "What is *that* supposed to mean?"

"It means you trust the wrong fucking people."

Was Imogen imagining something or did Kelly look a little frightened? No. No, she was just unhinged. That was all. She was probably high right now.

"You're not making any sense and I need you to leave my house." Imogen said firmly, turning for the door but she was stopped by Kelly grabbing her arm and turning her back round. "Get off!" She wrenched her arm from the other woman's grasp.

"Listen! I remember now. Annie told me! You have to follow the money." Kelly's eyes were wide as she stared back at Imogen. "The money."

Imogen's thoughts flickered to Annie's diaries and the argument with Sasha the other day. That couldn't be what she meant, could it? There's no way Kelly would know… but she said Annie had told her.

"What money?"

"*Sasha's* money."

* * *

Imogen was sitting on the couch in the living room, her legs pulled up, a glass of wine held lazily in one hand.

She had been going over and over Kelly's visit in her mind since she'd thrown the woman out and locked the front door firmly behind her.

All she had been able to think about was Annie and Sasha and money.

What money?

Why would Sasha need to give Annie money and why did it feel like it had been this big, huge secret. Why had Sasha gotten so defensive on the phone?

Why did Kelly suddenly bring it up? What had prompted it? Her thoughts flashed once again to the diaries that she had read recently, only finding out about the money then, and this stalker who kept texting and seemed to know everything…

Once again, she wondered if it was all just Kelly. Trying to throw her off.

Or was this money more important than Sasha led her to believe?

Imogen didn't like it but her thoughts were going to some very uncomfortable places.

Sasha had been supportive of Imogen's quest for the truth since she told her about it so she couldn't be involved, right?

It was just impossible.

Though she *was* in those diaries, and she *had* gotten so annoyed by Imogen asking about it.

Sasha had also been at the shop the day Annie's diaries had been targeted. She was the one who had led Imogen to Chloe.

Imogen lifted the wine glass to her lips and gulped down a mouthful.

This was crazy.

Kelly was just trying to make her question her best friend. She was trying to make her feel crazy and suspicious. Probably to get back at her for telling Lauren she was suspicious of her.

She rolled her eyes and stood up, setting her glass down on the side with a sigh. "You're being ridiculous."

Imogen headed upstairs, checking on Brooklyn before turning for the main bedroom.

Slipping into bed beside Eric, she sighed and curled up close to him. He woke momentarily to put his arms around her but Imogen didn't feel much comfort.

She lay there wide awake for most of the night.

thirty-two

It took Imogen three days before she got the courage to go round and actually confront Sasha.

The two hadn't spoken since that last phone call and Imogen was getting anxious. Did that mean Sasha was mad at her or did it mean something deeper? Did it mean that all her worrying over the past three days was closer to the truth than she'd like to believe?

She decided to walk, instead of taking the car. Just so it would take longer. To pace away the anxiety or something.

Imogen pushed Brooklyn's stroller as she went. She'd have liked to leave her with someone else but nobody had been available today, so she was along for the ride.

Anyway, maybe she'd ease the tension. Sasha loved her after all.

She knocked on the door four times but it started to look like nobody was home. Just as she was about to give up, turning away from the door, it was thrown open.

Imogen turned back, looking at Sasha's confused face. "What is it?"

"Can we talk?" She asked, stepping back up to the door.

"I'm a bit busy." Sasha seemed guarded, wary.

It didn't help stop Imogen's dark thoughts from twisting and turning and tangling together.

"Sash... come on. Five minutes."

There was another brief hesitation but then Sasha moved aside, holding the door open for Imogen to come inside.

She worked up a little smile as she pushed Brooklyn's pram into Sasha's place, hating feeling so estranged from her best friend.

And she hated that it was all over Annie.

"You okay?" Imogen wondered, as she moved to sit down on the couch.

Sasha was quiet for a moment, shrugging. "Yeah. Just got a lot on right now."

There was another awkward silence and Imogen sighed. "Look. We need to talk about this."

"Why?" It was Sasha's turn to sigh as she grabbed a pillow, hugging it to her as she looked over at Imogen from the other couch.

"Because obviously this stupid thing has gotten between us."

"Stupid thing?" Sasha blinked.

Imogen frowned. "Well, yeah..." She paused. "I didn't think it would upset you so much."

"You didn't think accusing me would upset me?" Sasha interrupted.

"What?" Imogen shook her head. "No, Sasha, I wasn't *accusing* you of anything. What are you--?" She trailed off, not sure what else to say.

"Yes, you were. You're on this crazy crusade to figure out who offed your childhood bestie and *everyone* is suddenly a suspect. Including *me*. I'm not having it."

"That's not what--"

"Yes, it is!" Sasha reached up and raked her fingers through her hair, frustrated. "You're taking every little thing you find or remember and turning it into something bigger. Something it isn't."

Imogen was quiet, staring at Sasha incredulously for a few moments. "You -- you're saying I'm seeing things?"

Sasha blinked and shook her head. "No... I mean, not like that, but.. God, Imogen, you're turning small things into big things." She said. "Something that means absolutely nothing is suddenly some big clue that's going to solve a murder. I tried to be supportive but it's going too far."

Imogen frowned again, shaking her head. "I--" But she didn't know what else to say.

She wasn't sure what she'd expected but it wasn't any of this.

The word *crazy* was spinning around and around in her head.

Was it possible that this whole time, Imogen had just been so wildly wrong and... crazy?

She went quiet, just looking at Brooklyn sort of despondently. She couldn't shut the feeling off. That niggling thing that ate away at her subconscious.

Imogen looked up again. "Just... tell me about the money."

Sasha's expression formed another frustrated frown. *"Imogen."* She sounded tired, irritated.

"Please, Sash." She sighed, knowing she wouldn't be able to let it go now that it had taken hold. "I won't say anything else about it. I just need to know."

Sasha looked like she truly couldn't understand what Imogen was getting at but she sort of looked like she was about to resign herself to the fact that she was just going to tell Imogen what she wanted to know.

"Fine. But, listen, Immy it's really not a big deal. And it was a long, long time ago." She shook her head, studying Imogen's face. "We were all just stupid kids."

Imogen nodded, sighing, because she knew that was true. She definitely wasn't the same person she was back then, that kid who would have done anything Annie asked her to do. That kid who asked how high when Annie said jump.

"I know." She told her, shrugging.

Sasha sighed again, rolling her eyes. "Okay, look." She started. "Annie and I didn't get along. That's no secret, right? The whole Harvey thing…"

Imogen bit her lip as Sasha said Harvey's name. She remembered the party where she'd taken Annie's lie at face value and told Harvey that Sasha had cheated on him. The dramatic break up in front of everyone. Then Annie magically getting her claws into Harvey, the two of them dating for a brief time. Which had been her plan all along, of course. To take what Sasha had just because she could.

Sasha had been so upset.

Imogen remembered Annie's diaries mentioning Harvey too. Sasha following him or something. Did that have anything to do with this?

"Annie just wanted to take him to let me know that she could." Sasha continued.

Imogen didn't like thinking of Annie that way but she knew that Annie hadn't been some angelic soul who could do no wrong. Still, part of her hated admitting that.

"After she had him, she kept taunting me about it. Even after they broke up." They didn't last long because Annie had simply been a way for Harvey to get back at Sasha, not that anyone thought Annie actually liked him either.

"She said she could make him believe anything." Sasha continued. "She told me she was going to tell him that I was *stalking* him or something."

Sasha shook her head and Imogen looked back at her, trying to put these pieces together. "But you weren't?"

Sasha frowned, her gaze locking on to Imogen's face. "What? Of course I wasn't!"

Imogen felt guilty. "Sorry, I--" She trailed off.

Sasha shrugged. "You know what Annie was like. She could twist things and make people believe things." She gave Imogen a pointed look. "She made you believe the whole cheating thing, after all."

Imogen felt her cheeks burn. She hated the reminder because she hated that she'd hurt her best friend that way in the past, over some lie Annie had made up. But Imogen had truly believed her.

"Anyway." Sasha continued. "I was naive back then. She was a bully, she made my life hell. So I believed her and she blackmailed me over it." Sasha looked up at Imogen again, though reached out to play with Brooklyn as the little girl crawled to her.

"That's what the money was for. She wanted me to pay her so she wouldn't tell Harvey I was stalking him…"

Imogen watched Sasha hesitate, like she wanted to say more. "What?"

Sasha sighed heavily. "She said she was going to make his new girlfriend think I was the one who attacked her in town."

"Clara?" Imogen asked, thinking back. They were still together today, right? Not that it mattered.

She nodded as the vague memory of an attack came back to her. Clara had been hit from behind and knocked to the ground but the attacker was never caught.

Sasha nodded too, seeing on Imogen's face that she remembered. "Yeah. She was going to say it was me… coupled with the obsessed stalker thing… I was just so sure she could do it, you know?"

Imogen nodded because, the more she was learning, the more she could believe. Annie hadn't been the angel Imogen had always held her up to be. It was a sad realisation to come to but she had to be realistic.

Imogen sighed. "I'm sorry. I didn't… I just don't understand. There's so much I'm trying to figure out."

Sasha shook her head. "I get it but, Imogen, you can't let this take over your life. The police are doing it. You don't have the training, you're just chasing after childhood rumours."

Imogen digested that for a moment and she felt the weight of it on her shoulders. It was true. She was running around town, digging up the past, harassing everybody who just wanted to move on with their lives.

She had been upsetting and alienating her friends. Running around digging up everyone's skeletons. Thomas, Hannah, Dakota, Kyle. She had gotten Kelly all riled up.

But she just couldn't seem to let go of the fact that somebody had been sending her texts. Someone had been pushing this whole thing and Imogen was sure they knew what had really happened that night.

And she *had* to know.

So she worked up a smile as she looked back at Sasha, watching her with Brooklyn.

"I know. You're right. I'm gonna leave it to the cops."

She knew that she was lying, and she felt guilty about it, but now that she had started this, Imogen had to see it through.

thirty-three

When Imogen got back to her house, Kelly Sharpe was once again standing outside on the front doorstep, waiting for her, pacing and looking like she'd taken something.

Which, knowing Kelly, she probably had.

Keeping tight hold of Brooklyn's pram, Imogen moved towards the front door. "What are you doing here?"

Kelly seemed to sort of jump when she spotted her, but in an excitable sort of way.

"Did you see her? Did you see Sasha? Did you ask about the money?"

Imogen rolled her eyes. "You're high. Go home, Kelly."

Kelly shook her head, frowning. "No. No, you did, didn't you? What did she tell you? She's a liar."

Imogen swung around. "Are you kidding me? You're standing here on my doorstep, high as fuck around my baby, accusing my best friend of being a liar. What is she supposed to be lying about, exactly?"

Kelly swiped at her nose with her hand. "Ask Sophie!"

Imogen stared at her, feeling the breath knocked out of her a little. She shook her head, sighing softly, the fight going out of her. "Go home, Kelly."

She didn't have the heart to say that Sophie was dead. Clearly Kelly was so dosed up that she wasn't even all there.

Imogen quickly moved Brooklyn and the stroller into the house, closing the door in Kelly's face and locking it quickly behind her.

* * *

Imogen sat bolt upright in bed, eyes ripping open from the nightmare she'd been stuck in.

She sat in the dark doing her best to catch her breath, her brain going over the images that had haunted her sleep.

Sophie's mangled corpse rising from the forest floor and dragging itself towards Imogen, who couldn't move a muscle.

Her head was hanging to the side, her red hair covering most of her pretty face. She was covered in blood, cut up and bruised.

She was a zombie.

It was like one of the hallucinations she had had when she'd suffered her schizophrenic break.

It was horrible.

She knew it had been triggered by Kelly's visit and her words *ask Sophie* and the subsequent thoughts of the redhead, but it wasn't easy to shake herself out of it.

Imogen turned her head, looking at Eric as he lay sleeping beside her. He stirred but she was careful not to fully wake him and he rolled over onto his side and soon she could hear his gentle snoring again.

Knowing she wouldn't be able to go back to sleep, Imogen carefully turned and slid her legs over the side of the bed, curling her feet into her slippers and padding carefully out of the room and down the hall.

She peeked into Brooklyn's room, making sure she was okay, and then she turned and made her way downstairs.

In the kitchen she filled the kettle and flicked it on. She wasn't always the biggest tea drinker but she liked the comfort of it when she couldn't sleep late at night.

Imogen grabbed a cookie from the tin nearby and took a bite, turning to lean against the counter.

As she stood there, chewing her bite of cookie, something out of the kitchen window caught her attention.

Her gaze was drawn to a flicker of movement.

Imogen froze, fear immediately coursing through her entire body. What was that? Was somebody… out there?

She hesitantly turned and flicked off the kitchen light, keeping her gaze on the glass.

As the room plunged into darkness, Imogen's blood ran cold. Without the glare of the light against the glass, she could more easily see out into the back garden.

Her eyes were quick to adjust and she could see the black shapes of the swing set, the playhouse… and the figure standing near the back door, hood up so she couldn't see their face.

Time slowed down as the two seemed to stare back at each other through the pale moonlight.

Imogen felt frozen in place, like she couldn't move. Fear had gripped her entire body and she couldn't fight against it.

It was four o'clock in the morning and there was somebody creeping around in her back garden.

Suddenly, the spell was broken and time seemed to start up again. The figure in the garden suddenly moved, sprinting across the grass towards the garden gate.

Imogen's heart was thundering in her chest as she spun around and ran for the stairs, rushing up and into the bedroom.

"Eric!" She shook him awake, panic still threatening to overwhelm her.

He opened his eyes too slowly for Imogen's liking but she was in complete overdrive.

"What is it?" He asked groggily, reaching up to rub at his eyes.

"I think someone was trying to break into the house!" Imogen hopped off the bed again and rushed to the window. If they went out the back gate, they had to come round this way, right?

"What?" Eric was up quick after he heard that, standing behind her at the window, peering out as he pulled on a shirt. "How do you know?"

Imogen turned. "I saw them in the back garden. Creeping around."

Eric frowned and turned away, heading for the door and rushing downstairs in a flash.

Imogen turned back to look outside but she didn't see anybody. Annoyed, she turned and rushed after Eric.

In the kitchen, the back door was flung open but Eric was nowhere in sight. She paused, standing in the dark, listening. She couldn't hear anything.

"Eric?" She ventured, taking a few steps towards the back door.

Imogen took hold of the door, peering out into the dark, scanning the garden but she couldn't see anything. Where had Eric gone? Had he run after them? She felt worry tugging at her at the thought. That was dangerous. The thought of him getting hurt made her feel sick.

"Eric?" She quietly called again, her voice just above a whisper.

Then, suddenly, she heard footsteps. Slow footsteps crunching towards her from around the side of the house.

Imogen froze again, fight or flight completely going out the window.

The steps came closer until she could tell they were directly to her left, right by the door. Imogen glanced towards the counter next to her, eyeing the large pan that was the only thing she could reach to use as a weapon.

Then suddenly Eric rounded the corner, almost walking straight into her.

Imogen let out a slight scream and fell back a little, but Eric caught her.

"Hey, hey, it's me! It's just me!" Eric wrapped his arms around her, holding her while she shook, waiting until the fear spike went back down.

"Jesus…" Imogen muttered, pulling back and looking up at him, relief flooding through her. "Did you see them?"

Eric shook his head, turning to close and lock the door again. "No. They must have made a run for it before I even got there."

Imogen looked at the window again, peering outside. She knew nobody was there anymore but in her mind she could still see the shadowy figure standing there, staring back at her.

"Hey." Eric touched her arm gently. "They're gone."

Imogen nodded, sighing as she turned away from the window, crossing her arms over her body. "It just scared me…"

"I know." Eric said, putting his arm around her and kissing the top of her head. "Come on, let's go back to bed."

Imogen let him lead her back upstairs but her mind was still fixated on what had just happened.

Who had been out there? *Why* were they out there? Was it a burglar? Was it someone with darker intentions?

No. No, surely they wouldn't have up and ran away when Imogen noticed them. Would they?

She moved quietly into Brooklyn's room, hurrying towards her bed and looking in at her. She was still sleeping soundly.

Imogen watched her for a few moments before she crept away again and moved back into the bedroom with Eric.

She glanced out of the window one more time, scanning the street but all was completely still.

Sighing, Imogen padded towards the bed and finally slid back under the duvet, curling up into a little ball. She was wide awake and unsure if she would be able to get back to sleep now. Not that she even really wanted to.

Nightmares when she closed her eyes, nightmares when she opened them. Her whole life seemed to be one big nightmare.

"You okay?" Eric asked softly, climbing into bed beside her, rolling onto his side to face her.

Imogen nodded, though she probably looked anything but. "Yeah, just… spooked."

"Yeah. Did you see what they looked like or anything?" Eric wondered.

Imogen shook her head. "No. It was too dark, I think they had a hood up or something. I don't know."

"They probably just wanted to steal the TV or something… thought we were asleep. Seeing you in the kitchen probably scared them off."

Imogen nodded. "Yeah. I know." She knew that he was probably right. It was just some prowler trying to find a place to rob. Maybe they'd hear about a house down the street getting robbed later on.

"Try and get some sleep, okay?" Eric kissed her gently and then closed his eyes.

Imogen watched him for a few moments, the rise and fall of his chest. She knew that he was right. It was a random prowler.

Still.

Part of her couldn't help but wonder if maybe - just maybe - this had something to do with the mysterious texts she had been receiving.

Annie's diaries flashed back into her thoughts. The entries about somebody *stalking* her. Following her and sending her weird messages.

Was this the same person? Were they now stalking Imogen? The thought made her shiver despite it being something she had thought many times already.

Thinking and wondering was quite different from actually experiencing it.

* * *

Hours later, Imogen was standing in the kitchen again. She had managed to get a few hours of restless sleep but she still felt dead tired.

She was even on the verge of giving in and forcing herself to drink a disgusting coffee in the hopes of having more energy.

As she walked around the kitchen, Brooklyn on her hip, Imogen couldn't shake the feeling of uneasiness.

She tidied up the kitchen table with her free hand and moved to grab Brooklyn some breakfast from the fridge, when something out of the corner of her eye caught her attention.

Imogen turned to the window, trying to make sense of what she was looking at.

There was something stuck to the glass and she frowned, turning to settle Brooklyn into her high chair at the table and set her breakfast of melon out in front of her. Chubby little fingers reached out greedily.

Then she turned and moved cautiously towards the back door, unlocking it and stepping outside. She felt braver in the daylight and she knew there was no chance whoever had been out there last night was still lurking, but the uneasiness had still settled itself into her bones.

Imogen moved to the window and reached up, peeling a piece of paper off the glass. It was taped to the window so it was obviously deliberately put there. It's not like the wind had blown it along and it had gotten stuck.

Imogen turned and hurried back into the house, locking the door behind her and then she leaned against the counter and looked down at the piece of paper in her hand.

Somebody had scrawled a message on the paper in red pen.

"Don't stop.
You're getting warmer."

Imogen stared at the paper, the words blurring together as she seemed to forget how to even blink.

When she finally regained control of herself, Imogen turned immediately to close the blinds, even though she knew there was nobody out there looking in… but she felt watched all of a sudden.

The message was so similar to the texts that Imogen couldn't convince herself that it *wasn't* put there by the same person.

The same person who seemed to know *everything* about That Night and about Annie's Secret Summer.

How could they… unless they were the one following Annie around. Stalking her. Sending her weird messages like they had been sending to Imogen.

This person had witnessed Annie's murder.

Or, perhaps, even carried it out themselves.

And now they were lurking around outside Imogen's house in the middle of the night.

The only thing Imogen didn't know was the only thing she needed to know most of all…

…*were they dangerous?*

thirty-four

It had been a week without any more incidents. No stalkers in the night. No texts. No messages stuck to the window. No surprise visits from Kelly.

Everything sort of felt normal again, apart from the fact that Imogen couldn't shake the thoughts away.

Still, it was a welcome reprieve from the chaos. She took Brooklyn to feed the ducks and she managed to sit out in the garden in the sun with a book and not jump at every sound she heard.

Then, on Thursday morning, she woke up to an envelope through the letterbox.

At first, it didn't arouse any suspicion. It was a normal envelope addressed to Imogen. She figured it was probably another bill she had to pay. She put it on the kitchen table with the rest of the mail until later that afternoon.

Imogen had dropped Brooklyn at her mother and Lauren's place. They had planned to take her to the park and Imogen could use the time alone.

Eric had gone into the paper because they had a massive deadline to meet for the next day and they'd been running a little behind, so Imogen had the house to herself.

She finally decided to turn her attention to the pile of bills on the table, going through them one by one.

When she came to the envelope in question, the contents came tumbling out, and it certainly wasn't a bank statement or a bill.

She frowned, staring dumbly down at the table for a few moments, trying to make sense of what she was seeing.

Polaroids?

Imogen reached out to pick one up, her eyes glued on the image that it showed.

"What the fuck?" She muttered, her expression twisting from confusion to fear.

In her hand, Imogen was holding a picture of herself. It was recent, she could tell from the jacket she was wearing. In the picture, she was pushing Brooklyn in her pram.

Imogen suddenly realised that it was taken the day she had gone to see Sasha the other week.

She thought back, recalling the fact that that same night had been the night she'd woken to find a prowler in the back garden.

Imogen dropped the picture and reached for another one. A picture of her standing on Chloe Pierce's doorstep, Chloe's face looking anxiously out at the street. Was she looking directly at the camera? No. She couldn't be. It had to be the angle.

Another polaroid showed Ruby and Imogen standing on Annie's old street, where she'd grown up. This was the day she found out Annie's body had been found. Imogen remembered it like it was yesterday.

This person had genuinely been following her since the beginning.

Why her?

What did they even *want?*

Imogen had spent the last few hours pacing the house, feeling anxious and on edge.

She felt paranoid and watched and didn't know what the hell to do.

Should she go back to the police?

No closer to answers than she'd been a few hours before, Imogen padded back into the kitchen, lingering in the doorway and glaring at the pictures on the table as if that was going to make them disappear.

Imogen moved back over, wanting to tidy them away before her mother dropped Brooklyn off.

As she lifted the envelope, something slid out onto the table. One more polaroid. She wasn't sure how she had missed it.

Imogen frowned, picking it up, her blood immediately running cold.

It was a picture taken of a mirror, a burst of a flash taking up most of the glass.

It was dark but Imogen could make out a face towards the side of the mirror, adjacent to the flash.

She squinted but the image was too dark and too grainy, too unfocused. The flash made it impossible to really see but Imogen figured that was probably the point.

She was pretty sure that she was looking at a picture of the person who was sending her these messages. The person who was following her. Who had followed Annie and seen what happened the night she went missing.

Imogen glanced away from the impossible-to-make-out face, giving up on trying to conjure up some features that would give her all the answers to this person's identity.

Her gaze flickered to the mirror, to the writing written upon it. The words written in red, made to look like blood but probably (hopefully) just in lipstick.

I SAW EVERYTHING

thirty-five

"Hey, kid." Brooke's voice called out as the front door to the house opened.

Imogen shoved the polaroids into the nearest kitchen drawer and moved out to greet her mother, putting on her best smile.

"Hey." She leaned down to scoop Brooklyn up into her arms. "Did you have a good day?"

"She had the best day." Brooke chuckled, moving to set down Brooklyn's bag of things by the coat rack.

Lauren walked in behind her, eyes glued to her phone for a few moments before she looked up and offered Imogen a smile. "Hey." She glanced at Brooklyn. "You'll be pleased to know she was very spoiled."

"Oh, good." Imogen laughed, amused. She moved to put Brooklyn down in the living room, letting her waddle over to her toys

"Thanks for watching her, guys."

"Oh." Brooke waved her hand. "Anytime, you know that." She watched her granddaughter with a besotted little smile that made Imogen's own smile brighten. The two really had the cutest relationship.

Imogen turned to look at Lauren, wondering if she should say something about the polaroids she had received. Part of her just wanted to dump all of this information she had onto the police and leave them to it.

Eric had reported the prowler in the garden, the supposed burglar that Imogen knew wasn't really a burglar, but nothing had come of it. Not that she'd expected it to.

Her phone buzzed in her pocket just as she was considering saying something and, distracted, she turned her attention to it.

"Do you guys want some tea or coffee?" She asked as she pulled her phone out.

"Oh, no, it's okay. Thanks. We're heading to one of Lauren's work things." Brooke replied casually, but Imogen's mind had already sort of switched off from the conversation, the text on her phone taking a front row seat.

"Say a word and her killer goes free."

Imogen's immediate reaction was to look towards the living room window, as if she would see a face peeking in at her with a menacing expression.

Of course, she saw nothing at all. Just the flowers beneath the windowsill and the sun shining down from the cloudy sky.

"Immy?" Brooke's voice brought her back out of her mild trance and she turned away from the window, working up another smile.

"Yeah?" She put her phone down on the coffee table, doing her best not to overthink it all. Obviously, this person still wanted *her* to be the one to follow the clues. They wanted to lead Imogen to what they knew. If there was a reason for that, she didn't know, but she wasn't going to jeopardise it now. She had already decided she was going to continue, the day she'd lied to Sasha.

"You okay?" Brooke wondered, now looking at her with slight worry on her face.

"Yeah, 'course." Imogen nodded back at her, moving to hand Brooklyn the stuffed bunny that was just out of her reach up on the sofa. "A bit tired." She continued, covering for any uncertainty that might have shown in her response. "I've not really slept too well since… you know."

Brooke nodded, giving her daughter a sympathetic look. "Yeah. I can't even imagine how scary that was. Waking up to someone trying to break in."

Imogen nodded, glad her bluff had seemed to work.

"I'm sorry we haven't been able to find them." Lauren chimed in.

Imogen shrugged. "It's okay. I'm sure they won't come back, it… was just a shock."

"Right, well. We better be off anyway." Brooke moved to give Brooklyn a little squeeze goodbye and then turned to wrap her arms around Imogen. "If you need us to watch her again just let me know."

"Yeah. I will. Thanks." Imogen hugged her back and turned to walk them both out.

She waved them off, glancing suspiciously down the street, before she turned and retreated back inside.

thirty-six

Imogen had been sitting staring at the polaroid for the past few hours, trying to make out something, *anything*, in the blur of the face reflected in the mirror.

She became more frustrated by the minute, the person as unrecognisable to her now as they had been when she first saw the picture.

It was maddening. Like they were taunting her with the fact they were just out of reach. They could see her but she couldn't see them.

Maybe having all of this information made them feel powerful.

She decided to go over all the old messages and see if she had missed anything. There must be somewhere else she needed to go. Imogen read over her texts, recalling her visits to Thomas, Hannah, Nina, Chloe, Dakota, and Kyle. The whole Sasha and Harvey thing.

Annie sure had had a jam-packed summer that year, leading up to one similarly jam-packed night.

Imogen sighed as she grabbed her phone and decided to just do it the old fashioned way and ask.

"Where do I go next?"

She placed her phone down on the couch beside her and reached for one of Annie's diaries, re-reading the pages again but she didn't get to read much (not that there was much of anything to read) because the reply was quick to come through this time, the vibration of her phone making her jump.

"Poppy Hart saw her in the woods that night too."

Imogen blinked down at the message.
Poppy Hart?
Imogen remembered seeing Poppy and her sister Jasmine at the funeral, two of the last people she would have ever expected to see there.

Though she was starting to feel like she was saying that about everybody who had turned up. Had *anyone* been there to lay her to rest or had everybody just gone to see off the witch, as it were.

She shoved those thoughts away and told herself to focus.

Jasmine Hart had been another of Annie's poor bullying victims and Poppy had done her best to make Annie's life hell for it.

Poppy wasn't like her sister. Where Jasmine was shy, reserved, and quiet, Poppy was brazen, bold, and angry. If you pushed Poppy, Poppy pushed back. Often twice as hard.

Imogen thought back to the night of the party, thinking she could recall Poppy being there but she couldn't be sure. Imogen had been too busy having fun with her friends that night.

She stood up, deciding that now was as good a time as any. She wasn't going to get answers sitting around on the couch, was she?

Imogen dressed Brooklyn and got her into her pram, though she started fussing because she wanted to be let out so she could wobble around, but Imogen didn't have the patience to watch her tumble her way around Baberton.

Thankfully, she eventually settled down and just watched her surroundings, gnawing away at a rusk biscuit.

Imogen didn't really know where to go. She didn't want to just march right up to Poppy's front door and demand answers. It would feel weirder than the others. Honestly, Poppy kind of intimidated Imogen, and she had since they were all younger.

Then there was the incident that same summer. When Poppy and Annie had gotten into that big fight in the middle of town.

It had been a hot summer day and so many other people they knew had congregated in the town centre, ice creams and shopping bags in hand.

Imogen remembered they had been talking about heading down to the river to swim so they could cool off.

Nobody was really supposed to swim in the river, not since a girl named Erin Hopkins had drowned there a few years previously. But people still did anyway, especially kids, and it was difficult to police.

Imogen couldn't remember how the fight even started but the next thing she knew, Annie and Poppy were at each other's throats and a crowd had gathered.

It ended with Poppy swinging for Annie, clocking her right in the nose, and being dragged away by a couple of people as everyone suddenly realised it had gone a bit too far now and they should probably step in.

Annie had been furious, blood dripping from her nose and down her chin, bleeding all over the pavement.

Leaving her mark on this town just the way Annie Pierce always had.

It was funny how poetic you could be after somebody was dead and gone, wasn't it?

Well. Not funny.

Imogen sighed, snapping herself back to the present, stopping abruptly in her tracks as she nearly ran Brooklyn's buggy into somebody.

"Oh my God, I'm sorry!" She gasped, pulling back a few steps. "Are you okay? I didn't get you, did I?"

"No... it's okay."

It took Imogen a moment to realise it was Daisy Ramsey in front of her. She hadn't seen the other girl in so long that she had nearly forgotten her existence entirely, which made her feel bad. Then she remembered that she'd seen her at the funeral and felt worse.

Daisy and her brother Austin had moved to town a few years before Annie went missing. Austin had fit in at school right away but Daisy had been a little bit weird and didn't really get along with anyone else.

She was just one of those people who had preferred to keep to themselves.

Imogen smiled politely. "Are you sure? I really should have been watching where I was going, I'm sorry."

Daisy shrugged. "It's fine." She worked up a smile of her own.

Despite being all grown up now, Daisy still had a lot of her old awkward air around her. Imogen felt kind of bad for her. It had to be hard being alone so much, right?

"I should let you get back to it anyway." She said, gesturing to the camera clasped in Daisy's hands. "Getting anything good?"

"A bit." Daisy shrugged again, looking down at the camera and then up at Imogen. "Some birds. Cats. You know... Baberton."

It was said in the way that everyone around here said it. *Baberton. Oh, nothing ever happens here*.

Imogen chuckled. "Yeah." She made a face. "You should try by the river. I bet you'll find a heron or something."

Daisy nodded, her smile brightening a little. "Yeah. Yeah, I might.... thanks."

"Sure." Imogen grinned, feeling better. "Hope you get something good." She said, moving to push the buggy again. "Good luck."

Imogen headed off, feeling, in a way, like she'd done her good deed for the day.

Ending up at the park, she sat at a picnic bench and allowed Brooklyn out for a little bit, letting her toddle around on the grass.

She smiled softly, almost forgetting what she was even out for, until she saw Jasmine Hart sitting on another nearby bench, scribbling away in a notebook.

Then her thoughts drifted back to Poppy and the whole reason she had come into town at all.

While she was looking away, Brooklyn fell and started crying, bringing Imogen's attention back to her. Along with Jasmine's as the other woman looked up from what she had been writing.

Imogen jumped to her feet and picked Brooklyn up. "Hey, you're alright." She could tell she hadn't gotten hurt and only given herself a fright. "Come on, silly, you're okay." She sat back down at the picnic bench, sitting Brooklyn up on the table part, reaching up to wipe her tears away. "See? All better, yeah?"

Brooklyn was quick enough to settle back down again as Imogen took a piece of melon out of her bag for her to chew on.

"She alright?" A voice from somewhere to her right drew her attention.

Imogen looked up, noticing Jasmine Hart was still looking her way.

She nodded. "Oh, yeah... yeah. You know." She glanced back to her daughter with a little chuckle. "Just a little tumble. All good."

"Kids are pretty resilient, I guess." Jasmine smiled in mild amusement.

Imogen nodded. "Yeah. Way more than I'd thought before ever having one of my own." She chuckled.

There was a silence for a few moments, Imogen wondering if she should ask if Jasmine knew where her sister was.

"How have you been otherwise?" Jasmine filled the silence first, which surprised Imogen a little.

"Uh, yeah." She nodded, offering a little shrug. "Fine… considering. What about you?" A pause. "How's, uh, Poppy?"

Jasmine looked a little surprised but she covered well enough and nodded. "Yeah. I've been fine, too." It was the sort of forced conversation that Imogen was used to so she just nodded along and smiled as Jasmine continued. "Poppy's been alright as well, yeah."

Imogen nodded. "That's good. She still working over at the bank?"

Jasmine nodded, though Imogen could tell there was some mild surprise in her expression that she'd continued asking about Poppy. "Yep. Four days a week."

Imogen nodded, not sure what else to say without sounding like she was pressing the issue.

She turned her attention back to Brooklyn, who was wriggling to get down off the bench, seemingly over her little tussle with the ground.

"Do you, uh, talk to her often?"

"Hmm?" Imogen looked up again. "Who?"

Jasmine shrugged. "Poppy."

Imogen shook her head. "Oh. Oh, uh, no. Not really. I don't really see her much. I was just… wondering."

"Oh." Jasmine nodded, but Imogen could hear the uncertainty in her voice.

"What?" Imogen asked after a beat.

"I just... I don't know. I wouldn't have thought... after everything..."

"After Annie?" Imogen turned back to keep her eye on Brooklyn.

"Yeah. They weren't exactly each other's favourite people." Jasmine said.

"So?" Imogen looked back up again.

"So, aren't you meant to be all loyal to her or whatever?" Jasmine looked uncomfortable. "Y'know. Not fraternise with the enemy and shit."

"I didn't realise we were all still in high school." Imogen found herself saying, though she felt bad the minute it was out of her mouth.

Jasmine turned her gaze back down to her notebook, shrugging. "We're not, I just..." She shrugged.

Imogen bit her lip. "Sorry, I--" She paused, sighing. "I just need to talk to her."

"To my sister?" Jasmine looked up again, surprise etching itself back into her features.

Imogen nodded. "Yeah. Do you know where she is?"

"Why do you need to talk to her?"

Imogen shrugged. She knew Jasmine was asking because of what happened that day in town, Poppy punching Annie. They hadn't exactly all been besties once that happened.

But things were a lot different now and Annie was dead and apparently Poppy had been in those woods which could probably mean two things.

That she saw something.

Or that she did something.

"It's complicated." Imogen eventually responded, expression guarded as she looked back at Jasmine.

Jasmine didn't look convinced and Imogen eventually sighed, relenting with a shrug.

"It's about Annie."

Jasmine's expression shifted and she shook her head. "Imogen." Her tone was almost a warning and Imogen understood.

The summer that Annie had gone missing, and people started to believe she had to have been hurt, Poppy had become suspect number one.

Everybody knew about the punching incident in the town centre. Nothing stayed under the radar in Baberton, especially not gossip.

If they'd had a local gossip magazine, it would have been featured on the front page.

The police had jumped on the incident, adamant that it had sparked another fight. Maybe one that had turned deadly, made worse and fueled by the alcohol at the party, and if Poppy would just come clean they would go easy on her.

Of course, Poppy stuck to her story. That she hadn't been anywhere near Annie since the incident in town and that was that.

Eventually, the police had no choice but to drop it. No Annie. No evidence.

No body, no crime.

By then, though, the damage was already done.

Poppy had another mark against her name, murder suspect number one.

Not that there was proof of an actual murder at that point in time but rumours ran rampant around the town. Even after the police concluded that Annie must have simply run away.

During this time, Imogen had sort of hidden herself away, and the four girls who were left drifted slowly apart without Annie.

Now, though, Imogen was ready for more answers. Yes, she may have been pushed in this direction by whoever was sending her texts but she also wanted to see it through.

"I don't think she did anything." Imogen said quickly, trying to put Jasmine at ease so she'd be more inclined to tell Imogen where Poppy might be right now.

Of course, she had no real idea. It's possible Poppy could have done something but it was also equally possible that she didn't.

Jasmine was frowning as she looked back at Imogen, like she was sizing her up, trying to figure out her motives perhaps.

Eventually, she sighed. "She's probably at the bowling alley." She said, shrugging.

"It's closed, isn't it?" Imogen frowned, confused.

"Yeah, but dad gives her the keys. She likes to hang out there by herself." Jasmine explained.

Imogen nodded. "Okay… um, thanks."

"Just… please don't make it worse." Jasmine said quietly.

Imogen looked at her for a moment and shook her head. "I won't."

Could she really promise that though? Imogen wasn't so sure.

* * *

Once Eric had finished at the paper, Imogen left Brooklyn at home with him, and then she set off again.

Imogen couldn't say that she went to the bowling alley too much. She wasn't that into the game, nor was she even very good at it.

When she was younger, the bowling alley was a more popular hangout spot for teenagers, and she remembered she and her friends would go just for the amazing milkshakes they sold, but she wasn't too sure how popular it was nowadays.

Imogen drove up to the bowling alley, hoping that Poppy would still be there by the time she arrived.

The alley was in the middle of the spot of town that locals called *The Entertainment Centre.* It was where things like the cinema, gym, swimming pool and ice rink were located. All together so you could make a proper day of it if you really wanted to.

Imogen parked in the Starbucks car park and walked the short way over the road to the bowling alley.

She tried the door but, of course, it was locked. That didn't mean anything, though. Jasmine had said that her dad, who owned the place, would let Poppy hang out there when it was closed and Imogen doubted that she would leave the door unlocked for just anybody to wander in.

She hovered there for a minute, peering in through the little window on the door, before she just decided to knock.

One knock. Nothing,

Three knocks. Nothing.

Five knocks. Nothing.

Imogen sighed, wondering how long she should try. It was possible Poppy wasn't even here anymore. Still, she didn't want to give up without knowing for sure, so Imogen lifted her hand again, knuckles knocking against the door.

Eventually, she saw movement from inside and a figure appeared.

There was the sound of a key in a lock. Then the door swung open and Poppy Hart was scowling back at her.

"What do you want?" Poppy took her earphones out as she blinked back at Imogen.

Imogen had almost forgotten how intimidating Poppy could be. She had an angry confidence about her, that was the only way to describe it.

"Sorry, um." Imogen stammered a little, doing her best to reign her anxiety in. "Your sister said you might be here, I... just wanted to talk to you."

Poppy's frown deepened. "Talk to me about what?"

"Can I come in?" Imogen wondered.

"Why?" Poppy shook her head.

"I just..." Imogen bit her lip, wishing she could just spit it out. "Please?"

Poppy stared at her for a few moments, silent, and then shrugged and stepped to the side so that Imogen could enter.

"Thanks." Imogen worked up as big a smile as she could manage, her heart finally slowing back to a normal pace. She'd half expected the door to be shut directly in her face. Okay, more than half.

She moved inside as Poppy locked the door again behind them, leaving the keys hanging in the lock, and followed her across the entrance area.

Imogen could see a sketchbook sitting out on one of the tables, gathering that Poppy was probably sketching and listening to music when Imogen interrupted her.

Poppy moved behind the counter to grab herself a coke. "Want one?"

"Sure." Imogen nodded, taking the can when it was slid across to her.

Poppy cracked open the coke can and had a sip, letting the silence stretch between them.

Imogen felt uncomfortable but she had a feeling that Poppy didn't.

"So, what do you want?" Poppy finally asked again, putting her drink down and hopping up onto one of the little stools.

"I just wanted to talk." Imogen started, shrugging. She took a sip of her own coke so that she could stall for a brief moment.

"About what?" Poppy asked before Imogen could continue. She was impatient, that much was clear.

"Annie." Imogen decided to just blurt it out. It was an awkward topic as it was these days and she might as well just throw herself in headfirst.

There was another deafening silence as Poppy stared at Imogen, making her wonder if she should have just kept her big mouth shut in the first place.

"What the fuck would you want to talk to me about Annie for?" Poppy sounded irritated.

Imogen shrugged. "I'm just trying to figure some stuff out."

"What, like if I killed her and buried her in the woods over a stupid high school rivalry?" Poppy asked bluntly, moving to pull a cigarette out of her pocket and lighting up.

Imogen was a bit surprised by the fact she'd just thrown that out there and shook her head quickly. "No. No, of course not, I just…" She shrugged. "You were at the party that night, right?"

Poppy shrugged. "Sure. So what? Everyone was there."

Imogen nodded. "Yeah. I know." It wasn't a big deal and she wasn't trying to say that it was but Imogen could tell that Poppy was defensive.

"What point are you trying to make then?" Poppy asked, again not waiting for Imogen to figure out how to awkwardly string the words together.

"Did you see her in the woods?" Imogen just threw the question out, fiddling with the tab on her coke can to occupy her fidgety hands.

Then she looked up at Poppy.

The other girl was staring at her through narrowed eyes, thoughtfully puffing on her cigarette. The smoke tickled Imogen's throat.

"What are you trying to say?" Poppy finally asked, blowing another cloud of smoke.

Imogen coughed. "Nothing. I just wanted to know… I wondered if you saw something."

"Look, I can hardly even remember that night. I was so trashed."

Imogen nodded. "Oh. Right. Okay."

Another awkward silence stretched between the two, though Imogen again felt like she was probably the only one who was feeling awkward.

"I'll leave you to it." Imogen said eventually, moving to stand up.

"I did see her at some point." Poppy said randomly, stubbing her cigarette out into an ashtray on the counter.

Imogen looked at her in surprise. "In the woods?"

Poppy nodded, looking thoughtful suddenly. "Yeah. I was so drunk I could barely stand up. I can't even really remember it, it's just… a whisper." Poppy shrugged. "I think she tried to help me up. I don't know. I fell asleep. When I woke up I stumbled home and passed out again. Then in the morning everyone was saying she was missing."

Imogen nodded, taking this in. It really didn't feel like too much information which put her into a downer just a little bit.

"Why would you ask anyway?" Poppy wondered, looking curiously at Imogen.

Imogen shrugged. "I'm just trying to understand what happened." She said. "That night, she sort of disappeared at the party and then… she was gone." Missing. Dead.

"Yeah, but the police are working on it, right?"

"Did you tell the police you saw her in the woods?" Imogen asked, looking up with an eyebrow raised.

Poppy went quiet then and shrugged. "No."

"It would make you look more guilty." It wasn't a question. Imogen wasn't stupid.

Poppy nodded. "Yeah." She blinked. "I still don't get why you'd ask." She said again. "There's no way you could know I was even in the woods. Is there?"

Imogen shook her head. "No. No, I didn't *know*, I just.." She couldn't tell anybody else about the messages, it was probably too risky. "I just guessed."

"Right." Poppy didn't seem convinced and she opened her mouth as if she was going to say something else, but suddenly a loud whistle echoed through the bowling alley.

The two girls immediately froze, gazes locked on each other, and a sickening silence stretched over the whole building.

"What was that?" Poppy finally whispered.

Imogen shook her head in a way that said *I don't know.* Maybe it was nothing. Maybe it was just one of those noises you hear in a big empty building without a crowd of people.

But then they heard the footsteps.

Slow, careful steps echoed through the alley. It sounded like they were coming from the lanes, like somebody was walking across them, coming from the other end of the building, and right towards them.

Another low whistle sounded. It was unmistakably from a person and Imogen could feel her heart jumping into her throat.

Somebody was in here with them.

Somebody had been listening.

It seemed like Poppy and Imogen unfroze at the exact same time as they both jumped and ran towards the front door.

"What the fuck?" Poppy snapped, tugging at the handle but it didn't budge.

Looking over her shoulder, Imogen could see that the keys Poppy had left hanging from the lock were gone.

The footsteps suddenly stopped and the silence settled back around them.

Then there was a burst of loud music. Imogen practically jumped out of her skin, grabbing Poppy's arm in terror.

The lyrics from the song *Teddy Bear's Picnic* suddenly flooded the building.

If you go down to the woods today...

"Back door." Poppy took off suddenly and Imogen forced herself to follow.

In her hand, her phone buzzed, causing her to nearly drop it to the ground.

For some reason, though it wasn't the best time, Imogen found herself looking down and opening the message.

"She saw something else."

Imogen suddenly stopped running as it dawned on her what was happening.

They had followed her here.

They were inside the building, listening.

But why were they terrorising them? She looked at the text again, wondering if it was simply that they knew Poppy was holding something back.

"Wait!" She shouted over the music, watching as Poppy came to a stop by the back door, which of course was also locked and there wasn't a key in sight.

"What?" Poppy snapped, gesturing for Imogen to follow her. "Come on! Help me find the keys!"

"What else happened in the woods?" Imogen asked.

"What?" Poppy stared at her like she had just sprouted two extra heads. "Are you serious? Now is not the time!"

"Now is the only time." Imogen said, moving quickly over to Poppy and thrusting the phone at her.

Poppy scanned the message with a frown. "What is this?" She asked, shoving the phone back to Imogen.

"Just tell me." Imogen pleaded.

"Imogen, there is somebody in here!"

"Just trust me, Poppy. Tell me what else!" Imogen was about to get down on her knees and beg at this point. She was scared too but what else could she do?

Poppy shook her head, seemingly not understanding what was happening here. Truthfully, neither did Imogen. The thought that somebody was in here blasting music, creeping around and spying on them, was pretty traumatising.

"What did you see?" She cried out again, looking over her shoulder as she thought she heard another whistle over the music.

"Sarah!" Poppy snapped back, turning around again, facing Imogen. "I saw Sarah Clarke!"

The music abruptly stopped, leaving the two of them standing there in complete silence, feeling exposed.

Imogen frowned, staring at Poppy in surprise. Sarah Clarke? "What? Talking to Annie?"

Poppy shook her head. "No. I don't know, she pushed her. I think she pushed her." Poppy frowned, looking thoughtful for a moment or two, as if something suddenly occurred to her.

"I think someone was whistling." She whispered the words and Imogen's thoughts went to that first whistle they'd heard before the music had started playing.

All of a sudden there was the sound of a door opening and then slamming shut.

Imogen jumped. Poppy looked over Imogen's shoulder and carefully moved back through to where they had been sitting minutes before.

The keys were hanging from the lock again, moving as though somebody had just put them back there.

When Imogen moved over, cautiously and slowly, the door easily swung open when she tried the handle.

Turning, she looked at Poppy, still shaking from the fear and the adrenaline rush of the whole situation.

"What the hell is going on?" Poppy asked her with a frown, moving over to where the lanes were and peering around the room, as if she expected somebody to still be lurking, but Imogen knew they were gone.

"It's a long story." Imogen shook her head, moving to grab her coat from the back of the chair she had been sitting on. "You're better off not knowing. Come on, I'll give you a lift home."

thirty-seven

"Do you want some coffee or something?" Sarah asked, but Imogen could tell she was uncomfortable.

"No, I'm fine. Thanks." Imogen worked up a smile, but didn't feel like she looked very reassuring.

Sarah hovered for a moment and then she sat down on another chair. She looked anxious.

"So, um." Imogen started, trying to keep the conversation going. From what she remembered, Sarah had always been quite quiet and reserved. Shy and awkward. The poor girl had always had problems.

"How have you been?" Imogen continued, offering her a friendly smile.

Sarah shrugged. "Fine." Was all that she said, much to Imogen's frustration. She knew it probably wasn't Sarah's fault but it was difficult to engage in a conversation with her. No wonder she had never had that many friends. Imogen felt mean as she thought it, immediately scolding herself.

"That's good." Imogen nodded, clasping her hands on her lap as the silence lapsed between the two of them once more. Sarah was looking down at her hand, picking at her nails. Imogen watched her for a moment before trying again.

"So, I just wanted to talk about something."

Sarah looked up, blinking at her, before shrugging. "Okay. What is it?"

Imogen felt bad for bringing this all up since she knew how sensitive everything was for Sarah.

Her suicide attempt, though so many years ago, was still quite a hot topic in the town gossip pool.

Imogen couldn't say she had ever been bullied but she knew that sort of thing had to have lasting effects through the years, right?

Her thoughts chewed back over Ruby's words a few weeks back, when Imogen had tried to defend Annie for the whole Sarah thing.

She just deliberately slipped the need for them in her already fucked up, fragile mind.

From the outside looking in, Sarah didn't help prevent herself from being a target. She was practically born weird.

Shy and quiet and full of insecurity made a great target for other teenage girls.

Especially if that teenage girl was Annie Pierce.

Imogen had always tried to see the good in Annie and she had ignored all the nasty parts, excused all the bad things she said and did, and the things she'd forced her friends into doing.

Imogen's most fatal flaw had always been that she was too naive. She could too easily excuse the bad things people did and imagine up the good in them, even where there was none. Especially when it came to Annie. Though Imogen still believed now that Annie had good in her. Somewhere deep down.

Sarah had been easy to target because she simply took it. She didn't often give much of a reaction and Imogen thought now that was part of the challenge.

Bullies wanted a reaction, right?

Not that she liked to think of Annie as a bully, but looking back on it all, Imogen could definitely see that eking out a reaction had been a big game to Annie.

A challenge she never tired of.

"It's about the night Annie died..." Imogen said finally, biting her lip as she watched Sarah's head snap up.

"What?" Sarah frowned. "What do you mean? I don't..." She shook her head.

"Look, I just..." Imogen sighed. "I know you were there, okay?"

"No, I... I wasn't."

Imogen shook her head, feeling like she needed to be pushy but she felt bad about it. Still, Sarah was obviously lying right to her face. Why?

"I know you were." She said as gently as possible. "Someone saw you."

She watched Sarah's expression change. Was that a little fear she recognised? The same expression Imogen had seen in the mirror a thousand times before.

"I just want to know if you saw something, Sarah."

"Saw something?" Sarah was frowning as she looked back up at her.

"In the woods."

There was a silence that followed. Sarah seemed to be having difficulty. Maybe she was trying to come up with some other lie to tell, some way to explain away her being there or continue protesting that she was there at all.

"Please, Sarah." Imogen sighed, not wanting to plead but this whole situation was feeling completely out of control.

"I didn't do it." Sarah whispered, keeping her gaze fixed down upon her hands, now balling up into fists.

Imogen felt uneasy. "I didn't say…"

"You're implying it!" Sarah snapped, her head lifting and her gaze landing on Imogen.

"No. I just…" Imogen couldn't say she had ever seen Sarah like this but she supposed she hadn't ever paid her enough attention. "I'm just trying to figure out what happened."

"Aren't the police doing that." It wasn't a question.

"Did you see anything?" Imogen pressed again, her tone a little pleading.

"I didn't do it." Sarah said again, only serving to irritate Imogen further.

"No one's saying you did." In her head she was wondering if Sarah had ever heard the saying *the lady doth protest too much*.

Sarah sat there for a few more moments, quiet and deflated. She'd wilted, like a flower that had been trodden on.

"I wasn't the only one who was there." She muttered, picking at her nails again.

"I know." Imogen nodded, thinking about all the things she had learned about that night so far and all the things she maybe didn't know yet.

It all sent a chill shuddering up her spine.

"Sarah, look. Just tell me what happened. I really don't care why you were there but if you saw anyone or heard anything… I just need to know."

Sarah looked away again, lifting her hands to cover her face. "I was just so sick of it." She said, shaking her head.

"Sick of what?" Imogen prompted gently after another pause.

"Annie." Sarah stated, opening her eyes and dropping her hands from her face. "I was sick of Annie." She said again. "I was sick of her shouting at me, I was sick of her throwing things at me, I was sick of her calling me names and belittling me. I was sick to death of her."

It was Imogen's turn to be uncomfortable as she glanced down. She knew that Annie hadn't been everybody's favourite person. She knew that Annie could be confrontational and, honestly, cruel. Still, she didn't ever spend too much time dwelling on it because, as always, Imogen only wanted to see the good and the beauty in her lost best friend.

Unfortunately, all of this kept on flinging the bad up into her face so there was no way that she could ignore it.

"What did you do?" Imogen asked quietly, though she wasn't sure if Sarah had technically *done* anything. But the way she was talking and the fact she'd been led here at all was enough to lean her thoughts towards the possibility.

"Nothing. Well." A pause. "I know it was nothing now."

"What do you mean *now*?" Imogen asked, looking at the blonde, though her mind went back to what Poppy had told her earlier.

I think she pushed her.

Sarah hesitated, looking like she was struggling with whether to come out and say it. Eventually, she seemed to decide that it was a good idea.

"I was just out walking." Sarah said quietly. "I didn't mean to end up near the party."

Imogen stayed quiet, just letting Sarah get her story out.

"Annie... she came out of nowhere, I didn't even know anybody else was around." Sarah continued. "She was drunk. She was a bitch."

Imogen wasn't sure she had ever heard Sarah say more than five words let alone swear. "What did she do?"

"She was just mean. Like she always was." Sarah frowned. "Looking at me like I was dirt. Like I was nothing. It was her tone of voice, the way she looked at me." Sarah paused. "After everything, I was... I was just sick of it."

Imogen knew that *everything* meant Sarah's suicide attempt and subsequent stay in the ward.

When they were sixteen, Imogen could remember Sarah being Annie's main target. Though she didn't like to use that word, that's exactly what it was.

Imogen had tended to lean towards the idea that Sarah was always troubled and maybe she was but she knew that Annie's constant berating and tormenting didn't help.

She remembered days when the group, led by Annie of course, would follow Sarah around for ages, never leaving her alone, shouting things her way.

It had seemed like harmless stuff at the time, though Imogen couldn't understand why now. Maybe it had something to do with the immaturity of youth or their brains not being fully developed. Truthfully though, she knew she couldn't excuse it.

Sarah had downed a whole bottle of pills one night and had been found on her bathroom floor by her mother.

Having a daughter now, Imogen could only imagine how traumatic and terrible that would have been for the woman. She felt guilty. She should have said something.

"I was just so… over it." Sarah spoke again, frowning. "So I shouted at her. Then I…"

Imogen watched her for a few moments, not sure whether to press Sarah to talk faster.

"I pushed her."

Imogen blinked in surprise, not sure she'd been expecting her to just admit it. But there it was. Confirming exactly what Poppy had said.

Sarah shrugged. "She laughed. She'd called me crazy." She frowned. "So I did it again and…"

"And?" Imogen had to prompt her to get her to continue speaking after a few long uncomfortably quiet moments.

"And she went down, she hit her head… I heard it…it was horrible." Sarah closed her eyes, looking like she was going to cry. "I ran away, I thought…"

"You thought what?" Imogen pressed again.

"I thought I'd killed her." Sarah's confession was startling. "I didn't see her move, there was a... a horrible sound when her head hit the ground. I really didn't mean it."

"What? So you ran away to get a shovel, came back, and buried her so nobody would find out?" Imogen was so shocked she could hardly get the words out. She had imagined a light shove that riled Annie up, not two hard shoves, one of which caused her to smack her head so hard that Sarah thought she was *dead*.

Sarah's gaze snapped up again, frowning at Imogen. "What? No. No! Of course not!"

"Then what-?" Imogen started but was cut off.

"I said I *thought* I killed her! I didn't say she was *dead*. I didn't *bury* her! I went home and I cried and I fell asleep." Sarah explained. "The next day everyone was saying she was missing... but she was never found lying in those woods. So it couldn't have been me."

Imogen frowned as she looked back at the other girl. God, this whole night was just a tangled mess that she couldn't unravel even if she wanted to. Which she did. Which she had been trying to do. Which whoever was texting her had been leading her towards doing.

The whole thing just kept getting more and more complicated.

She thought back to Poppy and remembered her saying she had seen Sarah and *then* she'd interacted with Annie. So, of course, Annie had still been alive, meaning Sarah couldn't have killed her.

I think someone was whistling.

"Did you hear whistling?" She asked, causing Sarah to look at her like she was mental.

"What? No. No, I--I don't think so."

They both fell silent for a few moments, neither sure what to say now that the confession was out there.

"Wait, yeah... yeah, I did." Sarah finally spoke again, voice so soft that Imogen almost missed it.

Imogen looked back up at her, waiting for her to continue. The look on her face was thoughtful, like she was trying very hard to remember something.

"There *was* whistling... from way behind, like, further into the woods." Sarah murmured. "I didn't pay much attention... I was just trying to get out of there." She continued, looking up at Imogen with a frown.

"But I swear... I heard the *same* whistling later. Same tune, same everything. It was like... months later. It brought the whole night flooding back." She explained, looking up at Imogen. "In the park."

"Did you see who it was?" Imogen asked, feeling frantic. "Who was whistling, Sarah?

"It was Jamie Kirk."

thirty-eight

Jamie Kirk worked up at the local gym. Imogen had to admit it seemed like a good fit for him. He'd always been the sporty, jock type, along with his friends growing up.

Jamie Kirk, Jason Wright, Thomas Playfair, Chris Marshall, and Kyle Flynn.

The Footie Five, everyone called them. Or the College Hotties, which was often preferred by Imogen's peers.

His car accident back when Imogen was still in high school was still a fairly hot topic around town even now, years later. Some people still whispered when he walked into a room.

It had been so shocking at the time. He'd nearly lost his life and the fact he'd walked away from the wreck was quickly thrown into the top ten Baberton Scandals.

Some people took the gossip too far, saying Jamie must have been drunk, that he'd paid off the judge to not get jailed for being over the limit. Some said he was simply driving too fast, showing off on the roads.

Whatever story people believed didn't really matter. Nobody truly cared about the truth of it, they just seemed to like being able to talk about it. So long as it wasn't about them, everyone always loved a good gossip. It was one thing Imogen was sure would *never* change about Baberton.

Moving inside the building, Imogen looked around. The gym was large. It was modern and clean and very popular. It was owned by Dominic Anderson, a local ex-boxer, and Kelly's brother Kane worked here as well, alongside Jamie.

Imogen spotted Kane first. She couldn't say that she had ever gotten on with Kelly's older brother. He'd always been a bit of a dick, to put it very lightly. Kane liked to think of himself as a playboy, a big ladies man. He always stank of weed as well, you'd be smothered in a cloud of it every time he walked past.

Imogen could remember the arguments Kane would always get into with his parents, particularly his cop father, who thought he was wasting his life and made no real secret of that fact.

Imogen turned away from Kane, who thankfully didn't seem interested in approaching her. The last thing she wanted to do right now was end up talking about Kelly.

She walked over to the counter, where receptionist Becky Tate was sitting. "Hey, is Jamie in?"

Becky looked up and shook her head. "Not yet, but he should be in about half an hour." She smiled. "You can wait for him over by the smoothie bar if you want."

Imogen nodded. "Yeah... yeah, sure. Thanks." She returned Becky's smile and turned to walk over to the tables around the corner, next to the little smoothie and snack shop.

Imogen sat down at one of the tables after ordering a mango smoothie, sitting for a few moments scrolling through social media on her phone.

Shutting her phone off again, Imogen looked up and glanced around, sipping her smoothie.

She noticed Daisy Ramsey was sitting at one of the nearby tables, dressed in leggings and a tank top, staring at her own phone while she nursed a water bottle.

When the other girl looked up and made eye contact, Imogen smiled at her. "Hey." She lifted her hand slightly, giving a tiny wave.

"Oh, hey!" Daisy smiled at her. Her gaze took in Imogen's jeans and boots. "You don't look kitted out for a day at the gym."

Imogen chuckled, looking down at her clothes and shrugging. "No… no, I'm not." She looked up again. "I'm just waiting for someone."

"Ah, gotcha." Daisy nodded, flicking her hair over her shoulder as she leaned back in the chair and lifted her water bottle to her lips.

Imogen noticed Daisy was in much higher spirits than the last time she had seen her. She'd been quiet and shy and today she seemed happy and confident. Maybe there was something to be said about endorphins after all.

Imogen wasn't really a big exercise person. She didn't like the gym, she didn't like being all uncomfortable and sweaty. She didn't jog or run or really work out at all, which always made her feel quite inferior and lazy but she did ride her bike when she had the time to.

After having Brooklyn, things like that had taken a backseat. She wasn't one of those yoga mums. Not that there was anything wrong with that, Imogen just felt like running around after Brooklyn was exercise enough and she would rather spend her free time reading or something.

Or chasing after her dead best friend's killer, apparently.

"Are you waiting on Kane?" Daisy asked, picking up the protein bar on the table in front of her and opening it so she could take a bite.

Imogen shook her head, frowning a little. "Uh, no. No." She supposed Daisy had asked because of Kelly. Despite the fact she and Kelly were barely friends anymore, everyone always still lumped them together. They lumped them all together, even their two dead friends.

"I'm waiting for Jamie." Imogen said.

"Oh?" Daisy tilted her head, looking at Imogen curiously for a moment.

"Yeah." Imogen shrugged. She wasn't going to get into it with Daisy. The girl was nice enough but this wasn't really any of her business.

Daisy took a bite out of the protein bar and then put the rest back down on the table, ignoring it as she took her camera out of her bag and started looking through the pictures like she always did.

Imogen turned her gaze away awkwardly. She supposed that was the end of that conversation then. Not that she could blame her, they weren't exactly besties.

"What you doing over here?" Kane's voice broke through the silence, causing Imogen to look up.

Great.

Imogen tried to work up a smile, failing miserably and ending up just grimacing at him

"Why? Is it illegal?" Imogen couldn't help but start with sarcasm.

Kane chuckled. "Chill out, I'm just askin'."

Imogen sighed. "I'm waiting for Jamie."

"Why d'you wanna talk to Jamie?" Kane frowned at her, looking surprised.

It was no secret around town that Jamie seemed to have problems with Annie's old friends, though Imogen didn't know why since she'd never done anything. Why hold a grudge for Annie over everyone else's head?

"None of your business." Imogen picked up her smoothie again.

Kane laughed, not looking offended, only amused. "Alright, alright, take it easy. It was just a question."

Imogen made a face, feeling a bit bad but it's not like she wanted to spill her whole story to Kane Sharpe of all people. Especially when she was still furious about Kelly, though she didn't know how close the two were now.

Imogen's phone vibrated on the table from inside her handbag. She reached in to check it as Kane went about wiping the tables.

A photograph of herself arriving at the gym not even fifteen minutes ago.

Imogen looked over her shoulder, as if she was going to see someone standing with a phone camera aimed her way. Of course the photo wasn't sent back to her in real time so she wasn't going to see anybody lurking.

She turned her attention back down to the phone in her hand, studying the picture as if the photographer would just jump out at her, nametag and all.

The picture was taken from the corner of the doorway and she could see everyone else in it too. Kane by the machines. Becky behind the desk. Imogen sighed, looking up and over to the side, where Daisy was still looking down, her focus elsewhere.

It felt a little bizarre that everyone around her was business as usual when Imogen had just received a photograph of herself from a stalker.

She didn't feel in danger, she just felt... anxious, uncomfortable and frustrated.

If they knew so much, why were they spending so much time following her around pushing her towards a killer instead of just going to the police?

"Are you okay?"

Imogen turned her head at the question, realising Daisy was now looking at her, concern plastered across her face.

She winced, feeling a little embarrassed. She obviously wasn't hiding it very well.

"Yeah. Yeah, I'm fine. All good." Imogen quickly replied, brushing off any worry Daisy might be feeling. "Just work stuff. I'm going back soon, it's a bit stressful."

Daisy nodded sympathetically. "Right. School teacher, isn't it?"

Imogen nodded, working up a little smile. "Yeah. Primary school."

"I don't think I could do that."

"It's not for everyone." Imogen agreed. It was harder than a lot of people seemed to think that it was but it had been Imogen's dream job since she was about ten years old and idolised her primary school teacher Mrs. McKenzie.

Daisy went quiet again and Imogen looked down at her phone with a sigh. She put it away in her bag, wishing she could shake the feeling of being watched.

When Imogen looked back up again, Daisy was frowning, looking around her as if she didn't know where she was.

"Are *you* okay?" Imogen asked, returning her earlier question.

Daisy glanced at her. "Um... what?" She shook her head. "Yeah. No. Yeah, I'm fine."

Daisy stood up, grabbing her camera and knocking her backpack off the table as she did, sending some of the contents spilling out onto the floor.

Imogen jumped up quickly and crouched down to help her gather her things back up.

Daisy shoved everything away and stood up, swinging her bag onto her shoulder.

Her face had turned bright red, like she was embarrassed. Some of the other people in the gym were looking and it was clear to Imogen that drawing attention wasn't Daisy's favourite thing.

Daisy mumbled a quiet *thanks* as she hurried for the door of the gym, head down, and disappeared down the street.

Well, that was weird.

So much for those endorphins.

The door opened again and, finally, Jamie Kirk was in the building.

Imogen fixed her gaze on him, Daisy forgotten as she turned her thoughts back to her task.

Jamie moved across the floor and put his things down behind the counter, talking to Becky - probably saying hello or something. Becky laughed and so did Jamie, then he moved back out onto the floor and scanned the people using the machines.

Imogen wasn't sure how to approach him. No matter how many times she did this, it never got any easier.

She thought back over what Sarah had said as she watched him moving around the gym. He had a slight limp so it was clear to Imogen that his leg was bothering him today.

Sarah had been so sure that it was Jamie whistling in the woods that night.

After a short while, she stood up and made her way over to where he was standing surveying the room.

"Hey."

Jamie glanced at her and nodded slightly. "Oh. Hey."

Imogen felt awkwardness instantly rush over her, unsure how she was supposed to keep the conversation going, and then steer it in the direction of That Night.

"Becky said you were looking for me." Jamie said, taking the first step for her.

Imogen looked over her shoulder towards the counter, but Becky wasn't looking her way. She wondered if that's what made the two of them laugh but she was quick to remind herself not to be so paranoid.

"Yeah." She turned back, glancing up at Jamie.

He was standing with his arms folded, leaning back against the wall, surveying the room.

The epitome of cool, the way every single one of the Footie Five had always been.

"What's up?" He asked, his gaze moving to her face.

"It's about--" Imogen started, but she wasn't able to get anything else out before he interrupted.

"About Annie?" His tone betrayed that he wasn't really asking because he already knew the answer.

Imogen blinked at him, surprised that he would immediately get it.

"Thomas told me you'd been running all over town asking people about it." Jamie explained, turning back to scan the room.

Imogen made a face. "Right." Of course he had. Imogen told herself it would be ridiculous not to expect them to all be gossiping with each other about it.

Though she wondered just how truthful they were being. Did everyone know about Thomas and Annie's affair? Imogen knew they were all still fairly close in some way but she didn't know just how open they would be.

"So, what about it?" Jamie asked.

Imogen looked up at him and then glanced around the gym. "Out here?" Just in front of everyone where they could all overhear?

"Why not?" Jamie turned back towards her with a slight frown. He raised an eyebrow at her but then shrugged and gestured for her to follow him through to the back room.

"Go on then."

Jamie was acting so casual about it all that it was kind of putting Imogen off a little bit. She didn't totally understand why he didn't seem more concerned.

Did it mean he didn't do anything so didn't have anything to worry about? Or did it mean he was trying hard to make it *seem* that way?

Or maybe she was just reading too much into it. As per usual.

"I mean, it seems like you already know what I'm here to talk about, doesn't it?" Imogen sighed.

Jamie smirked, looking amused as he sat down at one of the tables in the back room. He shrugged. "Vaguely. I don't know what you expect me to say. You're going around asking about the night she went missing, but of course I'm going to say that I saw her." He blinked. "I was at the party. Everyone was at the party. Everyone saw her." Jamie frowned again, lightly. "What are you looking for?"

"Was killed." Imogen said softly.

Jamie's frown deepened. "Sorry?"

Imogen shrugged, sinking into the chair opposite him. "You said the night she went missing… she wasn't missing. She was murdered."

"Right." It didn't sound like the difference mattered too much to him, however.

"Anyway, I'm not just vaguely asking about... that night." Imogen continued. "I wanted to ask you about a specific part."

Jamie shrugged. "Go on then."

"You were in the woods, right?" Imogen asked point blank.

Jamie shrugged. "I'm sure we were all in and out of the woods at one point or another that night."

"I mean, deep in the woods." Imogen added.

Jamie shifted in his chair. "I don't know. I suppose I walked through on the way home, yeah."

"Did you see anyone?"

"Did I see *Annie*, you mean?" Jamie tilted his head as he regarded her.

Imogen shrugged. "I mean, I didn't ask that but, sure... *did* you?"

Jamie shook his head. "Nope."

Imogen waited for him to say something else but nothing came. Was that it?

"What about Sarah Clarke?" She asked.

There was a longer pause this time and Jamie's expression changed. At first Imogen took this as a big, glaring yes, but as she properly looked at him, she realised that he just seemed confused.

"Sarah Clarke?" Jamie's frown deepened. "She wasn't even at the party, was she?"

"No. But she was in the woods. She's pretty sure you were there... around the time Annie would have been hurt."

"Whoa, hold on. Wait. Sarah fucking Clarke is saying she saw me in the woods? When Annie was done in?"

Imogen cringed at the wording but she let it go this time. "Not... exactly."

"What do you mean?"

Imogen made a face. "She was there. She and Annie argued. She... *heard* you whistling."

"She heard me whistling?" Jamie's expression was incredulous. "Is this some kind of joke?"

"No. Look, I know it sounds weird, but she heard you that night, she ran away, then she heard the same whistle later. She was adamant."

"She's also mental." Jamie stated, frowning again.

Imogen didn't say anything.

After another pause, Jamie shook his head. "Alright, look. I don't know about any whistling. But I did walk through the woods that night, I took the shortcut home. The trail. I didn't see Annie."

Imogen just didn't know what to believe anymore. Nothing about any of this was making sense.

"I know you didn't like Annie." Imogen sighed, shrugging, as if the statement would give her all the answers.

"Nope." The way Jamie shrugged as he said this irritated Imogen. It felt disrespectful.

"Right, but, why?" She frowned.

"Do I even really need a reason?" Jamie scoffed lightly. "She wasn't very likeable."

Imogen frowned. She didn't think that was fair but then she reminded herself of the reasons people had had their issues with Annie. Still, it left a bad taste in her mouth.

"She didn't even really do anything, I mean..." Imogen was cut off pretty quickly.

"Didn't do anything?" Jamie looked angry all of a sudden. "She *ruined* my fucking *life*."

Imogen blinked in surprise, staring at him. She was completely caught off guard by his statement. "What do you mean?"

Jamie shook his head, seeming to clam up as if he hadn't even meant to say anything at all. "Nothing.. it's nothing."

"You meant *something.*" Imogen insisted.

Yet another uncomfortable silence followed and then Jamie shrugged. "The accident."

"What?" Imogen shook her head as she eyed him.

"My accident, the car accident." Jamie continued.

"Uh... okay?" Imogen made a face. "What about it?"

"It was *her*, Imogen." Jamie snapped, impatient. "It was her fault. *She* did it. She screwed with my brakes."

Imogen stared at him as if he'd grown an extra head. "What are you talking about? No, she didn't... she... she wouldn't."

"That's not what she said when she visited me in the hospital the day after." Jamie shrugged.

"You're saying she caused your accident and then visited you in hospital and admitted to it?" Imogen relaxed just lightly. This whole story screamed bullshit. "Is this what you're going to be trying to get people to believe now we know she's dead? So they can stop talking about you and turn it on a poor dead girl instead?"

"A *poor*, dead girl with a serious psycho problem." Jamie shook his head. "Believe what you want to, Imogen, but I know what happened. You think she didn't threaten my sister so I'd keep quiet? She did it to make a point."

"What point?"

Jamie's jaw tightened briefly as he looked back at her. "That Annie Pierce gets whatever the hell Annie Pierce wants."

thirty-nine

Brooklyn was wobbling around the living room, looking for something to play with, uninterested in the many toys that were already scattered across the carpet.

Imogen hadn't been able to focus on anything since she had woken up that morning. She was pretty sure she had only managed to grab a few hours of sleep as well.

The visit to Jamie had been weighing heavily on Imogen's mind since she left the gym the other day.

She had learned so much more about Annie over these past weeks than she had known before, most of it not very nice and sort of shattering the rose coloured glasses she had always worn in regards to the other girl.

But could her best friend have been so beyond devious that she would try to get somebody killed? Would she mess with Jamie's brake line and risk his death? Maybe *hope* for it, even? Just to prove a point? A ridiculous point, at that?

Imogen didn't know anymore.

What she did know was that almost killing and ruining a man's chances of ever using his leg properly again, ruining his big dreams of becoming a professional footballer, was a pretty decent motive for murder.

Maybe the best motive that Imogen had heard so far from people she had talked to.

However, her thoughts did keep drifting back to Kelly. Kelly's obsession with Annie and how it could perhaps have turned deadly.

Imogen knew how teenage girls could get. Hell, she had been one. It was easy to fall down the rabbit hole of wanting what you couldn't have, of wanting the popularity and the fame that came with someone like Annie Pierce.

Kelly had followed and copied Annie like it was her job. Like it was what she lived and breathed for.

Thomas and Hannah and Kyle and Dakota had slipped further and further down her list as the time went on. They were still there, lurking in the recesses of her mind, but they weren't the highest priority.

Truthfully, she felt like hardly any of the people she had spoken to had given her a clear picture.

Not Thomas. Not Hannah. Not Dakota. Not Kyle. Not Chloe. Not even Nina.

Everyone had gotten defensive and argumentative the second Annie was even brought up.

Nobody wanted to talk about that night which made it seem like everybody was keeping secrets.

The only people she had fully written off were Charlie Baker and Poppy Hart.

She couldn't fully write Sarah Clarke off, just because she admitted to shoving Annie. Twice. Hard enough for her to fall and hit her head and injure herself. She could be lying about Jamie to cover her own ass. Imogen had brought up the whistling first, after all.

Brooklyn started crying and Imogen snapped out of her thoughts.

"What's wrong, baby?" She stood up and moved over, seeing that the little girl had broken the head off one of her dolls. "Oh, no.."

Imogen gently pried the doll from her hands and moved to pop the head back into place.

"See?" She wiggled the doll's hair in Brooklyn's tear-stained face, glad to pull a laugh from her. "All better."

Just like that, tears gone.

If only it could stay the way it was when you were a kid. Tears gone and forgotten in an instant. Mummy can make it all better and fix any problem.

If only mummy could figure out her own.

***

"Oh, give me a break."

Well, that wasn't the warmest welcome she had ever received.

Imogen was standing back in the doorway of Chloe's apartment. She wasn't fully certain what she was doing here but she felt the need to turn up anyway.

So here she was.

"Chloe, just... please." Imogen was relieved when the other moved aside to let her come in.

She followed Chloe through to the living room, pushing Brooklyn's pram with the sleeping little girl inside.

Soon she was sitting on the couch enveloped in yet another awkward silence.

"Was it you?" Chloe asked after a few more moments.

Imogen blinked in surprise. "What? Was what me?" Her mind jumped to the worst - this was the same question she had asked in her head over and over again, the more people she talked to.

Was it you? Did you kill my friend?
Was Chloe thinking the same?
Was it you? Did you kill my sister?

"Did you break into the shop?" It was unexpected and, honestly, Imogen had nearly forgotten all about that in the chaos that had followed.

The diaries.

She shook her head but it wasn't convincing so she shrugged. "How did you know?"

"You're poking around about Annie. I tell you about her diaries and then suddenly the shop is broken into but nothing is stolen?" Chloe actually looked a little amused. "Pretty clear cut to me."

"You gonna tell your mum?" Imogen sighed. She couldn't believe she was going to end up getting in trouble for something so stupid. She had barely even learned anything from the diaries.

"Nah." Chloe said it as if it was obvious.

Imogen gave her a look and Chloe shrugged. "It's not like you set fire to the place or robbed the till." She said. "Any of the diaries survive?"

Imogen wasn't sure what she had expected when she'd come here but it wasn't this.

She nodded. "A few... well, *parts* of a few." Imogen clarified. The diaries hadn't been fully intact. "There could have been more, I don't know, I didn't really get the chance to have a thorough look."

There was a silence and then Chloe spoke again. "Do you want another look?"

Chloe got up and a cardboard box was dragged from where it had been hidden behind the couch.

"Mum didn't want them there anymore but she still didn't want to throw them away." Chloe shrugged, looking like she couldn't understand why. They were ruined after all. "I don't want to touch them, really..." She looked up at Imogen. "You can look. If you think it will help."

Imogen wasn't sure if it would help or not but she knew she couldn't pass up the opportunity and she nodded quickly.

"Yeah. Yeah, it might. Thanks."

Chloe shrugged and then stood up. "I have to finish up some emails. Just... be careful with them."

Imogen watched her go, double checked Brooklyn wasn't about to wake up, and then moved to kneel on the floor beside the box.

Annie's diaries would have been an array of bright colours and patterns, full of life like their owner. Now it was a box of grey, of ash and gloom. Full of decay, like their owner.

Imogen pulled one out and flicked through the pages. Nothing could really be made out so she moved on to the next one. Then the next. Then the next.

Soon there was a little pile of charred notebooks sitting on the floor beside her, growing bigger by the second.

So far, she had only managed to find a couple of entries where some snatches of words and sentences were still visible. None of these entries seemed to hold anything of value.

Until, finally, she pulled out a diary where many of the pages were more crisp and white than burned and black.

She flipped through a couple of pages. There were no dates in this one, like Annie had decided the date no longer mattered.

Imogen supposed it didn't but she would have liked to know when it was written. It would help her in putting together a timeline.

She glanced up as Brooklyn stirred in her sleep, luckily staying that way.

Imogen looked back down at the notebook, turning past the first page where the ink had bled until it was unreadable.

The next page was Annie's swirly handwriting detailing the texts she had received from an anonymous number.

The "stalker" she had been talking about in her other diaries.

The same person Imogen believed had been sending her the texts... stalking her like they'd stalked Annie.

Annie's Diary

TEXTS FROM THE FREAK

Thursday - you better watch your back.

Monday - I see you Annie. I always see you.

Wednesday - I could have been your friend. You chose to make me your enemy. Not a smart move.

Thursday - Bet you wish Jamie died in that accident. I saw what you did to his car.

Monday - Don't worry about your diary. It's in a safe place.

Tuesday - (pictures of sasha stalking harvey)

Dear Diary.

This year, I got my first stalker.

Not a Gemma Harris type who follows me around and stares at me, or dreams about being included in my group, or dresses like me and wears my perfume.

Not a Kelly Sharpe kind of stalker, who copies every little thing I do and acts like my bestie but desperately dreams of taking my place.

A real, proper stalker.

Who knows how the fuck they got my number but they're obviously following me around town because they know things that nobody could know and have seen things that happened when nobody else was around.

Sending me texts and stuff like proper freaks. I keep looking around but I never see anyone.

-A ♥

Present

There was a little more but Imogen heard Chloe coming back down the hall and something made her shove the diary into her handbag, to finish later in private.

"Anything?" Chloe asked, moving back over to the couch.

Imogen shrugged. "Not really. But thanks. I should probably get going though."

"Oh, yeah, okay." Chloe nodded, standing up again so she could walk Imogen out. "See you later.

At the door, Imogen paused and turned to look at Chloe. "Hey, um... this is weird, but in some of her diaries, Annie said things like... you wanted her gone."

Chloe frowned and Imogen shrugged. "Is that... true?"

Chloe shook her head. "Of course not. She was the one who planted stolen jewellery on me hoping I'd get arrested. She was the one who attacked me and tried to kill me during one of her rages." Chloe looked sad as she spoke. "Annie was the one who wanted *me* gone."

Then she closed the door and Imogen trailed away down the street, thinking about Annie and all she knew - or didn't know.

forty
That Summer

"I see you, Annie. I always see you."

The first text.

Of course, Annie had no idea it was the *first* text, she thought it was a one off message from some stupid wannabe bitch who was jealous of her or something.

Probably Gemma Harris or Macey Cross or Sarah Clarke. It could have been a number of people.

She ignored it. When Annie received the message, all she did was roll her eyes and delete it. They saw her? *Great.* She wanted people to see her, after all. She wanted to be the only thing people saw when she was around.

All eyes on Queen Pierce.

After that, she forgot all about it. The text was irrelevant. Someone had gotten hold of her number and was trying to freak her out because they were jealous. So what? *Everyone* was jealous. Annie didn't care. She was much bigger than a text. It would take more than that to freak her out.

"I could have been your friend. You chose to make me your enemy. Not a smart move."

Annie hadn't been expecting a second message. She had genuinely believed that this person would disappear after the first one when she gave no response.

What was the point of this anyway? To scare her? Annie wasn't scared of a couple of texts. *I see you.* Well, everybody saw her and that was the way she liked it so whatever.

Honestly, it could have just been an admirer. But this second one wasn't from an admirer. Or maybe it was from an admirer gone crazy.

You chose to make me your enemy.

From the sounds of it, this person had wanted to be Annie's friend. Maybe she'd knocked them back, but she knocked people back on the daily so that didn't even narrow it down.

She deleted the second message too, not really wanting to dwell on it. Whoever this bitter person was... they would get bored. They would leave her alone eventually and that was all there was to it.

"Bet you wish Jamie died in that accident. I saw what you did to his car."

This one put Annie on edge.

When she had messed with Jamie Kirk's brake line, she had been very careful to be sure that there was nobody around.

Nobody had been there. Nobody had seen her.

She'd been in and out of his garage in a few minutes, and when she slipped back out, there had still been nobody there.

The street was empty. There was silence. No movement. No eyes.

She'd gotten away with it.

Or so she thought.

This message said otherwise and it came with a nice little photo attached of her sneaking out of Jamie's garage.

This one made her stop and think. Who was this? Were they going to spread this around? What did they want?

She text them back asking the very same thing and their response was simply *"to watch you squirm."*

"Don't worry about your diary. It's in a safe place."

That was the final straw. That was the message that caused Annie to start on her somewhat obsessive quest to actually track this person down.

Find the mysterious anonymous texter who was trying to torment her.

She kept her diaries in a box under her bed. A box with a lock on it.

This person had been in her house. In her bedroom. In her private things.

Annie was angry but she was also, in a strange way, curiously proud of whoever this was.

This was something very, very Annie-like and she wondered if perhaps she had misjudged this person. Brushed them off too quickly.

Maybe they weren't just another pathetic loser after all. Maybe they could be an asset to her, if she could figure out how to control them.

Annie stayed up late that night, coming up with a plan. A plan to find this person and, either get them on side, or take them down once and for all.

forty-one

There were plenty of things that Imogen could be doing. Dishes. Laundry. Tidying up after Brooklyn. Taking the dogs out. Hoovering. Cleaning.

Instead, she was sitting in the living room staring at the little diary that sat on the coffee table in front of her.

She had the horrible feeling that there was going to be nothing written in here that was going to be of any help in finding out who hurt Annie.

Annie didn't know who had been following her so she wasn't going to find a name written down in permanent marker, pointing the way like a beacon.

Imogen had read some of Annie's other diaries and some of the words in there had hurt or had chipped away at her perfect image of the Annie she knew… maybe that's why she was a little apprehensive to read any more.

Eventually, she forced herself to reach forward and grab up the diary, being as careful as she could not to ruin it. It wasn't completely untouched by the fire so it was still a little delicate.

Imogen flipped through a couple of pages. Annie had started to keep a detailed-ish account of her stalker. She'd written down texts she had received and it seemed like she had started her own investigation into who this person was.

Imogen read about how she had gone to Ashton Sherwood, the town computer nerd, to see if there was anything he could do to help, some way he could hack into her phone and find out who was doing it.

This must have hit a dead end because Annie started to sound frustrated and seemed to move on pretty quickly.

Next, she confronted Gemma Harris.

Then Macey Cross.

But she kept mentioning Sasha.

"Sasha was stalking Harvey and I busted her ass so she's stalking me now. It makes perfect sense, right?"

Imogen thought back to her conversation with Sasha. They hadn't actually talked since the last time, which was weird for them. They talked all the time. Imogen suddenly realised that she missed her.

Her thoughts drifted back to the last time Kelly had burst in, looking paranoid and going off about following the money.

Something was niggling at her, in the back of her mind, something vaguely connecting but Imogen didn't allow herself to touch it.

Then suddenly there was a loud knock on the door and the thoughts were banished.

She frowned, standing up as another few loud, sharp knocks. "I'm coming, I'm coming." She muttered to herself. "Take it easy."

When she yanked the door open, she came face to face yet again with Kelly Sharpe, who looked even wilder, if that was actually possible.

Her hair was a bird's nest, she was wearing clothes that were three times too big for her, her eyes were wide, her face was flushed. She had a painful looking scratch on her cheek.

"Kelly?"

Kelly pushed her way past Imogen and into the house.

Imogen hurried to pick Brooklyn up, still not trusting that it wasn't Kelly who let her get the cigarettes.

"What are you doing here? What's wrong?" Imogen stared at her. "Are you high?"

Kelly raked her fingers through her messy curls, shaking her head frantically. "What? What does that matter! This is serious, Imogen! We have to do something!"

"What do you mean?"

There were soft footfalls on the staircase and Eric appeared in the living room doorway, much to Imogen's relief. She moved over to hand him Brooklyn.

"What's going on?" He took a wriggly Brooklyn into his arms without question.

"That's what I'm trying to figure out." She told him, turning back to Kelly. "Kel--"

Kelly shook her head. "Look!" She pointed to her face. "Look what she did!"

"Who?" Imogen asked gently. "Let me see, do you need something for it?"

Kelly looked frustrated, as if she was annoyed that Imogen wasn't getting it - but, to Imogen, she really wasn't making any sense.

"She killed Annie!" She exclaimed, suddenly pulling a knife out of her pocket and waving it around.

"Whoa, Kelly…. Kelly, what are you--"

"Imogen, come here." Eric's worried voice to her left, concerned about Kelly's knife.

Imogen's thoughts flashed back to all the clues that had pointed to Kelly having some sort of obsessive mental break and hurting Annie... and now she was standing in front of her, brandishing a knife.

"She killed Sophie, too."

Those words froze Imogen in place, right from the tips of her toes all the way up to her brain.

"Wh-what?" The words felt sluggish coming out as she stared at Kelly. "Sophie fell."

Kelly shook her head. "Sophie was pushed." She thrust her phone out towards Imogen, who jumped a little as the knife was in the same hand.

Hesitating, Imogen took the phone and looked down at the screen.

"Sophie was clever. Sophie followed the money. Sophie paid the ultimate price."

A message from that freaky stalker.

Imogen shook her head, looking up. "No... Kelly, no, this is a trick. They're playing games. They're messing with you."

She was starting to feel a little dissociated. The talk of Sophie was bringing back those images again. The memories and the dreams.

"Come on!" Kelly suddenly bounded past her and back out the front door.

"Where are you going?!" Imogen yelled after her, hurrying to the door and watching her get into her car. Imogen was pretty sure she shouldn't be driving in her state.

"Imogen, don't." Eric said, not wanting her to run off after a crazy person brandishing a knife. "Call the police and let them handle it."

Imogen shook her head, throwing him an apologetic look as she grabbed her keys and her phone. "I have to, Eric… I'm sorry, stay with Brooklyn." She turned for the door. "Call Lauren!"

"You don't even know where she's going!" Eric's voice followed her down the driveway as she jumped in the car and started the engine.

"Actually, I think I do."

forty-two

On the way, Imogen checked her phone. She knew she shouldn't while she was driving but it was an emergency so she justified it to herself that way.

She noticed that the stalker had text her the same message about Sophie. About two hours ago.

They must have sent it to Kelly when Imogen didn't message them or do anything about it.

"Well, sorry for being busy, I have a life outside of you, stalker." She muttered to herself as she called Ruby, put it on speaker and chucked her phone on the passenger seat.

"Hello?" Ruby sounded like she was in a good mood and Imogen felt bad

"Hey, is Charlie home?"

"Uh, yeah. Why, what's-?" Ruby was cut off.

"I need you to meet me at Sasha's place, okay? As soon as possible."

Thankfully, she would have Charlie there to watch Hope because Imogen felt this was no place for children.

"What do you mean? Immy, I'm really busy, I've got--"

"Kelly's gone mental and she has a knife, okay? Just meet me there! Now." She hung up the phone and sped up a little, hoping no cop cars were around to catch her.

Eventually, she pulled up outside Sasha's place. Kelly's car was outside, parked haphazardly half across the pavement, half on the road. The door was still open.

"What are you doing, Kel?" Imogen muttered as she got out of the car and made for the front door.

Another car pulled up behind her and Ruby got out. She lived much closer than Imogen and she was glad to see that the other had showed up and taken her call seriously.

"You said she had a *knife?*" Ruby rushed up to her side and Imogen nodded.

"Yeah, she came by my place, ranting and raving, saying crazy stuff... she's high."

Ruby gave her a look and shook her head. "We should call the police."

"Eric's calling Lauren." Imogen told her, hurrying inside when they finally reached the door.

Sasha was standing in the middle of her living room, hands in the air, Kelly in front of her waving the knife around and ranting incoherently.

"Kelly!" Imogen exclaimed, distracting the other girl for a few seconds. "You have to stop, what are you *doing?*"

"She's going totally mental, that's what!" Sasha shouted, obviously distressed and Imogen couldn't blame her. Not when someone had broken in with a knife, no doubt accusing her of ridiculous things. Imogen had told Sasha her suspicions about Kelly being dangerous so she had to be nervous - this would only be confirming them.

"Do *not* call me that!" Kelly snapped.

"Hey, Kelly, hey... come on..." Ruby took a step forward now, holding her arms out carefully. "Look at me, Kel. It's just me. You need to put the knife down, okay? We're gonna get you some help."

"I don't need help, I need this bitch to confess!" She jabbed the knife Sasha's way, the tip nicking Sasha's palm, causing the other woman to jump back.

"Ouch! You bitch!" She snapped, grabbing an ornament off the mantelpiece and throwing it directly towards Kelly's head.

"Hey!" Imogen lunged forward and grabbed Kelly's sleeve, dragging her out of the way just in time. "Stop it! Everybody stop!" She was dizzy with confusion and anger and frustration.

"Tell them." Kelly snapped, ignoring Imogen, her fiery gaze fixed directly on Sasha.

Sasha shook her head. "Tell them *what?* You're mad!"

"You *know* what, you crazy bitch!" Kelly rushed towards her again but Imogen and Ruby were quicker this time, holding her back. "You *killed* her!"

Sasha stared at her. "The only one acting *crazy* and like they could *kill* anyone right now is *you!*"

Kelly shook her head. "You were there, you were in the woods that night. You hurt her. You hurt Annie and Sophie figured it out, didn't she? She was too clever!"

Imogen was frowning. She didn't know what she was supposed to do. Maybe she should have just called the police, maybe Eric and Ruby were right.

"Can we just talk about this rationally?" Ruby tried to play mediator.

"No freaking way!" Sasha snapped. "Not with psycho bitch. There's nothing to talk about."

"Why do you think she was there?" Imogen suddenly asked. "Why do you think she was at the party?"

"Look in my pocket." Was Kelly's only reply.

Imogen hesitated before she moved to reach her hand into the pocket of Kelly's hoodie.

"You can't seriously be entertaining this." Sasha said, rolling her eyes.

Imogen didn't say anything, her fingers grasping something glossy.

She pulled out a polaroid picture and frowned. Ruby was looking over her shoulder. They both took in the image of Sasha standing in the woods with Annie Pierce... who was wearing that purple glittery top she was wearing the day she died.

"Sash..." Imogen frowned, looking up at her. "What is this. What..." She paused. "You were *there?*"

"Of course not." She moved to snatch the polaroid but Imogen pulled it out of her reach.

"Then explain this." Imogen snapped, holding the polaroid up so she could clearly see the image.

The other polaroid flashed into Imogen's mind, the one which showed the stalker, though hidden, with the message *I saw everything*.

Then she suddenly had a random flash of another memory. The other day when she had gone to talk to Jamie Kirk at the gym, Daisy Ramsey had dropped her things all over the floor and Imogen had helped her pick them up.

One of those things was a polaroid camera.

She was suddenly caught by the shock of it. Why hadn't she noticed that at the time? What were the chances? How many people carried polaroid cameras around with them these days?

"It's fake, Imogen. Obviously! Not even a decent fake."

As if right on cue, the front door was flung back open behind them and in walked Daisy Ramsey herself, looking confident as the empire state building.

"I don't need to fake anything, Sasha, honey." She cooed, tilting her head as she smirked.

She didn't look like Daisy, it was as if somebody had taken control of her, making her walk and talk and act... very un-Daisy-like.

Like Imogen had seen a couple of times the past few weeks.

"Get out of my house, Ramsey." Sasha snapped, though her eyes flickered back to Kelly and the knife.

She looked worried but it could just be because of the knife, Imogen told herself. Of *course* it was because of the knife.

"It's you." Imogen murmured, turning her attention back towards Daisy.

Daisy flashed a grin her way.

"You're the stalker."

"I prefer *the watcher*." Daisy responded, flicking her pin-straight hair over her shoulder.

"You were stalk -- *watching* Annie. Then you were watching me." Imogen continued, piecing it together.

Daisy nodded. "Uh huh." As if it was no big deal. As if it was totally normal to stalk people and take pictures of them and send them creepy messages.

"I saw everything." Daisy echoed the words on the polaroid Imogen had been sent, her gaze turning towards Sasha with a funny little smirk. "Everything."

"What happened?" Ruby looked from Daisy to Sasha and back again, finally having wrangled the knife from Kelly's hand somehow and was holding it behind her back.

"Do you want to tell them?" Daisy asked, tilting her head again in that eerie way. "Or should I?"

"There's nothing to tell." Sasha snapped at her, shaking her head. "You're making it all up, this is some sick joke."

"Oh, honey." Daisy twirled a strand of hair around her finger, putting on a fake pout. "The camera doesn't lie."

She took her phone out of her pocket and held it up so everyone could see. On the screen was a video, a shot of the woods.

Annie Pierce stomping through the leaves and the twigs, wearing that sparkly top of hers.

"What the fuck is this." Sasha moved to grab the phone out of Daisy's hands but, surprising herself, Imogen moved in between them.

"Sasha..." Imogen felt like her heart was starting to break but she still didn't want to admit it to herself.

"You do not wanna do this." Sasha's attention was back on Daisy, irritation flooding through her. She felt like she was being completely pushed. Sasha did *not* like being pushed.

On the phone screen, another person came into view. Sasha. Walking towards Annie. There was an argument. About money.

"Didn't think I'd be seeing you again until it was time for you to pay up."

The words *'follow the money'* and *'Sasha's money'* danced around in Imogen's brain as she stared at the screen.

Annie was sneering. She looked completely drunk which didn't surprise Imogen or Ruby considering how much she'd had to drink that night. She'd gone harder than any of them, she always did.

They watched her turn away, watched Sasha's recorded figure bend down and pick up a large, jagged looking rock.

Imogen, Kelly, and Ruby watched in absolute horror as Sasha Miller struck Annie on the back of the head with the rock, sending her sprawling to the forest floor.

Ruby had let go of Kelly and by this point she had grabbed hold of Sasha's wrist in a vice-like grip, preventing any escape.

Daisy was smiling but nothing about this was funny. Ruby was crying. Imogen felt like she was floating away, up, up, up and out of her body.

How could this be happening?

"Someone else found out before you did." Daisy said suddenly, looking solemnly from person to person. "Sophie was very clever. She didn't even need me to point the way."

"Sasha." Imogen's eyes were sparkling with tears, thinking of the moment she stumbled across her best friend's body in those woods. "What did you do to Sophie?"

That Other Night

That night had been dark and cold. The ground damp from the spring shower that had fallen from the sky earlier. The woods were quiet until suddenly they weren't, as two girls went storming across the leaves.

"Oh my God, *stop!*" Sasha was practically screeching at this point, too drunk and angry to really care about anybody hearing. Not that anyone was really in the woods at this time of night. She was by herself, drinking, smoking... right on top of the spot where Annie's body had been buried. It held a sort of sentimental value for Sasha.

After all... she was one who buried the bitch there.

It hadn't been premeditated. She'd been drunk from lurking at the party unnoticed, and pissed off, and Annie had been pushing *all* of her buttons.

Much like Sophie Baker was right now. The redhead had come across her smoking in the woods.

The other girl had figured it out. Apparently Annie had told Kelly about the money - that stupid, *stupid* money - and Kelly had let it slip to Sophie. Now, thanks to her stupid cleverness, Sophie knew *everything*. She figured out exactly what Sasha had done to Annie.

"It was an *accident!*" Her protests, her explanation, didn't sound good with the way her voice slurred and her head spun, making her sound confused and making her talk in circles.

The alcohol was making her feel heavy and dizzy. God, was it too much to ask to just be left alone?!

Sasha had tried to disagree with Sophie. Tried to laugh it off but it was too late for that. The girl *knew...* so Sasha told her everything.

Why not, right?

She was completely out of it by now. Alcohol... maybe some pills, she didn't know exactly what she'd taken, but she was so completely off her face, Kelly Sharpe style, that she barely knew where she was.

When Sophie started raving about going to the police... Well, Sasha just couldn't have that!

She panicked, grabbed the other girl's arm and tried to reason with her. In her drunk state, it probably felt more like she was trying to attack her but it wasn't Sasha's intention - it really wasn't!

It hadn't even been with Annie, she'd panicked then too. Not that it was much of an excuse but it was the truth. Or at least, it was the truth that she told herself.

She almost couldn't believe it when she yanked Sophie's arm to turn her around and the other girl lost her balance as she yanked back in return, to try and shake Sasha off.

Then Sasha pushed out, shoving Sophie away out of nowhere.

That was when Sophie lost her footing in the dark and disappeared down the bank beside the river.

Which wasn't exactly a short drop...

For a few long, deathly silent moments Sasha stood there.

Shocked.

Frozen.

Unblinking.

This wasn't real, right? This was a dream, there was no way that had just happened...

Everything was so blurry and she tripped, almost catapulting herself over the same edge the redhead had slid down, but managed to hold on as she lay on her stomach and squinted down through the dark.

"Sophie?!" She called down, feeling like the world was spinning around her.

Nothing.

Completely panicked, with tears rolling down her face, she stood and backed away.

God, she wished she could think properly.

What should she do? Call for help?

By the time she realised she was even running, she was already in the middle of town.

Far away from Sophie Baker, lying in the woods. Was she unconscious? Was she hurt? Was she even alive?

She went home.

She should have gone to the police station, she knew that, but she went home.

Curled up in her bed, under her thick duvet, and lay there shaking, staring into the dark for the rest of the night as the gravity of what just happened really hit her.

Sasha had killed Annie Pierce... and now she'd just killed Sophie Baker.

Present

Tears were rolling down Imogen's face as she stood there, staring at Sasha.

She felt sick.

She felt more than sick.

What was more than sick? What was more than shock? She didn't know anything anymore.

Sophie had figured out that Sasha had attacked Annie the night of the party.

Had she seen something? Had she just put it together because of the money that Kelly had known about Annie blackmailing? Had she suspected Sasha for long?

Imogen would never get to ask her any of this because now she was gone. She'd broken her neck in that fall but it hadn't been from tripping in the dark and losing her footing like everyone thought... it was from a push.

A push from Imogen's current best friend.

A push from a girl Imogen wouldn't have suspected in a million years.

A push that had broken Imogen's heart into a million little pieces.

"Why... how..." None of the words that she wanted to say came out. None of the questions she wanted to ask unstuck from her throat. They all just sat there inside her, festering. Eating away at her like maggots.

"You killed them." She whispered, her heart shattering into fifty million different little jagged pieces.

That was when the police sirens sounded down the street, coming to a stop directly outside.

Eric had called Lauren after all.

epilogue

"Did you remember the sunscreen?" Imogen asked as she shouldered the bag of towels and beach toys.

"Of course." Eric smiled, leaning in to kiss her lightly. "It's in the bag."

She smiled, shaking her head. Of course he had. He remembered everything. It was Imogen who was the forgetful one of this marriage.

"Come on then, Brookie." She smiled, hauling the little girl up into her arms as Eric took the bag off her shoulder and swung it up onto his own.

They left the house and moved towards their car, getting the toddler in before heading off.

They were going for a nice day at the beach to kick off Imogen's last weekend before she went back to work.

Ruby and Charlie were meeting them there with Hope and Imogen couldn't imagine a better way to spend the day.

It wasn't far and Brooklyn was all impatient and wriggly before they'd even stopped the car.

Imogen laughed as she got her daughter out of her car seat and grabbed the cooler with their lunch in it from the back. Eric grabbed the other bag and followed her down across the soft sand towards the spot Ruby and Charlie had already picked out.

"Hey." Imogen smiled, dumping the cooler down and spreading out a towel, sitting down with Brooklyn who reached out immediately to touch the sand.

"Hi." Ruby smiled back, chuckling as she watched Charlie swinging Hope around down by the water.

"Wanna go join in?" Eric asked Brooklyn in a baby voice before he pulled his shirt off and swung her up into his arms, hurrying down towards the water where he and Charlie let the girls get their feet wet. They all looked happy so Imogen decided she would remind him about sunscreen later.

Charlie looked good and Imogen was glad about that. It had been tough, after Sasha was arrested. The whole Sophie revelation had reopened a lot of old wounds, picking at scabs until they were bloody and raw again.

Imogen had been watched like a hawk by Eric and by her mother, which did nothing but piss her off quite honestly.

They were afraid this whole thing was going to prove too much for her, that she would have another psychotic break or something.

But she took her pills and she went to therapy and she processed what she'd learned about Sophie and about Sasha and about Annie.

She didn't think she would ever be over it, any of it, but she felt like she could maybe feel better about moving forward now.

Annie's family had the closure they needed, and so did her friends... and Sophie's had the closure they hadn't known they'd even needed.

That had to count for something, didn't it?

It turned out that Daisy wasn't well herself. She suffered from something called Dissociative Identity Disorder. Basically, there were two people living in her body.

There was Daisy, the shy bullied little new girl who Annie hadn't liked.

Then there was Lily, confident and precocious, the one who followed people around and sent the creepy messages.

She had targeted Annie due to her relentless bullying of Daisy. Lily's whole job was to protect Daisy, though she perhaps went a little far with it.

Daisy didn't even have a clue that any of it was happening. She had been suffering from headaches and loss of time but she'd just assumed she was overworking herself.

When they finally pulled her in for a psych evaluation, after Imogen and her friends told the cops she'd been stalking Annie and also them, the doctors eventually figured it out.

She had suffered some pretty heavy abuse in her childhood, before she even moved to Baberton.

Lily had been there the whole time, protecting Daisy's fragile mind.

Daisy's watcher.

Watching everything.

Honestly, Imogen felt bad for her and she didn't really hold much of a grudge towards the girl.

Well, not Daisy anyway. She had bone to pick with Lily considering it was *her* who had given Brooklyn that nicotine. Not Kelly.

Lily had wanted to throw Imogen off a little, make her suspect her old friend of being the killer and of poisoning her daughter.

She supposed Lily held a grudge against all of them for not standing up to Annie. For sitting idly by while she bullied and harassed and tormented.

Imogen supposed she could understand that, even if she couldn't quite forgive.

Sasha had been arrested and she was now in prison, charged with one count of murder and one of manslaughter.

It had been difficult to watch Sasha get hauled away in handcuffs that day. Imogen felt like she had floated up out of her body and was watching it all from high up on the ceiling.

She was aware people were asking her questions. The police wanted to know everything.

She was aware that Eric showed up at the police station, along with her mother, and that they were fussing over her.

It had simply all been too much for her. She trusted Sasha. She trusted her with everything. With her daughter. With her thoughts.

Imogen hadn't visited her, though Sasha had written a couple of times. She'd thrown the letters away without even opening them.

She didn't want to know what Sasha had to say. She'd killed her two best friends and lied to her face for years.

Kelly had volunteered to go and visit her just so that she could finally punch her in the face but Imogen and Ruby had both thankfully talked her out of that one.

For now, at least.

Kelly was actually doing a lot better now, too. She was going to a rehab facility in a few weeks, hoping to finally get sober and straighten herself out.

Hannah had, surprisingly, decided not to press charges for the assault. Imogen thought that was pretty decent of her.

The deaths of Annie and Sophie had affected the remaining girls in different ways.

They'd all broken in different places, but now they could all really start to rebuild and move forward, knowing that they'd gotten justice for their friends.

Annie wasn't the perfect little angel that Imogen had wanted to remember her as, but that didn't mean she deserved to die.

To be beaten with a rock and buried in the woods for six years.

Imogen had given Annie's diaries back to her family. She didn't need them anymore and the things written in there? Well, it didn't matter.

She still loved Annie and she was pretty certain that Annie had still loved them too.

At least most of the time.

Annie had been a spoiled teenager navigating the world, flawed and ugly, but beautiful too.

Imogen didn't want to excuse bullying and attempted murder, she knew now that Annie had done some pretty nasty things, but the Annie she knew, the Annie she chose to remember... that Annie would always matter to her. That Annie didn't deserve what happened to her. That Annie deserved to grow and change, not become worm food for six years.

And as for Annie's secret summer... well, some secrets are meant to stay buried.

Printed in Great Britain
by Amazon